The
Irish Manor House
Murder

Also by Dicey Deere

The Irish Cottage Murder

The
Irish Manor House
Murder

Dicey Deere

St. Martin's Minotaur ☙ New York

www.minotaurbooks.com

Library of Congress Cataloging-in-Publication Data

Deere, Dicey.
    The Irish manor house murder / Dicey Deere. — 1st ed.
      p. cm.
    ISBN 0-312-20606-2
    1. Americans — Ireland — Fiction. 2. Women translators — Fiction. 3. Ireland — Fiction. I.   Title.

PS3554.E3553 I66 2000
813'.54 — dc21

                                    00-035268

First Edition: August 2000

10 9 8 7 6 5 4 3 2 1

To Marijane and "the Crowd" at Ashawagh Hall

1

It was a horror. First, Torrey heard the horse's hoofs pounding; it was like a thudding in her heart.

She was coming from the old groundsman's cottage in the woods to take the shortcut across the Ashenden meadow to the village. October, three o'clock, bright sunlight.

She drew in a breath of the fresh-cut grass as she reached the fence that enclosed the meadow. A hundred feet to her right, on a hill, rose Ashenden Manor with its four stone chimneys.

Then Torrey saw a figure. Someone was crossing the meadow, coming from the manor and going toward the woods at her left. She recognized the spare, upright figure of Dr. Ashenden, who must have just arrived home to the manor from his office in Dublin; he was still in city clothes.

Then suddenly the *pound, pound, thud, thud,* shaking her —

A great gray horse came galloping across the meadow toward Dr. Ashenden, the girl astride him crouching low on his neck, her red hair wild, lips drawn back, Reaching Dr. Ashenden, the horse reared, neighing, eyes rolling, frantic. But the girl on his back, gripping the reins, fiercely forced him to do her bidding, and his great hooves rose and came down like giant hammers on Dr. Ashenden . . . then again . . . and again. All the while, the girl in the saddle was screaming down at the man's fallen body. Then abruptly she wheeled the horse and was gone.

"No!" Torrey moaned, stunned, sickened, "*No!*"

On her knees, Torrey brushed dirt and crushed grass from Dr. Ashenden's face. He lay on his back, jacket torn, his white shirt ripped, his tie twisted. His face was dirty and bruised, his eyes closed; his silvery hair was globbed with mud. Dead?

"Dr. Ashenden . . . ?" But now he moaned. He opened his eyes, heavy-lidded eyes under thick, gray-white eyebrows. His dazed look, unfocused, met Torrey's. He moved his lips and said faintly, "My shoulder . . . broken, I think. Or maybe . . . I rolled aside just in —" his gaze sharpened in recognition of Torrey in her faded navy turtleneck and jeans. "Ah, Ms. Tunet." He took a breath, gasped in pain, then in his elegant clipped style, he said quickly, irritably, "That damned stallion! Rowena can't control him! I've warned her again and again, but she doesn't listen!"

Torrey gaped, stunned. "Yes, yes." She saw that Dr. Ashenden was trembling. He must be in terrible pain and, of course, shock. He was in his late seventies. And this murderous attack! Was he out of his head, thinking the hellish attack was an accident?

Confused, she gazed at a dark red bruise covering his cheek. Then blinked. Odd that it was already swollen. Something off.

". . . or if not broken, possibly sprained." Dr. Ashenden was probing his shoulder with trembling fingers.

Definitely off. But clearly he didn't want anybody to know that his granddaughter Rowena had tried to kill him. Torrey shifted her knees in the grass and looked down at Dr. Ashenden. "Can you get up? I'll help you."

"No. No thank you, Ms. Tunet, I can manage." He raised himself on an elbow and shook his head as though to clear it. "I'm all right."

But a hearty Wicklow-accented man's voice at Torrey's shoulder said, "Here, let me, Dr. Ashenden."

Only then did Torrey realize that she and Dr. Ashenden were not alone in the meadow. Someone else had witnessed Rowena's murderous attack on her grandfather.

She looked up at Sergeant Jimmy Bryson.

2

So that's when I arrested Rowena Keegan," Sergeant Jimmy Bryson said to Inspector Egan O'Hare at six o'clock in the glass-fronted room that was the Ballynagh police station, "When I got Doctor Ashenden back to the manor, by luck Dr. Padraic Collins was there. He'd dropped in, as usual. Between us, we got Ashenden upstairs. Sprained shoulder, contusions, and some undetermined kind of blow to his face. Abrasions and so on. I'd've sworn he'd be dead."

Sergeant Bryson pushed his cap up off his forehead and looked over at his neatly typed report on Inspector O'Hare's desk. He was twenty-two, narrowly built, and loved a bit of excitement, which ordinarily was in short supply in Ballynagh. Still, the ugliness of what he'd seen in the meadow a bare two hours ago had rattled him. "What a shocker! I was coming back from O'Shaugnessy's when I saw it. Jesus! Rowena Keegan galloping into the meadow and riding her grandfather down like a crazy woman. She meant to kill him. *I saw her face!*" —

Inspector Egan O'Hare glanced at the report, then leaned down from his desk chair to give Nelson, the black Lab, his six o'clock biscuit. Nelson took it delicately between his teeth and settled down by the Coke machine. O'Hare said to Bryson, "Well, now, Jimmy, you say that Ms. Tunet was crossing the meadow. Torrey Tunet. So presumably she'd be a witness. But she denies — "

"Absolutely, Inspector! Swears she didn't see a thing! Looked me right in the eye and said she'd accidentally stumbled over Dr. Ashenden's body."

Inspector O'Hare sat back, pursed his lips, and for a moment regarded the wall behind Sergeant Bryson. "Ms. Tunet may not be the soul of truth, considering that she and Rowena Keegan have become such fast friends. Walking the woods and hills, tea at Miss Amelia's Tea Shop, feeding acorns to squirrels. Keep an eye out, Jimmy."

"That I will, Inspector."

O'Hare tapped a finger on Sergeant Bryson's typed report. "This, about O'Malley's pub. Sean O'Malley says Rowena Keegan's hardly ever been there before." He frowned down at the report. According to Sean O'Malley, Rowena Keegan had come into O'Malleys and started drinking heavily about an hour before her attack on her grandfather. Straight whiskeys. Leaving the pub, paying Sean, she had muttered under her breath, "That bastard! That inhuman bastard! He belongs in hell!" Sean had sworn those were her words. He said the girl was crying.

"That's it, then, Jimmy?"

"Everything, Inspector. Except that Sean O'Malley said that for a pretty girl, Rowena Keegan looked a sight, her red hair wild and those green eyes all bloodshot. Made me think, Jesus! What's happened? Them always so thick before, Rowena and her grandfather."

Inspector O'Hare, reading the report and listening to Sergeant Jimmy Bryson, was wondering the same thing. He was fifty-four years old and had been Inspector in Ballynagh for the past twenty-two years. There was little he didn't know and much that he remembered. He was recalling now that from the time Rowena Keegan was three or four years old, she'd been her grandfather's darling. Dr. Ashenden taught the child to ride, to swim, to fish, to play tennis. By the time she was twelve, they rode together daily when Dr. Ashenden returned from surgery in Dublin. Whenever Rowena Keegan caught a cold, had an earache, or cut a finger, Dr. Ashenden treated it like a major emergency. In the village, they laughed about it, what with Rowena Keegan being such a bloomingly healthy young woman.

In any case, the bloomingly healthy young woman was at present not in residence at Ashenden Manor. She was, instead, in the only cell that the police station in the village of Ballynagh possessed, exactly twenty-five feet away from where Inspector O'Hare now sat. At half past six o'clock, Sergeant Bryson would go across to Finney's to get her dinner. It was Friday night. Baked shad, mashed potatoes, spinach.

3

The cottage was chilly when Torrey woke up. She hadn't known about October in Ireland. Shivering, she took her morning shower; the water was lukewarm as usual and only a frustrating dribble. Back in the damply cold bedroom, she put on a gray woolen skirt and her heaviest cotton jersey, a red turtleneck that she'd bought two months ago back home in North Hawk, just before going on to the Boston airport. "Have a nice trip, Ms. Tunet," the elderly clerk had said, taking her credit card. "How I do envy you!"

"Thanks." But this time it wasn't her usual trip. It wasn't an interpreting job, staying in Europe's luxury hotels, speaking Danish or Italian or any of her dozen other languages, wearing her tailored suit, her time-sweep efficient watch on her wrist. No conference rooms and occasional evenings of polite formal dinners, wearing glittering earrings and discussing political and European Union problems.

No. This time it was the dilapidated old groundsman's cottage in Ballynagh. The Children's Language Institute had offered her a contract: a three-language series of books for kids. She hadn't been able to resist. Kids and languages! Four months of hard work and she'd deliver the first book in the six-book series. "Half payment in advance," they'd stipulated cautiously about this first book, "the other half on delivery and acceptance."

Hardly enough money to scrape by on. She had no savings. Having grown up poor, she enjoyed spending. So now it was back to her early days of half cans of tuna, dried beans, powdered milk. But irresistible. Kids and languages!

She'd thought back to the time in North Hawk when she was twelve and won that prize of twenty-five dollars translating for little kids from Spanish-speaking countries who didn't speak English. She'd learned Spanish from tapes she took out of the library. Why? "I don't know," she'd told the *North Hawk Weekly* reporter. These days they said it was genetic, her peculiar language ability. Her Romanian father had been the same. So had two other interpreters she'd met at the United Nations. Yet how she had slaved for years to learn! She was now twenty-eight and had a passport stamped with exotic foreign destinations and an unflattering, rather wistful-looking photo showing her dark, wavy, short hair, her narrow chin, and her gray eyes that somehow looked better without mascara. She was five feet four, slim, and addicted to pasta and chocolate bars with almonds. She was also helplessly fascinated by other people's lives. Nosy, some people called it.

Fingering the check from the Language Institute, she'd thought at once of the old groundsman's cottage in Ballynagh. It would be a cheap rental. There was blood in its recent history, she knew that well enough. She'd been in Ballynagh four months ago, when she'd worked at the conference in Dublin. The Ballynagh villagers still shuddered and steered clear of the cottage in the woods, in spite of a low rent. So, cheap. Hopeful, she made a long-distance call to the owner, Winifred Moore of Castle Moore, and pinned down a six-month lease of the cottage. Already she'd been here two months.

Still shivering, she picked up her jeans from the chair beside the bed. They were muddied and grass-stained at the knees from when she'd knelt in the meadow beside the body of Dr. Ashenden.

Still holding the jeans, she had a sudden, flashing vision of Rowena Keegan astride the stallion, the upraised hooves, Rowena's enraged face.

Torrey gazed down at the jeans. She saw herself yesterday afternoon standing in the great hall at Ashenden Manor with Sergeant Bryson in his blue uniform and cap. She heard her own smoothly lying voice, protecting Rowena. Then, footsteps: chubby, balding Dr. Collins, Dr. Ashenden's old friend, coming down the staircase in his familiar olive-green tweed jacket, bringing the reassuring news that Dr. Ashenden's main injury was a sprained shoulder. Dr. Collins's kindly voice and his honest blue eyes made her feel ashamed of her lying.

Stay out of it.

But of course she wouldn't. She never could. Besides, having lied to the police, she was already in it. And Inspector O'Hare was not one to let sleeping dogs lie. He'd kick them awake. Or more likely lure them awake with a biscuit held under their noses. Better not underestimate the paunchy, comfortable-looking Inspector O'Hare.

But above all, Rowena! There had to be an explanation for that horrifying scene in the meadow, that scene of madness.

What could have happened to turn Rowena so murderous? Rowena was not that person on the galloping, plunging horse. The Rowena Torrey knew was a warmhearted, loving young woman who was studying to be a veterinarian. Rowena had a gentle hand with horses, dogs, cats, and any living thing. A week ago, she'd crawled on her stomach through a rotting, maggot-ridden log to rescue a frightened kitten.

Torrey felt a stab of hunger. Breakfast was in order; it was already past eight o'clock. Sun flickered through the trees and shone through the small bedroom windows. Torrey went into the fireplace kitchen with its pine chairs, and table, and shabby couch. She'd have coffee and buttered day-old brown bread.

9

Passing the table, she switched on the little radio that she kept tuned to RTE, Ireland's national radio and television network. Slicing the bread, she heard the weather report. There was a break-in at Brewley's on Grafton Street, thieves making off with two sides of bacon and a turkey. A fracas near Trinity College over a soccer match.

Then the commentator's voice said: "Dr. Gerald Ashenden, Ireland's justly famous thoracic surgeon, late yesterday afternoon suffered a riding accident at the Ashenden estate in Ballynagh. An expert horseman, Dr. Ashenden faults a broken stirrup that resulted in the fall that sprained his left shoulder. A speedy recovery to you, Dr. Ashenden!"

Torrey, holding the coffeepot, said softly, "Well, bless me for a bloody lie!"

"Yes," Rowena said, from the open doorway.

Rowena was standing just outside, on the lintel. The sun flickered on her red hair, which was short and curly. She came in. She wore a parka and jeans and well-scuffed brogues. A thick brown muffler hung from around her neck. Her tanned face was pale. Her eyelids were heavy and tinged with pink.

"Coffee?" Torrey said, with a great sigh of relief. "I've only one egg, but I can make us French toast." She turned off the radio.

Rowena shook her head. "Nothing, thanks. I had breakfast at the jail. Sergeant Bryson sent over to Finney's. He said breakfast'll be covered by the Ballynagh taxes we pay. Can you imagine? It made me laugh." She walked aimlessly across to the sink and back to the table. Her unzipped parka hung open, her hands were thrust into the pockets. "I came to thank you. I saw Sergeant Bryson's report, what you said. You lied, didn't you? You *saw*."

"Actually, I didn't see what happened," Torrey said, lying again. There was something so strange and troublesome about Rowena standing there, so unlike the Rowena who was always whistling, laughing, speaking Gaelic slang to Torrey for kicks, or showing her how to feed a baby guinea pig. "Except it was a horrible accident."

Rowena gave a skeptical, under-her-breath sort of laugh, "Oh, come on, Torrey! I wish you *hadn't* seen what happened. You're my friend. But there's something I can't tell even you. But thanks for sticking by me. Lack of evidence freed me, what with my grandfather raising hell with Inspector O'Hare: 'An outrage, arresting my granddaughter . . . the damned stallion out of control, my granddaughter shouting at me, "I can't stop him! Get out of the way!" Altogether, an accident . . .' And now, as you just heard on the radio, my grandfather's revised official version."

Torrey nodded. And waited.

"Anyway, this morning after I had breakfast at the police station, I sneaked home. I went up a back staircase and changed my clothes. Then I came here. I can't stay at Ashenden Manor. Can you imagine me having dinner across the table from my grandfather, with his sprained shoulder in a sling? Both of us pretending that in the meadow I didn't try to kill him! Pretending to my brother Scott and my mother and her new husband that it was all a mistake, an accident that Sergeant Jimmy Bryson misconstrued!"

Torrey was thinking, *Why, Rowena, why?*

"And Inspector O'Hare keeping me overnight in the Ballynagh jail."

"Poor Rowena." *Rowena's wild, contorted face, the rearing stallion.*

"So for now," Rowena went on, "I'm moving into the old horse trainers' quarters above the stables at Castle Moore. Later I'll find a place in Dublin. I exercise the two horses at the castle, and I know it'll be all right with Winifred Moore. She's not in residence, anyway. I'll phone my mother this morning to pack some clothes and have Jennie bring them to Castle Moore. Thank God my mother wasn't home yesterday afternoon! By now she must think the world's gone upside down."

"I shouldn't wonder. And your brother, Scott." The boy with the deformed leg.

Rowena went still, then she shrugged and turned out her hands in a helpless gesture. "Yes. Scott."

"There's nothing you can tell them? Your mother and Scott?" *And me?* But Rowena's green-eyed gaze slid away, her lids lowering. She rubbed the bridge of her nose, a characteristic habit when she was upset.

Torrey said, "Rowena? If there's anything, I'm here, at my hot little computer. Keep it in mind."

At that, Rowena hesitated, then abruptly she flicked her fingers good-bye. She smiled, but her green eyes were strained. "I'd better get on. Bye, Torrey."

Troubled, Torrey watched Rowena walk toward the open door. Rowena's walk was . . . what? Different, somehow, heavier these last weeks, and something else. What? A bloom, a blossoming. Something. Torrey rubbed her forehead. What? What? And as though seen in retrospect minutes ago, yes, the unfamiliar tightness of Rowena's favorite plaid shirt straining across her breasts. Torrey, guessing wildly, called out, "You're pregnant, aren't you, Rowena?"

4

At Torrey's words, Rowena stood still. Her figure, half turned away, seemed to shimmer in the sunlight reflected up from the lintel.

Stunned at her own discovery, Torrey said, "None of my business. I'm sorry. If you'd've wanted me to know, you'd've told me."

Rowena turned fully around. Her face was pale. "I wish you hadn't guessed. Nobody else knows." She slid her hands deep into her pockets, thrust out her chin, and looked squarely at Torrey. She said carefully, distinctly, "I'm going to abort it."

In the small silence that followed, they stood looking at each other, then Torrey said "Oh?" as though Rowena had merely said *It's a nice day.* She had an odd feeling that Rowena would otherwise shatter into pieces. Then, "Sit down. You can't just tell me you're going to abort your baby and then walk out the door."

Rowena's look softened. She came back and sank down at the table. Torrey pulled out the chair opposite and sat down. And waited. Then without looking up, Rowena said, "I don't want to kill my baby. But I'm going to. If I could tell anybody why, it would be you." Now she did look up at Torrey. "But I can't. So that's it. That's the whole tale. The end. *Finis.*"

Torrey said, reasonably, "Just tell me this, Rowena, just tell me, so I won't feel so obtuse: Exactly what are you talking about? You're pregnant. You don't want to abort your child but you must. Well, as a friend, is there anything I can do?"

Rowena slanted a green-eyed glance at her and managed a half smile. "You *are* a caution, Torrey. Thanks for wanting to help me. But you can't. The subject isn't up for discussion either." She got up. Against her plaid shirt her slender neck looked white and vulnerable. "I have to do it."

"*Have* to? Oh, please!" Suddenly impatient, Torrey too stood up. She leaned across to Rowena, both hands on the table. "Come *on*, Rowena! You have a choice. I under*stand* that you're dying to get your degree. You've put in four years — five years? — of backbreaking work. And you're *not* married, but — " She stopped. Something about the way Rowena was standing there told Torrey that she wasn't hearing. She was in some other place, some far-off dimension from which she now said, so low that Torrey barely heard, "It would be a crime to let this baby be born."

Torrey felt a chill. She looked at Rowena, who now lifted her gaze. Her green eyes stared at Torrey from that other place, wherever it was. "Forget it, Torrey. Don't try to help me."

"But — the baby's father! What about *him*? Doesn't *he* have any say?"

"The father." Rowena stared at her. "The father? No. No say at all. Torrey, please! Have done with it! I'm going."

"Rowena, wait! Let me help."

"*Stop* it!" Rowena said fiercely. "*Don't!*" And more quietly, "Do me a favor. Forget all this."

But it was too late to forget. It had been too late from the moment Torrey had guessed so wildly and accurately as Rowena had walked toward the open door of the cottage.

"All right," Torrey said, "not another word. I promise. It's not my business. But . . . just one quick question?" She didn't wait. "How many months pregnant are you?"

Rowena gave an exasperated laugh, "You *are* a bulldog, aren't you, Torrey? You never give up. Is it too late for an abortion? Still not the second trimester. I have about three weeks left before it'll be too risky."

"I see. I was just asking." Risky. A better word was *dangerous*. And in any case, not legal in Ireland. Rowena would have to go to England or elsewhere.

"So I have to hurry."

"Yes," Torrey said. "Before it's too late."

5

At ten minutes past eight that Saturday morning, Inspector O'Hare abruptly jerked his hand holding the coffee mug. Coffee spilled across his desktop. "Turn it off! Turn the damned thing off!" he said, and Sergeant Jimmy Bryson turned off the radio on top of the Coke machine. The news commentator's last words still hung in the air. "A speedy recovery to you, Dr. Ashenden."

Inspector O'Hare, jaw tense, blotted up coffee with a paper napkin. "The Ashenden family's making us look like fools, Sergeant." He looked at the wall clock. "I give it ten minutes."

They waited. Sergeant Bryson meantime put vinegar on a bit of a rag and wiped the front windows of the police station. Inspector O'Hare drew triangles. Nelson lay just inside the front door, nose between his paws. The morning sun shone on the still-empty street.

Twelve minutes. The phone rang. O'Hare picked it up. "Inspector O'Hare here."

"Good morning, Inspector. Hold for Chief Superintendent O'Reilly, please," Chief O'Reilly of the Murder Squad at Dublin Castle. The Dublin Metropolitan Area comprised Dublin city and the greater part of the country and portions of County Kildare and Wicklow.

"Good morning, Egan," came the cultivated voice of Chief

O'Reilly, "This about your report. Attack on Dr. Ashenden by his granddaughter? And your detaining of the young woman? What's going on, Egan?" The chief superintendent's ordinarily pleasant voice was somewhat less than pleasant.

Five minutes later, Inspector O'Hare hung up, a taste in his mouth bitter as an unripe orange. He looked over at Sergeant Bryson. "Dr. Ashenden is not happy at Inspector O'Hare's action in imprisoning his granddaughter on suspicion of attempted murder."

"Isn't he, now!" Sergeant Bryson said. "He's not happy? Doesn't like what's going on here? What went on *there* was attempted murder! And them all buttoned up about it, Including *her*. That's the crux, Inspector. Ms. Torrey Tunet! Collusion! Snake in the grass! Lying for her friend, Rowena, swearing she saw nothing!"

"Collusion," O'Hare repeated; he was making more triangles.

"She and Rowena Keegan! From the time Ms. Tunet found that dog the gypsies left and brought it to Rowena Keegan, you'd've thought they exchanged blood."

Inspector O'Hare made another triangle.

"Not that they're lesbians, mind you," Jimmy Bryson said. "I'm not saying they're gay. Leastways, Ms. Tunet's got that fellow from Cork. Since last month, anyway. Fixed a leak in her roof's the story. Him on a bicycle trip's the story, Dún Laoghaire to Clifden. He as good as lives with her."

"Collusion." O'Hare gazed out through the plate-glass window at Butler Street, so empty. "Right, Ms. Tunet had to've seen it. That stallion's as big as a mountain."

"Bakes bread, I've heard," Sergeant Bryson said, "Cock-a-leekie soup. Beans with a bit of smoked pork. Fancy stuff, too. Good as a chef. From Cork. Just turned up at the cottage, time she had the flu, right? Jasper O'Mara, from Cork. Looking for a bed-and-breakfast. Stumbled on the cottage."

"Collusion," Inspector O'Hara repeated the charge.

"Jasper O'Mara, from Cork—he got hold of Dr. Collins on Ms. Torrey Tunet's phone and Collins came and gave her some, uh . . ."

"Antibiotics."

"Antibiotics. Right. Could've been a love potion. Her and Jasper O'Mara since."

"Collins?" Padraic Collins. Yesterday, Dr. Collins had treated the bruised and injured Dr. Ashenden at Ashenden Manor. Collins was Ashenden's oldest friend, closest friend. Played chess every Saturday evening at Ashenden Manor, so he'd heard. Still occasionally rode together, too, the spare, still-handsome Dr. Ashenden and the balding, belly-pouting, round-shouldered little Dr. Collins.

Inspector O'Hare felt a faint twitch, more like a flutter, in front of his ears. An optimistic sign. Had on his "thinking cap," as his mother used to say.

Friends. Through propinquity rather than predilection. Collins Court and Ashenden Manor were the two biggest estates in this mountainous corner of Wicklow, barring Castle Moore. Local Anglo-Irish society. No surprise that Gerald Ashenden and Padraic Collins had known each other since boyhood, gone shooting and riding together, though Ashenden was maybe a year or two older than Collins. By chance, both young men had chosen the medical profession and begun practicing in Dublin. Gerald Ashenden a surgeon, Doctor Collins in family practice. Padraic Collins had never married. One rumor had it that a boyhood skiing accident had made him impotent. Another was that, Protestant though he was, he was inclined toward the priesthood and celibacy. Or perhaps he had been disappointed in love? Not to anyone's knowledge. But Inspector O'Hare, who more than once had occasion to ponder the subject, knew that Padraic Collins indeed had an eye for women. O'Hare had wondered if Collins arbitrarily—and perhaps admirably?— refused to be coerced into marriage by society's expectations. Altogether peculiar, folks thought. There had been evenings when, seeing Dr. Collins in O'Malley's having a quiet small whiskey, Inspector O'Hare had quoted to himself Dickens's "secret and self-contained as an oyster."

Kindly, though. Three years ago, Collins had given up his practice in Dublin. "I'm a country man," he liked to say. In Ballynagh, a call for help to Collins Court always brought him out even if it was pouring torrents. He wore country clothes and had a taste for checked vests under his tweeds. Sentimental, too; he wore a tweed cap that had belonged to his late father.

"You want me to do the November budget now, Inspector?"

"Right, Jimmy."

So, close friends, Collins and Gerald Ashenden. Might Padraic Collins be able to shed some light on why Rowena Keegan tried to murder her grandfather? Sergeant Bryson had half carried the injured Dr. Ashenden back to Ashenden Manor. "No one was about," Jimmy Bryson had reported, "except the maid, Jennie O'Shea, and — thank God! — Dr. Collins. He'd dropped in at Ashenden Manor for a visit, like he often did. He helped me get Dr. Ashenden up to his bedroom. Uff! Collins himself looked in shock, Inspector. His fingers were shaking like dry peas in a pod when he treated Ashenden's shoulder. I left them there in the bedroom."

O'Hare gazed into space, seeing the two old friends in the bedroom, the door closed. He imagined Ashenden looking into his friend's questioning face and confiding. Confiding . . . justifying . . . confiding. Confiding what?

O'Hare tapped a pencil on his desk blotter. Surely Ashenden and Collins must have shared many a confidence through the years. He wondered if Ashenden knew about the hookers in Cork who had their hooks into the good Dr. Collins, not impotent but needed a little fancy work to get him going. Amazing the odd bits of information that reached one's ears.

A whiff of blood supplied by Dr. Collins, innocently, will-ingly, or unwarily, and he'd be on the scent. Rowena Kee-gan's motive. And the back of my hand to you, Chief Superintendent O'Reilly at that mahogany desk at Dublin Castle.

Inspector O'Hare picked up the phone.

6

It was a ten-minute walk. Then an immense hedge, and around the next bend, Inspector O'Hare saw the great circular drive, and at the apex, the six white Palladian pillars that fronted the entrance to Collins Court. He walked up the sun-dappled drive. Magnificent yet somehow chaste, the simplicity of Collins Court with its rows of windows, glittering now in the morning sun. Off to the left was the entrance to a walled garden, a curved oak door in a vine-covered stone wall. A bit away from the wall, and edged with tall, feathery greens, was a pond dappled with flat-leaved water lilies. On the right, he could see, far back, a corner of the stables. O'Hare imagined generations ago the jingling of harnesses, scarlet-coated horsemen and their ladies up on horses that jostled each other, dogs barking, servants handing up stirrup cups to the riders. But certainly not in Padraic Collins's time. Dr. Collins was an animal rights advocate who disapproved of hunting.

Helen Lavery, Dr. Collins's housekeeper and cook, let him in. "A bit of luck, Inspector, Dr. Collins being home this morning." She had taken his call; she always answered the telephone for Collins, who disliked doing it. She was a bustling, round-faced woman in her midfifties with small, kindly blue eyes. She wore a red-checked apron over a navy cotton dress and had a smudge of flour on one cheek. She cooked for Dr. Collins and was known to be one of the best bakers of pastry in this corner of Wicklow. In Inspector O'Hare's opinion, Helen Lavery was in love with Padraic Collins. It was an accepted fact that governesses and middle-aged housekeepers were in love with the widowers or single men who employed them.

"This way, Inspector, and mind the step at the end." She led him into a long-windowed drawing room. "I'll call Dr. Collins."

O'Hare looked around and raised his eyebrows, surprised. Roly-poly Dr. Padraic Collins! Unexpected. Padraic Collins, who wore his father's old tweed cap and a worn woolen vest, Collins, who rattled along in his eight-year-old Honda at late hours to this or that cottage where a man lay sick, or a frightened mother wrung her hands over a coughing or bloodied child.

The books, the pictures, that elegant piano. O'Hare approached the piano. He had never seen one like it before, with its delicate, shell-like finish that of course was not shell but a kind of whorled wood. Not varnished. Buffed. Buffed! A pile of music books, well thumbed, lay on the stand. The carpet was thin, worn, with an oriental look. The bookcases that ranged around the room were a mellow oak.

Waiting, Inspector O'Hare ran his hand over a row of leather-bound books. *Morte D'Arthur*. Lancelot. Galahad. Queen Guinevere . . . and thought: *lost loves, brave encounters, dragons slain.*

Footsteps. Then, "Well, Inspector! Sit down! Sit down! Glad I was here when you called. Helen will bring us some tea. A midmorning cup, eh? What with this chill in the air. Almost like November. And we'll have some tarts, baked this morning. Already had two at breakfast, but I'm peckish. This weather, and . . . and . . ." Dr. Collins's voice ran out of its frenetic, forced cheerfulness. He sank down suddenly in a chair beside a gateleg table, his plump face pale, dark puffs of sleeplessness under strained-looking, reddened eyes. His voice shook. "A shock. Altogether a shock. I happened to be right there, you know, at Ashenden Court when Jimmy — when Sergeant Bryson got Dr. Ashenden back from the meadow. Thank God for that!"

Inspector O'Hare sat down. He looked curiously at Dr. Collins in the chair across the gateleg table. Lancelot, Galahad. *Morte D'Arthur.* Secret romantic, wearing a sweater-vest and well-worn tweed trousers, and resorting to hookers in Cork.

"What I'm interested in," O'Hare said, moving his knees so Helen Lavery could more easily put down a tray with tea things and delicious-smelling tarts, "and knowing your close friendship with Dr. Ashenden, Did Ashenden ever say anything to you? Maybe while playing a game of chess of a Saturday afternoon? Maybe something he might've mentioned just lately? About anything not going well between himself and his granddaugher? Some difficulty? A problem that might have arisen . . . ?"

"A problem?" Padraic Collins looked uncertain. "No. Oh, no!" He shook his head. "Definitely not." He reached out and picked up a tart. He said unhappily, "I'd remember if he had. That dreadful — out there in the meadow, it was some kind of mix-up, what happened. Rowena would never have — *never.*"

Three fruit tarts and two cups of tea later, and having phrased the question obliquely in as many ways, Inspector O'Hare gave up. Waste of time. What the devil had he expected, coming here?

"Well, then," he said and stood up. Best get on with the other arrows he had in his quiver.

On his way out, Helen Lavery pressed a bag of still-warm tarts into his hands. "Cherry, apple, and blueberry. I use the canned fruit. It comes out just as good."

7

Ten o'clock Saturday morning. "The black nylon traveling bag," Caroline Keegan said to Jennie O'Shea, coming into the kitchen where Jennie in her striped kitchen apron sat at the table polishing the silver. "It's in the box room. Bring it up to Ms. Rowena's room, Jennie. I'm packing a few of her things." At Jennie's alert look of curiosity, she added, "That was all a misunderstanding last night, Jennie, Ms. Rowena being overnight in the Ballynagh jail. Inspector O'Hare had her released early this morning . . . as you've probably already heard?" And at Jennie's confirming blush, "Inspector O'Hare somehow . . . anyway, Jennie, the bag."

"The black nylon with the red stripe, is it, ma'am?"

"Yes, Jennie. Ms. Rowena's going away for a few days."

Upstairs, the morning sun slanted across the tapestry-covered window seat, sun-faded but beautiful, in Rowena's bedroom. Caroline closed the tall arched door behind her. Even that was an effort: this was one of her weaker days, her legs aching, those friable bones, and today that familiar, enervating pain at the back of her neck. She wore her usual flat-heeled shoes, a shirt, and pants and had pulled on a somewhat raveled navy cardigan against the morning chill. She had found an old barrette of Rowena's under the Sheraton chair on the landing, and not knowing what to do with it, she had used it to clasp her thin, fair hair back from her forehead. A skinny, overage Alice in Wonderland, she thought and made a face, then shrugged and smiled. She was forty-seven and was four months into her second marriage, in love with Mark Temple, her new husband. Wildly in love was how she thought of it.

Rowena's telephone call had come some twenty minutes ago, dismaying and exasperating her. "Pack some clothes? You're going to live above the stables at Castle Moore? But *why*? Just because you lost control of Thor in the meadow? Oh, for God's *sake*, Rowena! Your grandfather —"

"Later, Mother. Please," and Rowena had rung off.

Caroline looked around the bedroom. Of the nine bedrooms at Ashenden Manor, Rowena's was the biggest and most beautiful, with its marble fireplace and tall arched windows. Rowena was sixteen when her grandfather had had the room redecorated and gave to her for her birthday. Dark gold wainscoting, blue-green walls, and a frieze of ivory plaster horses prancing around the ceiling. The sleigh bed was buried under a luxurious peach-colored down comforter that Gerald Ashenden had had especially made in Munich where he'd been giving a lecture on thoracic surgery. At the Munich factory, he had himself selected the quality of down. A gift for Rowena's seventeenth birthday. Seven years ago.

Caroline felt the barrette sliding through her thin hair. She reclasped it, remembering when during her childhood this had been a heavily curtained dark mahogany bedroom with a big carved black bed where her father and mother had slept. The black bed, a dark night, moonlight falling across the bed . . . A memory surfaced, she saw herself coming crying into this room one moonlit night when she was about eight: saw herself shivering and barefoot in her flannel nightgown, neck aching, that painful aching, frightening her. At her weak cry, her father reared up in that black bed, such a fierce, angry, repudiating look on his face, glaring at her, that she stumbled back, frightened. And her mother?

Her mother lying there on her back, asleep, tangled dark hair strewn on the pillow, one beautiful white arm hanging over the edge of the bed. Even then, Caroline had known her mother was drunk. Her mother, who loved her, yet was locked away in some secret place within herself, helpless.

"Ma'am? Here's Ms. Rowena's carrying bag." Jennie O'Shea came in and put the black nylon bag on the bed. "I gave it a good brushing."

Caroline packed the clothes. They were mostly worn and stained jodhpurs and boots. When Rowena wasn't at her vet classes in Dublin, she mucked out the horse stalls at the manor and at Castle Moore and exercised the three horses at the castle a mile west of Ashenden Manor. Winifred Moore paid her thirty pounds a month. But Rowena would have done it for free. She was a lover of animals: dogs, horses, pigs, cats. She didn't mind getting dirty, mucking out stables. Besides, she was active, vigorous; she loved exercise.

Caroline zipped the nylon bag closed. The simple act sent a twinge of pain through her shoulder and made her gasp. Pain, since the beginning, since babyhood, always pain. She sank down on the bed. When she caught her breath, she'd take one of the pills. Pain . . .

Pain . . . and always her father, the already-famous surgeon, Dr. Gerald Ashenden, looming like a giant, hating the very sight of her. A pitiful-looking thing, with bluish-white skin, fair hair, and bewildered hazel eyes. She whimpered in her sleep, rocked by her mother. Aching bones, thin legs, pains in her neck when she turned her head. School could not be considered. She was tutored at home. Afternoons, when her father returned from his surgery in Dublin and happened upon her, she hardly dared look at him. She shrank into corners. She was afraid of him and ashamed of being the pitiful little thing she was, so that he could not love her. She knew her mother loved her, but her mother, her beautiful mother, would go off to the village. The two maids whispered about it; Caroline sometimes caught the murmured words, "O'Malley's pub," and once, "staggering on the access road." She heard other whispers. Her mother had been Kathleen Brady: she'd been a girl, eighteen, come from Galway to live with a spinster aunt above a shop in Ballynagh. She'd gotten a job as a waitress at a pub. Whisper, whisper, the young intern, Gerald Ashenden, heir to the Ashenden estate, had one evening dropped into the pub . . . whisper, whisper. "Milk and honey," Father Donovan said to Father O'Neal. "No Catholic girl has a right to look like that." Whisper . . .

When Caroline was eight, her mother somehow managed to arrange a birthday party for her. Neighboring children came. The party was ending in the late afternoon, and on the west lawn three or four children, departing, began roughhousing, playfully pushing each other around, faces getting red and sweaty, shirts being pulled out. In the midst of this, her father appeared, arriving home from his office in Dublin. He stood watching the children, smiling. And with a stab of misery, sharp as a knife, Caroline saw that her father liked children who had glowing health — active, shouting children, the kind who liked to play violent games and weren't afraid to ride horses.

The phone on Rowena's bedside table buzzed. Caroline picked it up. "Hello?" No answer. Instead, after an instant, a click. Disturbing, that sort of thing. If it had been a wrong number, the person could have said. She put down the phone. The pain in her neck was lessening. She rummaged in the pocket of the raveled cardigan, found her little plastic bottle of pills, and swallowed one without water; she'd long since gotten used to the art of pill swallowing. In a few minutes she'd be fine. What had started her thinking about those childhood miseries? Poor little wren that she'd been!

And then, worse, when she was eleven, something dreadful happened.

It was July. There was a drought. For six weeks no rain fell. Rushing streams in the valley where Ballynagh lay became trickles, then dried up altogether. Foxes, squirrels, rabbits died, snakes became bolder. High on the mountains among the gorse and heather, sparkling streams were diverted to supply the valley with water, but already in the woods, dry branches rustled in dry winds. Then one early evening in the woods in sight of Ashenden Manor, there was a burst of fire like an explosion, a brushfire, crackling, then roaring. Ballynagh's volunteer firefighters fought it: reinforcements arrived from surrounding villages. In a four-hour battle they conquered the fire. Dying, its thick smoke rose and drifted like a fog over Ashenden Manor. Two hours later, the firefighters, cautiously walking through the still smoldering woods to put out any last vestiges of fire, came upon the body of Kathleen Brady Ashenden. Later it was established that Kathleen Ashenden had left O'Malley's pub, and as she sometimes did, must have been taking the shortcut through the woods to get home.

For weeks after her mother now belonged to *them*, as Caroline confusedly thought of it—belonged to those other Ashendens lying within the iron-railed Ashenden cemetery—Caroline lived inside of books, reading, reading. In some strange way it was as though she was searching for her mother somewhere in the pages. The other odd thing was that she felt she had lost a child, that her mother had been a child who had run away.

But then, two months later, a miracle happened. It was September, about five o'clock in the afternoon. She was sitting on the broad stone steps of the manor, reading *Ivanhoe*. She looked up and saw her father, just returned from his day in Dublin, coming as usual from the stable where he kept his car. He came toward the steps, tall, handsome, fair-haired, his dark, heavy-lidded eyes concentrated with thought. At sight of her, the frown, that familiar faint repudiating twitch, appeared between his brows.

That's when the magic happened.

As though released from some kind of bondage, she suddenly no longer cared. Gone was the ache of being unloved, gone the shame that she was such a hateful sight to her father. She did not care. *She did not care.* From the stone steps, she looked composedly back up at him in his city clothes. She even smiled. And she saw instantly that he knew.

From then on, she did as she pleased. When she was twenty, wearing a Queen Guinevere circlet to hold back her fair hair and with the smell of marijuana on her breath, overcome with love she married Tom Keegan, guitar-playing rock star. "A darling man, besides," they said of Tom Keegan, who was then thirty-one, with recordings that were at the top of the charts. And when he was thirty-six and died in the van accident at Galley Head, "It took a piece out of Ireland, a main missing piece," they said of him. Caroline thought at first she would die of the loss. But at least by then she had the children, Rowena and Scott.

"Ma'am? I've finished up here. Should I bring Ms. Rowena's bag downstairs for you?"

"Hmmm?" She swam up from the past. "Oh, yes, Jennie. And didn't I say? You're to take it to Castle Moore, just leave it with Rose. You can use Ms. Rowena's bike, it has a big enough basket."

Alone, Caroline raised her head and looked up at the frieze of plaster horses, mares and stallions, manes flying, hooves upraised. She shivered. Something terrible had happened in the meadow, why lie to herself? And something terrible between her father and her daughter had caused it. Something beyond dreadful. But what? The *what* loomed like a giant wave. *What?* Who could tell her? Scott? She would sound out Scott.

She drew a breath of relief. Scott would know. He and Rowena were unusually close. He was two years younger than Rowena. But Rowena had always loved and protected her little brother. And Scott, maybe because of his deformed leg, seemed to have compensated by developing an intuitive sense.

Yes, Scott. He would know.

8

Jennie heard Dr. Ashenden come into the front hall behind her. She recognized his definite step, the crack of his heel on the marble floor. She was putting on her three-quarter-length coat. She'd meantime put the black nylon bag on the settle beside the front door. It was already eleven o'clock.

"That bag," Dr. Ashenden said, his voice sharp, "belongs to my granddaughter. Why's it here? What're you doing with it? What's she up to?"

Buttoning her coat, Jennie looked at Dr. Ashenden, one long, shocked, fascinated glance, then down at her buttoning fingers. His face! Scratches, purple bruises around his bloodshot eyes. One cheek was swollen from chin to cheekbone, a dark red. It was so painful to see that it made Jennie flinch. One of his shoulders was heavily bandaged. The left. His arm rested in a dark blue sling.

"Well?" Authoritative. It made her jump.

"The bag?" She was taking it to the stables at Castle Moore . . . Clothes, yes, some clothes . . . No, she didn't know . . . Mrs. Keegan — that is, Mrs. Temple — had packed them . . . A telephone call, she thought, from Ms. Rowena.

"I see."

Out the door with the bag, shivery somehow. Closing it behind her, she heard a sound, at first she thought a hoarse and strangled cry, but the door, a massive door, squeaked like a human in pain. It got that way in the wet of October, the wood expanding; it was oak.

A half hour before lunch, the smell of pea soup with curry wafted into the hall where Caroline at last found Scott. He was standing by the hall table, flicking through the morning's mail, resting his weight on his good leg. Caroline stood watching her son, smiling, but with that inevitable ache in her heart. Scott was twenty-two years old. Like her, he was too thin, and not tall. He had a thatch of fair hair and blue eyes with a tinge of gray that made them look so light as to be almost transparent. "See-through eyes," Caroline had heard a youngster in Ballynagh call them. In any case, Scott was undeniably a handsome young man.

Right now, he was in a navy shirt and yellow sweater. He wore dove-gray trousers that as usual he'd bought from a catalog to spare himself the mortification of buying trousers in a shop, exposing his pathetically narrow leg in the steel brace. Caroline thought: *My bones, my son's bones. Not like Rowena's. Did Scott envy Rowena that, her health and vitality? How could he not?*

Scott looked up. "Hello, Ma." He was separating catalogs from the regular family mail. "Smells like something with curry."

"Pea soup. Where's your muffler? The new one, the brown that I knitted, there's such a chill in the air. And wind. Leaves blowing all about."

"My muffler? Don't know, Ma. Last I saw, Rowena was wearing it. Sneaking out of here early this very morn, her worn-out parka and the muffler, old brogues. Looked like a refugee from *War and Peace.*"

"Rowena *here*? This morning?" She felt somehow betrayed. "What's going on, Scott? Two conflicting . . . My father saying he was out riding and his stirrup broke and he fell off of Thor. And Inspector O'Hare's *different* version.

And Rowena last night in jail! What's *going on*, Scott? If a mother may be so bold as to ask?"

"Hmmm?" Scott was tapping the pile of catalogs on the the table to even them, his fair-haired head bent down. "Am I my sister's keeper?"

"Scott!"

He looked up, contrite. "Sorry, Ma. My wicked tongue. But I was in Dublin. I got home late last night. Haven't got it straight yet, that meadow affair."

Caroline felt a familiar apprehension. In Dublin. One of those parties. A lot of drinking, gay young men, some nights not even coming home. It had started two years ago. Where did he get the money? He had no money of his own, no job, only the small royalties she'd made over to him, royalties from his late father's guitar recordings. So where did the money come from? She looked at the catalogs in his thin fingers. Catalogs for the expensive things he bought lately: the Renaissance lyre chair for his rooms at Ashenden Manor, gifts of perfume and leather and recordings for friends who were young men Caroline had never met. And having his favorite books specially bound by Erasmus House in Geneva.

She put a hand vaguely to her hair as a wisp fell across her eyes. Her poor Scott. She hardly dared think what she suspected.

"Ma?"

She looked at him blankly. She was seeing a morning twenty-two years ago, when Scott was born and she looked down at him in her arms and sensed that something was wrong and felt danger like a dark halo around his still-damp head.

"Maybe at lunch," Scott was saying, and his tone was gentle, "we'll ask your pa, the good Dr. Ashenden. He'll sort it all out for us, don't worry. All right?"

"Yes, darling," Caroline said, with total disbelief. "Your grandfather will explain it. That's best."

Scott watched his mother cross the hall. His gleaming little red Miata convertible was parked outside on the gravel near the stable. He longed to escape the ordeal of Saturday lunch. These hellish weekend lunches. *Charlatan!* The word, so contemptuous, though not actually spoken aloud, was in the curl of his grandfather's lips and in the angry glare of his dark, heavy-lidded eyes when Ashenden looked across the soup and noontime cold meats at the thickly built, fifty-year-old Dr. Mark Temple. That Ashenden's daughter Caroline had married a chiropractor! Fakes, all of them! A travesty to call them doctors. It made for a disagreeable and indigestible lunch. Scott had heard his grandfather expound on the subject of Dr. Mark Temple, ranting to his friend Padraic Collins one evening in the study, "The Ashenden name, damn it! Associated with that bone man's name!" Outrageous that he, Dr. Gerald Ashenden, whose name was preceded in medical journals and weekly newsmagazines by the word *eminent,* now had a son-in-law who pushed around people's bones. In Ashenden's view, Mark Temple had pushed around Caroline's bones in his expensive office in Dublin, full of charts of people's spines, until he had pushed her into marriage. Caroline believed totally in Dr. Mark Temple, who presumably adjusted her bones and who massaged her neck and back and limbs. "Believes in him! Damned fortune hunter! After her money!" Infuriating. And she loved him.

Scott knew that at lunch his grandfather would be silent about Rowena's murderous attack on him in the meadow.

As for his mother—"The Lady of Shallot," Scott said under his breath. Not weaving at a loom, no, but knitting; knitting mufflers and gloves and sweaters for him and Rowena, blue, brown, rust, red. He smiled, thinking of it. And then he stopped smiling, because his mother was bewildered and frightened for Rowena and wanted to know. But anything he could tell her would break her heart.

34

9

At four o'clock it was quiet at Ashenden Manor except for the murmur of voices and clatter of china in the kitchen, where Jennie O'Shea and Molly, the second maid, were fixing a high tea.

On the second floor, in the west bedroom, a Brahms concerto played softly. Broad latticed windows were open to the view of Wicklow mountains and the high hills dotted with grazing sheep. Below, fields spread from the manor to the woods and the beginning of the bridle path.

Mark Temple stood beside the massage table where his wife, Caroline Ashenden, lay facedown, naked, a towel across her buttocks. He briskly rubbed his hands together, warming the lotion. Then he put his palms on Caroline's naked back just below her neck. Then downward, long, slow strokes, putting gentle pressure on the strokes where they ended at Caroline's waist.

"Heaven," Caroline said drowsily, eyes closed.

Mark said nothing. He was frowning, his hands resting lightly at Caroline's waist. So delicate, so thin boned. And those pains. Shoulders, neck. He wondered if Caroline was aware that one of her legs was slightly thinner than the other. He thought of Scott's thin leg. Caroline was lucky to have come through childbirth so well, first with Rowena, then with Scott. When she'd appeared in his office in Dublin a year ago, hoping he could help her, he'd been surprised that her father, Dr. Gerald Ashenden, had been unable to diagnose the cause of Caroline's bouts of pain. Would gentle massage help? In his office on Merrion Square, Mark Temple had examined Caroline Ashenden Keegan, widow of Tom Keegan, the rock star. Then, listening to her low voice, he had looked at her untidy fair hair and delicate pale mouth, her hazel eyes with the heavy white lids. He had, lastly, in a final check, put his hands gently on her clavicle that linked the scapula and sternum. And unable to help himself, he had fallen in love. He was fifty years old, had been married twice, and was just divorced.

And now here he was, temporarily domiciled in Ashenden Manor. It would be another month before renovations on the elegant little Georgian house in Dublin would be completed and they could move in.

He had come to love Ashenden Manor. Slum child that he had been, born in a squalid section of Limerick, as a small boy he'd sometimes daydreamed of having been born to landed gentry and perhaps been stolen from a country estate. Then, just four months ago, driving with Caroline in his Bentley through the iron gates and up the drive of Ashenden Manor and seeing for the first time the broad, gracious Georgian manor, he'd thought, *Yes. There it is. At last.* At last he was coming home.

With his creamed hand, he slicked back a tendril of Caroline's fair hair that had fallen across her nape. He was thinking how, these last four months of being married to Caroline, each late afternoon when he'd left his office in Dublin and come home to Ashenden Manor, he imagined all over again that this was the estate he had been born to, grew up in. He'd had a pony, then a horse. He'd worn good clothes, slept in a soft bed, breakfasted on porridge, eggs, and sausages. Warm rooms in winter, crackling fires in fireplaces, servants.

So here he was at last. Ashenden Manor.

But alas, there was a snake in this paradise: his father-in-law. It spoiled everything.

"Mmmmm, heavenly," Caroline murmured, eyes closed, Mark could see her right profile as she lay with her face turned sideways. White eyelids, a touch of rose in her cheeks. The tiny lines of pain around her mouth were gone; the massage always helped. "I've good news," he said. "Carey Construction called. They'll be done in about ten days. Then they only have to pave the terrace. But we can start moving in."

The white lids flew open, Caroline turned on an elbow, alarm in her hazel eyes. "Oh, no! Not yet!"

"What?" He was startled. He'd expected her to be delighted.

"Well, I don't . . . I'm not ready! I mean, there are so many things—" Her voice broke, she turned her head from his gaze and lay facedown. "Oh," her voice was muffled, "it's too soon!"

He was bewildered. Caroline had never been happy at Ashenden Manor. She'd told him as much. She'd had a wretched childhood. Yet now she didn't want to leave. Too soon? Why *too soon*? It puzzled him. And something in her voice. Almost as though she feared to leave Ashenden Manor.

"Well, no rush," he said comfortably. "They might as well finish the terrace first." And under his broad hands on Caroline's shoulder blades, he felt the rise of her breath in a relieved sigh and a relaxation of the sudden, surprising tension in her shoulders. He sighed. So, weeks longer, living with that cold-faced, scornful bastard, Dr. Ashenden. Looked down upon. Bad accent. Limerick slum boy. Easy to guess, too, that the eminent Ashenden had little use for a chiropractor.

But at least he'd succeeded on his own. Slaved and saved. Waiter, doorman, valet parking attendant, all the dirty work.

Ashenden, though, had had the silver spoon. Generations

of landed Anglo-Irish Ashendens before him. And he an only child, heir to the estate.

Enviable, too, Ashenden's looks. An early photo in the library downstairs showed him to be extraordinarily good-looking. A crisp wave in his thick, fair hair, dark eyes under strong brows. Now at seventy-six his crisp hair was gray, his eyebrows were gray-white. But his tall frame had hardly thickened—he still wore the same dinner jacket he'd worn in his twenties.

Mark Temple, five feet eight, thickly built, and with rusty hair, tightened his abdominal muscles. Dr. Ashenden was also admittedly in enviable physical shape. Even though he got to his Dublin office at seven o'clock each morning and operated two mornings a week, he rode every evening at six o'clock. There were two horses in the Ashenden Manor stable. The bay mare he'd given to Rowena on her twenty-first birthday and Thor, the steel-gray stallion, the one he himself rode.

Damn it! Rowena's strange violence in the meadow yesterday, Rowena on Thor. Unfair that Caroline should now have this frightening worry about Rowena.

"I'm getting a chill." Caroline sat up. Drooping water lily, too thin, stretch marks on her thighs, but lovely.

"I'll close the windows."

Closing them, he looked out. The sun was setting. At dusk, around six o'clock in this fall season, he often glimpsed Gerald Ashenden on the gray stallion, cantering or galloping along the bridle path, an upright, handsome figure in breeches, riding boots, and cowl-necked maroon jersey; he never wore a riding jacket despite rain or cold autumn weather. Enough to make one shiver and long for a pint by a blazing fire. But would Ashenden ride today at dusk with an injured shoulder? Very likely, the bastard. In an hour or so, with the sky turning violet and the woods darkening, he'd be cantering along the bridle path astride Thor.

"Sweetie," Caroline said, "my book. The Eavan Boland, I

left it downstairs in the library, on the writing desk, I think. Would you mind? I'm going to take a shower."

Mark nodded. "Right. Which book? What's it called?"

"*In a Time of Violence*. Poetry."

At half past four, Mark Temple picked up the book from the desk in the library. A slim volume. Why was poetry always called a "slim volume," he wondered. A "slim volume of poetry"?

He turned to leave — and collided with Dr. Ashenden just coming in. "Sorry! Sorry!" Christ! Ashenden had staggered back. Bandaged shoulder, face grotesque with damage . . . Deservedly — or not? Took a beating there in the meadow; he looked terrible, not just the physical damage, but something, some inner devastation had taken place. Mark felt a surge of pity. But Ashenden was looking at the book in his hand. "Caroline leaves her things about." Then, nastily, "Wasted your time marrying my daughter, Temple. I'm revising my will next week."

For a moment Mark gazed at his father-in-law. Then abruptly he strode past him, just managing not to strike him with the slim volume, *In a Time of Violence*.

10

I've rented the groundsman's cottage to Torrey Tunet," Winifred Moore said to Sheila Flaxton. They were on the sunny, wind-protected west terrace of Castle Moore. They'd arrived from London a half hour ago, and after a quick washup were having a reviving tea of liver pâté, rolls, sweet buns, sliced peaches, Stilton, and water crackers. In Winifred's case, this was preceded by a double vodka, zestfully downed.

"Torrey Tu*net*?" Sheila said, "Back again in Ballynagh? Id've thought she'd be shy of Ballynagh — what the villagers know about her. Embarrassed."

"Nonsense. Everybody has something shameful to hide about his past. At least it wasn't murder. Besides, people forget." Winifred rattled the ice in her glass. "Torrey will be all right. Just as long as she doesn't tread on Inspector O'Hare's toes."

Winifred Moore was fifty years old and big-boned, with little fat. Her face was square-jawed, her cheeks had a high russet color, like a stain. Her hair was reddish gray, and she wore it short and pushed behind her ears. There was a look of suppressed humor about her mouth and in her hazel eyes. She had on comfortable, large-sized corduroy jeans and a pullover.

"Another thing, Sheila," Winifred said. "Rowena Keegan. Rose says that this morning when she was doing the ironing,

Rowena Keegan showed up here. Moved in above the stables, the old trainers' quarters. Then Jennie O'Shea came at noon on a bike, bringing some of Rowena's clothes. She's welcome, of course — she knows that. What d'you make of it?"

"How can I *make* anything of it?" Sheila was always petulant after the trip from London. She hated travel. She was forty and had light blue guileless eyes in a somewhat squishy-looking, pasty face. She cut her own hair to save money; it was mixed blonde and gray and cut somewhat unevenly to above her ears and with a few artistically arranged bits of fringe on her forehead. She was the editor of London's well-known *Sisters in Poetry* magazine and both Winifred's friend and the publisher of Winifred's sometimes prize-winning poetry. She had on two sweaters and a woolen skirt, as she was thin and wispy and felt the cold more. "For a poet of your caliber, Winifred, I really — "

"Easy enough to find out," Winifred said, and grinned, showing strong white teeth. "Did you see Rose's face? Bursting with Ballynagh gossip, I know that look by now. But I'd prefer Rowena's version. We'll ask Rowena to dinner, ply her with booze, and the tale will out. Something significant is my guess." She glanced up as Rose, the round-faced maid, came out onto the terrace bearing a fresh pot of tea. "Here's our messenger now."

Rose having gone to the stables with the message, Sheila got up. "I'm going to wash my hair, it's so *dusty*. It feels absolutely un*clean*." She fingered her fringe. "And a bath and a nap before dinner."

"Do," Winifred said. Sheila loved a bath in one of Castle Moore's enormous marble bathtubs.

Alone, Winifred leaned luxuriously back and gazed over the fields and woods. Hers, inherited a year ago from her cousin, the late asinine Desmond Moore. No more scrimping, boiling the same tea leaves. No more depending on the few pounds from her poems in literary magazines. Castle Moore. Six hundred acres. Mountains and streams, glens and bogs, pastures and woods with bridle paths, one of which she could see now, north beyond the ancient stone wall that separated Castle Moore from the Ashenden estate: In the distance she could see the four great chimneys of Ashenden Manor itself.

It was turning chilly: The sun had become a flat, dull-gold disk in a lavender-tinged sky. Almost six o'clock. So in a few minutes Dr. Ashenden astride his stallion would go cantering as usual along the bridle path and around the stand of beeches, to disappear. An oddly dramatic sight: Dr. Ashenden rode as though he were casting a challenge to time and the elements. He'd named the stallion Thor. Thor, the god of thunder in Norse legends. Was there a romantic side to Ashenden? If so, it was well hidden.

"Ms. Winifred?" Rose was back, breathing hard from the stairs; she was getting plump, "Her things, Ms. Rowena's things. They're all there in the quarters above the stable. She left them on the bed. And I saw her just ten minutes ago—she was stabling Gravy Train. But now, she must have gone out."

Winifred looked again at her watch. A few minutes to six. Dinner would be about eight-thirty. She'd even have time for a bit of racewalking to stretch her jet-cramped muscles. "I'll write a note, Rose. You can take it over. Leave it under the door."

"Yes, Ma'am."

11

Wear something warm," Jasper O'Mara said.

Torrey looked up from the laptop on the card table in the corner. The late sun was slanting through the kitchen window and across the kitchen table and the dish cupboard. While she'd worked, hours had passed without her noticing.

Jasper was leaning against the sink, smiling at her. She'd been vaguely aware of his chopping herbs and then the mouthwatering smell of sauteeing onions, garlic, and tomatoes, and of lilting Irish music playing softly on the radio. There'd been the clink of a bottle against a glass and a cold beer set down beside her laptop. The glass was empty, so she must have drunk it. The kitchen table was already laid for their dinner.

She stretched, smiling at Jasper. He was wearing, heavy trousers, a black flannel shirt, and an oatmeal-colored sweater. It was time for their before-dinner walk. Almost six o'clock. Up over the hill, down into the woods, past the bridle path, and along the edge of the pond.

She closed the laptop and pulled off the bandanna she'd tied around her head, the good-luck bandanna she wore when she worked. It was turquoise with a motif of peacocks, so beautiful she'd caught her breath when her father, Vlad Tunet, had given it to her. Given it to her the afternoon of her eleventh birthday, the day he'd gone off for good, leaving her and her dressmaker mother alone, as though he'd never appeared at all in North Hawk, it was all a dream of her mother's. Except that there *she*, Torrey, was. Vlad Tunet. So loving, then gone. Tunet, "thunder," in Romanian.

Thunder . . . Thor. For a flashing instant she saw Rowena on the stallion galloping across the meadow.

"And wear this, it covers your ears." Jason took her knitted navy cap from the hook on the back of the door and tossed it to her.

"If you say so." Stallion. Thunder. It had surprised her that Jasper hadn't mentioned the excited village gossip about Rowena's attack on her grandfather. He knew she and Rowena were close friends. And he must've heard about Rowena being in the Ballynagh jail last night. He did, after all, occasionally drop in at O'Malley's pub. And he was living at Nolan's Bed-and-Breakfast above the needlework shop down the street from the Ballynagh police station.

Funny that Jasper wasn't living here in the cottage with her. They were lovers, after all. Six weeks ago she'd awakened one morning with a throbbing head and a rasping throat. The cottage was cold and she'd dressed quickly, shivering, and started a fire in the stove. It was drizzling outside, but she thought she'd better bicycle to the village and get some cold medications. She couldn't afford to waste time on being sick. Outside, she'd wheeled her bicycle past the little pond and through the hedge to the road. Then she just stood, weak and trembling, blankly reading the patent number on her bicycle over and over. "Anything wrong?" A bicycle on the road had skidded to a stop. "You all right?" A man's voice, warm and concerned. Torrey couldn't answer. She could feel perspiration breaking out on her face. Bile was rising in her throat. "I . . . ," she began and waved a weak, helpless hand, then turned away and threw up.

"That's answer enough." The man's resonant voice was sympathetic but held a hint of laughter. He'd helped her back to the cottage, got on the phone while she sat slumped on the old couch, and the next she knew she was looking up at the round face of Dr. Padraic Collins. The doctor turned her arm palm upward and at her inner elbow she felt the prick of a needle. She slept then and woke to the delicious smell of bacon and fresh-baked scones. The stranger was there, wearing her checked red apron and whistling under his breath. He made an omelet with a tang of Tabasco and a pot of hot coffee.

His name was Jasper O'Mara, he told her. He was a rare-book dealer on a bicycling trip, searching out old books in castles and village cottages. And unmarried. Stopping at bed-and-breakfasts along his planned route. He'd been bicycling toward Ballynagh on the access road when he'd seen Torrey standing on the road, "looking green around the gills." He was booked to stay at Nolan's Bed-and-Breakfast in Ballynagh.

Lovers. First friends, for all of three weeks, while Torrey slowly got well, her convalescence helped along by savory meats and delicately seasoned soups and poached eggs in aspic, dishes created by Jasper O'Mara. Then to Torrey's amazement, after an incredibly delicious dinner of a casserole of veal scallops with ham and cheese, they became lovers. *Am I doing this? Is it really me? Am I seduced by puff pastry and honey-roasted chicken? Ensnared by mouthwatering grilled salmon with fresh thyme? Suborned by gigot farci, rôti á la moutarde?* Alas, yes.

Besides, Jasper O'Mara could talk endlessly about the books she loved. He was also intrigued by her being a gifted interpreter and children's book writer. He was black-haired, white-skinned, and comfortably overweight by a good dozen pounds. He had a longish face and a narrow nose whose nostrils would twitch when he said something he thought was funny. A kind of silent laughter. He had arrived wearing tan jeans, serviceable boots, and a windbreaker over his shirt and sweater. He was traveling coast to coast, Dún Laoghaire to Clifden, with all the necessities of life, to his mind: a bicycle pack of underclothes, a razor, an extra woolen shirt, camera, thermos, brimmed canvas cap, sweater, a two-by-six-inch notebook, pencils, and the *Larousse Guide to Food*, unedited edition, weighing in at seven pounds.

To her surprise, Torrey found herself sporadically revealing bits of her past to Jasper O'Mara. It seemed to her that he was somehow "safe," that he would not judge her. So Jasper knew that she had once been a thief. He knew that her theft had resulted in a tragic death back in North Hawk. "Inspector O'Hare discovered it last year when he and I were on opposite sides in a murder case here in Ballynagh. The whole village knows of it now. But I bested O'Hare in the case. He'll never forgive me for that. And he'll always be suspicious of me. And determined to get even." She added, "Inspector O'Hare and I—we're two enemy beasts meeting in a forest."

But one thing she did not confide in Jasper O'Mara was Rowena's pregnancy and Rowena's wanting to abort the baby. Rowena's secrets, Torry felt, were not hers to confide.

Altogether tempting, this Jasper O'Mara, to whom she'd confided so much else. But of course not to live with. Torrey had learned earlier in life that, working, she had to live alone. No semiconnubial bliss for her. Not if she wanted, as in this case, to deliver a completed three-language kids' manuscript, ready for illustrations, to Spindling Press within the next three months. It was a deadline she couldn't afford to miss. Neither morally nor financially. She was thankful that the rent on this cottage that she paid to Winifred Moore of Castle Moore was so low.

"All set?"

"Yes." She zipped up her jacket and pulled the knitted cap snugly down over her ears.

12

J̲ust to the bridle path and back," Torrey said, shivering. "It's getting too cold. Damn! I should have worn my padded jacket." They were in the Ashenden woods, had been walking for fifteen minutes. The setting sun flickered like a scattering of diamonds; a small, brisk wind had sprung up.

"Right — Christ!" Jasper had abruptly stopped. "My wristwatch! I looked at it two minutes ago. Must have dropped it. You go ahead. Meet you at the bridle path marker." And he was gone, disappearing back through the woods.

Torrey walked on. Thankfully, the wind was lessening, but she was anyway glad of her muffler.

Five minutes later she reached the marker, a granite slab that marked the boundary between Ashenden Manor and Castle Moore. It was perhaps three feet from the bridle path. Torrey sat down on the slab and waited. The granite slab was cold as an ice cube and the sun was setting.

Ten minutes, fifteen minutes. Where are you, Jasper? She was getting hungry for dinner. She wasn't a Spartan. She'd walk back and meet him.

She got up and started back along the bridle path. At the cottage, they'd make a fire and have a hot rum, plunging the red-hot andiron into the mug to make the rum sizzle. Jasper had some sort of French stew, Provençal-inspired, with white beans, keeping warm on the stove. Stove in

Greek was *therma'stra*, she had once counted twenty-six *therm* prefixed words in her dictionary, all meaning heat in some way. After the stew, apple crisp, warm from the oven. And with the crisp—

Pound, pound, like a thudding in her heart. For a moment, again she had a déjà vu of the meadow, of Rowena's red hair and wild face. And there—

There, on the bridle path heading toward her, she saw the galloping stallion, and astride him, Dr. Ashenden, left shoulder bandaged and arm in a sling. She stumbled back and felt the wind of the passing of the plunging horse, saw his stretched neck, heard the creak of leather, the jingle of harness. Breathless, she turned and looked after horse and rider. And then—

A terrible, unforgettable sound as the horse screamed, then reared, and she saw the rider go flying back. Then the horse sank back on his haunches, wavered, slipped onto its side, stomach heaving, and lay still.

13

They stood about. It was not yet dark. Jasper was beside Torrey, hands in his pockets. A few feet away, Winifred Moore stood whistling softly between her teeth. Winifred had been taking a before-dinner racewalk on the bridle path. Like Torrey, she had witnessed the accident and made the call to Inspector O'Hare from the cell phone that was always nestled at her belt.

Rag doll, Torrey thought. Dr. Gerald Ashenden. Like a thrown-away rag doll in riding breeches and maroon jersey, the body that had been Dr. Gerald Ashenden lay on the stones and twigs beside the bridle path.

"Here they are," Sergeant Jimmy Bryson said. Across the field they could see the flashing blue and red lights of the ambulance. The attendants would have to come on foot with the gurney.

Twenty minutes later, when the sound of the departing ambulance grew faint and was gone, Winifred Moore said, "Who's to tell them at Ashenden Manor?" She wore a brimmed cap with a green emblem that read NATIONAL RACEWALKERS ASSOCIATION. No one answered. It was, anyway, a rhetorical question.

Inspector O'Hare, in his dark blue, circled the stallion, stumbling over twigs on the edge of the bridle path. Hard to take in: Dr. Ashenden dead, terrible, such an accident. The vicissitudes of horseback riding, one lived with it. And sometimes, like now, died of it. Inspector O'Hare gnawed his lip.

"Heart attack?" suggested Sergeant Bryson doubtfully, hands on his hips. "The horse, I mean." He blushed.

"Gogarty'll tell us," O'Hare said. The vet was coming straight from the Sheehens' barn where he'd been seeing to a newborn calf.

Torrey walked slowly toward the dead beast. His silvery gray coat shone. He looked immense and tragic. Torrey went closer. The stallion's head was stretched up as though in agony, his unseeing eye glared, his lips were drawn back in final terror. Torrey thought of Picasso's *Guernica*, the agonized horse, victim of men's battles. The stallion's silvery gray coat — something caught Torrey's eye. On the stallion's thigh, a tiny scar.

She leaned closer. No, not a scar. Something like a dark flaw on the silvery gray. She squinted. The dusk made it harder to see. But, no, it wasn't a flaw. Not a flaw. More like a tiny . . . puncture? And a spot of blood, red on the silvery gray. Blood.

Torrey straightened. She stood very still. She could not move away. The cold that she felt was not from the damp. The woods around the path seemed to darken. She suddenly thought of the grammar school pageant in North Hawk when she was ten, with two boys humming and two boys singing the remembered refrain, *When I was young I used to wait / On my master and give him his plate / And pass the bottle when he got dry / And brush away the blue-tail fly.*

"Torrey? What is it? You all right?" Jasper, beside her.

It was humming through her head, *One day he rode about the farm / The flies so numerous they did swarm / One chanced to bite him on the thigh —*

"Torrey?"

The devil take the blue-tail fly.

50

Yes, and the rest of it, the fourth graders in the pageant, the two boys singing, two humming. *The pony run, he jump, he pitch / He throw'd my master in the ditch / He died and the jury wondered why / The verdict was the blue-tail fly.*

"Torrey, you look so —"

But she was turning her head, looking around. The dry woods, crystal air, a wind moving the leaves of the bushes beside the bridle path; there could be no flies.

14

Ah, no!" Torrey whispered involuntarily, kneeling there by the dead stallion in the crisp, dry air. Somehow hoping that the blood spot might nevertheless be from an insect bite. Because otherwise . . . otherwise . . .

Low as her whisper was, Inspector O'Hare was instantly standing over her. "What's that you — ?" And then he was looking down past her shoulder at the spot of blood on the stallion's thigh. "Well!" he said softly, after a moment. "Well!"

Torrey stood up. Jasper came over and cupped his big hand on the back of her head. "You all right?" he asked again. She nodded, and he gave her a grin and for an instant pulled her head close to his chest.

Winifred Moore gave a yank to the brim of her race-walking cap and stepped nearer to the dead stallion. "Got something on the hob?" she said to Inspector O'Hare, looking curiously from him to Torrey. "You and Ms. Tunet?"

"Possibly, Ms. Moore." Inspector O'Hare glance glanced at Torrey and smiled at her in a way she hated, a shark's smile. "Very possibly, Ms. Moore."

They waited in the darkening woods for Liam Gogarty, the veterinarian, Torrey shivering with cold but stubbornly hanging on. Winifred Moore, alive with curiosity, Jasper whistling between his teeth. But by the time Sergeant Bryson on his cell phone learned from Liam Gogarty that the lamb's birthing at the Sheehens' had developed complications, it was full dark with a sliver of a moon. On Gogarty's instructions, the dead horse was to be covered with a tarp overnight. Gogarty would be there at seven in the morning.

On the way back to the cottage with Jasper, Torrey said determinedly, "So will *I* be." She hated what she knew O'Hare was thinking. *Rowena. This time Rowena had succeeded.*

15

It was the biggest pair of tweezers Torrey had ever seen. She stood watching Liam Gogarty probe the thigh of the dead horse. Gogarty was skinny, bespectacled, sure-handed. Last night it had rained; water dripped from the leaves of the trees along the bridle path. It was by now seven-thirty, and the sky was clearing. Torrey was conscious of Inspector O'Hare breathing heavily. He stood beside her, bulking large in his police uniform.

"This is an official investigation, Ms. Tunet," O'Hare had said irritably fifteen minutes ago when he'd arrived and seen her already there and chatting with Liam Gogarty who was pulling his nose and contemplating the dead horse.

"I know, Inspector," she'd answered, trying to keep a chip-on-her-shoulder tone out of her voice. "I'm taking an interest. My presence isn't illegal, I believe."

At that, a muscle in the inspector's jaw had jumped, a sign of his exasperation. Torrey in the past had seen that muscle jump more than once. Well, too bad, Inspector Egan O'Hare. Here I am again. A fly in your soup.

"Hello, hello, *hello!*" Winifred Moore came striding up. Amusement made her lips twitch at Inspector O'Hare half-suppressed moan at sight of her. "Had to know what strange thing did Dr. Ashenden's horse in. Might be a poem in it. That a *tweezers*, Liam Gogarty?"

"*Got* it! *Got* it!" Gogarty drew something from the horse's thigh and held it up in the tweezers. A small, narrow object.

Blood on it, but a dull shine. "Aluminum," Liam Gogarty said, turning the object slowly this way and that, looking at it curiously. "Huhh! Must've been cut off of one of a longer pair. This piece is maybe an inch and a half. About."

Mystified, Torrey gazed at the narrow object.

"Longer pair of *what*?" Inspector O'Hare, impatient, squinted at the object.

"Longer pair of knitting needles," Liam Gogarty said.

For a minute they were all silent. The veterinarian, still kneeling, rummaged in his bag and found a plastic envelope. He dropped the piece of knitting needle into it. He stood up and handed the bag to Inspector O'Hare. "Your bailiwick, Inspector." He took off his glasses and wiped raindrops from them. "Got to get to Donovan's. A calf." He put his glasses back on and looked at Torrey. "As I was saying before, Ms. Tunet, seen you about with Rowena Keegan. Helping her at the animal center. Her giving shots and all." He looked down at the dead horse, than back at Torrey. "Understand you spotted it?" She nodded. "Hadn't been for you, then, I'd've thought the horse had died of a heart attack. Saw that kind of death more than once. Including last year at the Kerry Gold. The winning horse, Daisy Belle, a minute after her victory, jockey still astride, dropped dead. Embolism."

"Thank you." She wanted to cry. She'd been hoping desperately that by some kind of miracle a real insect had stung the stallion, all right, *not* a blue-tail fly, but there were other insects in these woods, weren't there? She stiffened her jaw, aware suddenly that Inspector O'Hare was looking at her.

"Well, *now* we're getting somewhere," Inspector O'Hare said. He was holding the plastic envelope with the knitting needle and smiling at her, a smile that chilled her.

"I'm off," Liam Gogarty said. "Nice to've met you, Ms. Tunet. Fascinating this police work, isn't it? A knitting needle! Somewhere out there a murderer!"

"Yes, fascinating." Somewhere out there.

16

At half past eight, in the Ballynagh police station, O'Hare picked up the phone and called the Murder Squad at Dublin Castle, Phoenix Park. Five minutes later he hung up. The van with the Garda Siochana technical staff and their equipment would arrive from Dublin within the hour. The murder scene.

O'Hare stretched. Getting somewhere. Finally. He smiled. Something to tell his wife tonight. Noreen had been complaining about such poor mysteries on television lately. Noreen liked a good mystery. Well, here's one for you, my lass. And an odd one indeed. Ashenden dead. And the irony of it. Brought down the temple on his own head, trying to protect his granddaughter. O'Hare frowned, puzzled. Something Dr. Ashenden hadn't wanted to come out.

Peculiar. Something altogether odd about the Ashenden family. He'd always sensed it. But difficult to make out. One thing he could swear to, in any event: Dr. Ashenden's death was a family affair.

"Morning, Sir." Sergeant Bryson. Fresh-scrubbed, shiny face, wet hair still showing signs of the comb.

O'Hare said, "Feed Nelson, Jimmy. Then you're coming with me." In the woods around the bridle path, the technical squad from Dublin would inch over the ground covered with clotted, dank leaves after last night's rain. They'd take photographs, they'd find something. A strand of red hair that had caught on a branch? Or, say, the print of a narrow boot, fitted, in the end, like Cinderella's slipper, to Ms. Rowena Keegan's foot?

17

Inspector?" The shorter garda, Daly his name was, came up, red-faced from having climbed up to the bridle path from the gully. "Here's something. Notebook. Wet from the dew, overnight." The notebook was already encased in a clear plastic bag that Daly had zipped closed. "Found down in the gully. Have a look."

Torrey quickly stepped to O'Hare's side. She saw through the plastic the smeared, inked words on the cover: *Horse diseases. Notebook #2.* and under it: *Rowena Keegan.* Her mouth went dry.

"Take your time, Ms. Tunet, take a good look," Inspector O'Hare said sarcastically. What the *hell* was she doing here? Always on his heels! He handed the notebook back to Daly who would take it to the crime laboratory in Dublin. The technical crew from the Garda Siochana was already packing up, getting into the van. They were done with searching the murder site and surrounding woods. They'd been here an hour. They'd found no footprints, no abandoned weapon, nothing—except, down in the gully, this notebook, an empty half-pint bottle of Bushnell's, and some long-rotted prophylactics.

Inspector O'Hare gave a half salute to the departing van with its crew and, with a final triumphant look at Torrey, strode off through the woods.

18

At two o'clock, a fax of the notebook, clearly dirty and water-stained, lay on Inspector O'Hare's desk.

Rowena Keegan stood beside the desk. She had refused to sit down. She wore a white turtleneck jersey, a big, heavy brown cableknit sweater, and an old pair of stained jodhpurs. Her curly red hair was pushed carelessly behind her ears. She held a can of diet Coke from the Coke machine beside the door. Inspector O'Hare was irritated that Nelson was nudging Rowena's leg, his tail wagging.

"No, I don't know how my notebook came to be in the gully," Rowena said. "I can't imagine. Unless someone—" and she hesitated and looked off into space. "It could have been taken from . . . from . . ." She shrugged and took a sip of Coke.

It was obvious to Inspector O'Hare: Rowena Keegan was suggesting that someone had been setting her up for the murder of her grandfather. O'Hare slanted a glance toward Sergeant Bryson. Bryson was standing nearby rocking back and forth from one foot to the other. Exasperating. Would he never grow up?

And could Ms. Keegan remember where she was at the time of her grandfather's murder? O'Hare tried to keep sarcasm out of his voice.

"I was walking about." Walking about? Walking about,

exactly where? "Oh . . . through the fields, the woods, near Castle Moore."

Evasive, a lie. The lie rang like a gong, the way Rowena Keegan's green-eyed glance slid away, the flush that rose and stained her pale face, cheeks to brow. Trickles of perspiration slid down from her temples, darkening the red hair that framed her face. So familiar to him; he'd seen her grow up. Only—he blinked, as though to clear his vision—only wasn't there something a bit different about her? More . . . solid? A creamy softness, a richness. Puzzling. Reminded him somehow of his wife. Not that Noreen looked at all like Rowena Keegan.

In any case, a liar. She'd been in the gully and dropped her notebook. But not enough evidence to arrest her for murder. O'Hare's jaw was beginning to ache. He'd been gritting his teeth again.

Leaving the police station Rowena Keegan put the can of soda on top of the machine. "I only drank half," she told Sergeant Bryson. "It's diet, no sugar in it. That's okay for Nelson's teeth. In case he'd like the other half."

19

"*Gully,*" Torrey said to Jasper. They were in the kitchen at the cottage. "Short for 'gully knife' in English dialect. As in, 'He cut the bastard with a gully.' "

Jasper didn't answer. His back was to her. He was putting prunes and apricots around the pork roast that would go into the oven for tonight's dinner.

"Just *why* Rowena's notebook was found there, what about this?" Torrey hesitated. Was she telling Jasper too much?

"What about what?" Jasper shook out a skimpy handful of brown sugar and sprinkled it into the roasting pan.

"Well, *suppose* someone put Rowena's notebook there, setting her up. Or she was in the gully to meet someone and doesn't want to say who." The gully. That hidden pocket in the woods. The thought was irresistible: Rowena, the pregnant Rowena, meeting her . . . lover? Because, *Where did you come from / Baby dear?* A lover. Alive and somewhere out there. If only it were so.

But she was revealing too much. She slanted a glance toward Jasper. He was sliding the pork roast into the oven.

"That's the last of the cloves." Jasper's head was turned away, his voice muffled. "What? Oh, sure. A possibility." He closed the oven door, straightened, and set the timer for the roast.

20

At eight o'clock Wednesday morning, Padraic Collins, his nose red from an unexpected morning chill, parked his old Honda in the drive at Ashenden Manor. He found Caroline pacing the vegetable garden, wearing a moldy old chinchilla coat. She was frowning in apparent intense concentration.

"I was passing," Padraic said. "I'm on my way to O'Doyle's. Touch of flu, the O'Doyle kids. Thought I'd stop by, see if there's anything I could—"

"The *will*, Padraic," Caroline said. "My father's will. I distinctly remember him saying to me—it must've been two years ago?—he'd just come from his lawyers, Wickham and Slocum, in Dublin. 'I've made a new will,' he told me. 'Had to make a change.' He looked so... is there an expression 'quiet rage,' Padraic?"

"Dryden? Something about swelling the soul to quiet rage?"

"Hmmm? So anyway, now I've no idea who's inheriting what. I know I was to've gotten the Ashenden Manor estate. I hope so. Mark seems so... so *enchanted* by it. But it's Scott. Scott has so little income of his own, just those bits of royalties of his father's. And his crippled leg..."

Padraic said, "What about Kildare? Your father once mentioned some Ashenden property in Kildare. Three hundred acres, a Georgian house, stables, good grazing land, a—

what's the matter, Caroline?" She had gone quite pale. Padraic felt a rush of concern.

"I haven't had breakfast." Caroline drew her coat closer. "I wanted some air, first. Yes, Kildare. Supposed to go to Rowena. It was promised . . ." Her voice faltered. "But as for Scott . . ." She shook her head, her hazel eyes anxious. "I'll call Wickham and Slocum and arrange for the reading of the will this week, definitely."

Puzzled. Padraic frowned. Caroline out here in the cold, distracted, worried, hadn't even had breakfast. She wasn't strong enough for such nonsense. He remembered the frail little thing she'd been. The nurse fed her with an eyedropper, like a baby squirrel. It was no wonder Gerald refused to have more children. A pity for Kathleen, Catholic and anyway hungry for babies. But Gerald was a rock. "Look at that child!" he'd grumbled angrily to Padraic when Caroline was an aching, whining two-year-old. "Does Kathleen want another one like that?"

So, only the one child. Caroline. Thin-bodied, big-eyed, this fragile, frightened child, Caroline. But an unexpected spirit had suddenly surfaced in her. She couldn't have been more than ten or twelve when she'd abruptly cocked a snoot at her father. And a couple of years later, when she was barely fifteen, she audaciously went her own way, an adventurous way, as it turned out: Dublin, London, Rome. A bit part in an Italian film, some cross-legged, meditating nonsense in India, then Dublin again, and finally marrying that guitar-playing Irish rock star, Tom Keegan. A Catholic! Ashenden had tried to pay the fellow off. No good. To Tom Keegan, Caroline Ashenden, with her hazel eyes and her long, straight, fair hair, was the heartbreaker of the world. Without her, Tom would have no world, only ashes. He made that plain.

Padraic said, "I'd better get on to the O'Doyles. And *you'd* better have Jennie O'Shea make you a solid breakfast. Fruit, eggs, scones, tea."

Caroline suddenly leaned forward and kissed him. "I'll walk you out to the drive."

It was cold and windy, but the sun was strong. Padraic Collins had a skin so fair that five minutes in the sun turned his face bright red. Overnight, the redness faded, only to surge up again at the next day's sun. He was never without the protection of that old tweed cap that had belonged to his father. He drove off in his dusty Honda, turning his head and waving back. He was an abominable driver; Caroline closed her eyes so as not to see, should he go into the hedge. It had happened twice before. A few seconds later, when she opened her eyes, he was already out of sight, fair-skinned Padraic in his father's old tweed cap.

Tweed cap. She stood there on the stone steps. The world quaked. Rain-wet, that old tweed cap. It was just before her supper. It was raining, and she was seven years old, standing at a window, frightened. Rain spattered on the window, a sudden, end-of-April storm, the weather turned wild. Her mother was somewhere out there. Where? Blasts of rain against the windowpane. She knew where her mother had gone. But now her mother could be coming home. She saw her on the road, soaked with rain, blinded by the rain, *staggering on the access road*, falling, falling down, a truck coming, headlights, blinding rain, or a car, something would come and run over her. Get the big umbrella, hurry, *hurry*! She ran.

O'Malley's pub. Someone sloshing out — "Christ Almighty! A kid, in this rain!" — and going off, hawking, spitting. A car stopping, a familiar car, "Get in the car, Caroline!" Padraic Collins, in his wet tweed cap, hurrying into the pub, coming out, pulling her mother along, ducking and splashing through the rain. The car starting up the street, she in the backseat, so safe the sound of the windshield made her feel. There was a smelly dog blanket; it comforted her, somehow. In the front seat, Padraic Collins and her mother, her mother's black hair soaked so that Caroline could see the white tips of her ears. Padraic's voice saying, "It must break Gerald's heart, Kathleen, that you're in the pub, always the pub. Don't keep on, Kathleen! For his sake! Ah, don't!" But her mother didn't answer. In the backseat, nestled in the dog blanket, Caroline arrived slowly at a thought: *Something wrong.* There was something wrong that Padraic Collins didn't know about her parents. She knew it. But what it was, was a mystery to her.

21

Torrey watched from the edge of the woods. It was ten in the morning. She could see, on the hill, the group of strangers and the Ashenden family and Dr. Collins within the iron-railed Ashenden cemetery. The ceremony was short: Caroline Temple turned over the first shovelful of earth; then Scott; lastly, Rowena. The square black box with the ashes of Dr. Gerald Ashenden was lowered into the earth. Now the —

A rustle in the woods to Torrey's left. She glanced around. Nobody. Beyond was the stretch of woods and fields to the bridle path, nothing there but more woods and a gypsy wagon she'd glimpsed earlier. Or maybe it was a tinkers' wagon; they moved about, "travelers" they were sometime called. Unattached to land, they roved about, footloose as her Romanian father who'd departed North Hawk when she was barely eleven.

Rustle. Only the breeze. She looked at her watch. It was getting on to ten-thirty. Rowena had phoned this morning, sounding worried. "Torrey? Can you meet me at the Castle stables around half past eleven?"

Torrey got off her bicycle in the stable yard at Castle Moore. Eleven-thirty. Smell of horse, smell of fresh hay. She could hear a stamp of hooves in a stall. Rowena would have watered and exercised the two horses. Cutting it close. Where was she? Maybe showering in the room above the stable.

Torrey sat down on a bale of hay beside the stable door. She looked up at the window of the room above the stable. Was Rowena up there? And what did she want? She'd sounded so anxious. Unnerved.

Five minutes. Ten minutes. Cool breeze, pungent smell of sun-warmed hay. Waiting, Torrey pulled a straw from the bale and nibbled it. She thought of Rowena standing in the groundsman's cottage barely a week ago, face pale, green eyes desperate. So short a time ago. It was now only two and a half weeks before an abortion would be dangerous.

"Hello, there!"

Winifred Moore, denim-clad, looking like a robust farmer ready to do morning chores. "Looking for Rowena?"

"Hello. Yes, we're supposed to meet here about now."

"Ah," Winifred said, "she's gone. Been a change of plans, I guess. Gone off with her brother, Scott. He picked her up in that little red car of his—a Miata?—silly little bug, holds only two people. Romantic, I suppose, *if* one's life is open to romance. Which is why I have a Jeep."

"Oh? I'll get on then to Ashenden Manor. Find her there." She got up from the bale of hay.

" 'Fraid not. They were off to Dublin."

Torrey bicycled slowly back to the access road. Rowena not even leaving a message for her! And going off with Scott on a day's jaunt to Dublin.

No. Rowena wouldn't do that. Scott must have phoned her at the stables, then had come and picked her up. Or at that ceremony on the hill, had he, then — No use to suppose. Anyway, Scott was taking Rowena to Dublin.

Why? What purpose?

The bike wobbled. Did Scott know that Rowena was pregnant? His transparent looking, gray-blue eyes were sharp as was his mind; she'd met him enough to know that.

He was in Dublin a lot, parties, clubs, he got about, knew people both savory and unsavory. If ever Scott needed to know something, whatever, it needed only a whisper here, a few pounds there —

No. Torrey stopped the bike. She stood on the road, a foot planted on each side of the bike. An appointment. For when? And it would be done in a room down some wretched side street. An illegal abortion. Risky. Occasionally a girl's or woman's body washed up in the Liffey. But it wasn't possible for Rowena to get to Europe for a legal abortion. Not while the eye of the Gardai was on her.

22

W ell, well!" Scott Keegan, alone in the library at Ashenden Manor, raised his eyebrows. He was standing over his grandfather's desk looking down at a blue document that lay on the desk, folded in thirds: *Last Will and Testament of Gerald Ashenden*. He picked it up.

"Here you are!" His mother, in the doorway. She came in. She was carrying a measuring tape and some sort of brochure. "Scott! I've been wanting to measure you for a vest, this new pattern. A bargello, not that easy to knit. But stunning." She unwound the tape. "Where've you been all morning? It's two o'clock!"

"Dublin. Doing this and that. At which I'm expert." With Rowena, down narrow, squalid streets.

"Stand still." His mother came close, holding the tape, surveying his waist. Her cardigan did not conceal how slight she was, her bony shoulders. Yet fair of face, and with an odd quirky humor to spare. Lucky Tom Keegan, lucky Mark Temple. She looked at the blue document. "What's that you've got?"

"This? Your pa's will." He waved the document at her. "I was just—hey! You all right, Ma?"

"Yes, nothing's the—" But she had gone quite pale. "That will, it's dated when?"

He looked at the document. "Two years ago."

"Oh." She was gazing at the blue document as though it were a cobra or possibly a tarantula. "I called Wickham and Slocum. I thought it was time we had a reading. They said any time this week would be fine."

"Sure, Ma. But we don't have to wait for lawyers' offices, all the heirs sitting around, smug smiles from the lucky inheritors, cries of indignation and outrage from the deprived. We can read it now." He began to unfold the blue document.

"Is that *legal*, Scott? I thought wills were read in lawyers' offices."

"Who says so? I'll read this now, Ma. Then let's see if we can rustle up all the mentioned lucky and unlucky." His leg was aching; the brace felt like an iron weight. Dublin with Rowena had been exhausting.

"Well, then, I guess it's all right."

23

Upstairs in her bedroom, Rowena slung the black nylon carrying case onto the bed. No need now to live above the stable at Castle Moore. From the doorway, a footfall. Torrey came in. "They said you were back."

"Yes." Rowena zipped open the bag. "The reason I phoned you this morning, I was getting frantic, and you lead such a cosmopolitan life, you *know* things, maybe even, uh, places. Anyway, it's all right now. Sorry not to've left a note for you at Castle Moore. Scott turned up at the stable in his Miata and he had the motor running, and he'd thought—"

"An abortionist, right, Rowena?" She sat down on the window seat and stuck her jean-clad legs out in front of her and crossed her ankles. Smell of pine cleaner in the room; Jennie O'Shea must have had a go at the furniture. She looked soberly at Rowena, who stopped taking clothes from the black bag and turned to face her.

Rowena's gaze met hers. "Yes. But then, Scott knew somebody who had a friend who . . . Anyway, Scott got an address and we went there, a place off the Finglas Road, back of the Glasnevin Cemetery. I made an appointment. He's supposed to be good. Safe. Anyway, Scott's friend said that—"

"Safe?" Torrey, imagining globs of blood on a not-too-clean floor, made a skeptical face. "When?"

"He's . . . busy. But he can do it the twenty-second."

This was what? The fourteenth? Eight days from now. Any later — frightening.

Rowena abruptly raised her hands and pressed them hard against her cheeks. After a moment she dropped her hands, leaving white welts on her cheek. She drew a deep, determined breath. "Two o'clock. In Glasnevin. Scott will take me. Then he'll wait."

24

At seven o'clock, a blue dusk, striated orange fading over the mountains, smell of wood fires in Ballynagh fireplaces. At the cottage, Jasper said, "Ruination!" and at the stove wiped a drop of gravy from the cover of his new *Cooking with Herbs* cookbook.

Just coming in, Torrey said, "Hmmm?" It was cozy inside, and she pulled off her sweater and walked about. "What's this?" She lifted a cover from the iron pot on the stove. Awful-looking stuff, smelling heavenly. She stood absentmindedly holding the cover, thinking: *Scott.*

Scott. How long ago had Scott found out that Rowena was pregnant? Had Rowena told him? And was Scott helping Rowena with this illegal abortion only because he was her brother? Scott was a dark card.

Torrey frowned, then shivered involuntarily. *Whisper.* That scandal sheet in Dublin. There had been innuendos in yesterday's *Whisper*, salacious hints about Rowena, since a little girl the darling of her grandfather. The sexually used darling? And now, finally, an explosion of rage culminating in the murder of Dr. Ashenden. Hints in the gossip column. Nothing outright, but —

"That ladle on your right, hand it to me, will you. Torrey? Torrey! Wake up!"

"Oh, here."

Salacious *Whisper*. Speculation. The sort of rumor that, burgeoning, had led to the conviction of many an innocent in a case of murder.

"If I snap my fingers, will you come out of it and be with *me*?" Jasper said loudly. "And rule one: Never lift a cover from another cook's pot without asking."

No, of course not. It was Rowena's pot. Her secrets were her secrets. Pregnant Rowena. Pregnant by whom?

And worse—

"Move over, my pretty. I want to warm the plates in the oven."

Worse, Inspector O'Hare must be hearing and reading the speculations. O'Hare was no fool. Behind the scenes he was industriously building a murder case against Rowena. Incest. O'Hare would seize on it. Revenge. *Whisper* had mentioned a case of a forty-year-old woman in Longford who'd axed her stepfather for using her thirty years earlier.

But Dr. Gerald Ashenden's killer could have had any of a number of possible motives, right? There was murder because of psychotic imaginings. And murder out of jealousy. Hate. Lust. And the most common of all: murder for money. Money.

Torrey paused her pacing. Money. She was seeing Jennie O'Shea coming into Rowena's room just as Torrey was leaving. "A meeting in the library before dinner, Ms. Rowena. No, Ms. Rowena, I don't know, Mr. Scott didn't say. But he called Dr. Collins to come over. Something about a will, Dr. Ashenden's will. I was coming from the pantry."

"Chervil," Jasper said. "Smell this." He was holding something green and pungent under Torrey's nose.

"Very like . . . parsley? The Italian kind?" She smiled unseeingly at Jasper. Under the circumstances, Dr. Ashenden's will would be very interesting.

25

It was chilly and damp in the stable at Castle Moore, making the smell of hay and horse more pungent. It was ten in the morning. In Fast Forward's stall, Torrey watched as Rowena pulled the hackle again and again through the horse's tail, ridding it of bits of straw and loose hairs. Rowena looked tired. Twice, she'd stopped to rest her arm and just stood, blowing out a breath. Her face was strained. The red curls that fell across her forehead were wet with sweat, and sweat glistened on her neck. Yet it was cold enough in the stall for the horse, snorting now and again, to breathe out a white vapor. And Rowena was wearing only jeans and an old blue shirt.

"What I meant was," Torrey said, "if your grandfather left a will, it might indicate something. Or somebody that —"

"I know what you meant," Rowena said tiredly. Her hand holding the hackle stopped. Her green eyes were bloodshot. "Look in my jacket on that nail. Left-hand pocket. We all met in the library for a reading. Scott had made copies of the will for each of us, like some kind of festivity, with him handing out party favors."

Torrey took the document from the jacket pocket and unfolded it. Only two pages. She read it carefully: To Caroline Keegan, Ashenden Manor and all the Ashenden estate with the exception of the Ashenden property in Kildare. To

Rowena, the Kildare property of four hundred acres with its Georgian house and stables. To Padraic Collins, the prized, carved ivory Chinese chess set. Ten thousand pounds to a Dublin hospital foundation for research in thoracic surgery. Small keepsakes to four former medical associates, one now in Montreal, another in Galway, one in Copenhagen, one in Edinburgh. And lastly, "to my grandson, Scott Keegan, ten pence."

Torrey looked up. Rowena, head bent, was cleaning horsehairs from the hackle with a kitchen fork.

"I'm rich now." Rowena sounded exhausted.

"Yes, I see."

Rowena said, "I've always had only an allowance. And my vet schooling at Dublin University paid for by my grandfather. Now, because of this inheritance, Inspector O'Hare'll have more reason to think I did my grandfather in. Money, money, money! O'Hare'll figure that I couldn't wait. Grist for O'Hare's mill. Planning to grind me exceeding small."

"Hmmm?" But Torrey was thinking of something else. "What did your grandfather have against Scott? It's so cruel leaving him ten pence."

No answer. Torrey looked up. Rowena was standing with her forehead resting against Fast Forward's flank, her hand with the hackle hanging down. She was crying.

"What?" Torrey asked. *"What,* Rowena?"

A shake of Rowena's head, then a broken, indrawn breath. "Oh, *God*! It goes back and back and *back*!"

"What? Back to what? *What* goes back? Rowena? What are you talking about?"

No answer.

26

On the west lawn, in the chilly midmorning, Caroline walked around the big oval of rhododendrons, her nose buried in the collar of her motheaten chinchilla coat. The coat had been in the Ashenden Manor attic for more generations than anyone could remember. It smelled faintly of perfume and mice. It had always been Caroline's comfort in times of stress. In childhood, in the late afternoon, when she worried about her mother who was off at the pub in Ballynagh, she would climb to the fourth floor and take the old chinchilla from the closet and wrap it around herself and huddle on the floor. Sometimes she would fall asleep in the soft fur and awaken with a stiff neck and then a growing feeling of panic that her mother might not have come back, might never come back.

She stopped walking as Mark came toward her. He was on his way to get his car from the stable garage. He'd be late getting to his office in Dublin, but they'd been up talking half the night, lying there in the great oak bed in the bedroom that had once belonged to Caroline's great-grandfather, oil portraits of earlier Ashendens on the walls and above the fireplace.

"My father murdered!" Caroline had said. "The killer could've been the husband or wife of one of my father's patients! A thoracic operation gone wrong and the patient dying. And a wife or lover or husband blaming my father! People do get crazy." She told Mark that yesterday she'd gone to Inspector O'Hare, and O'Hare had agreed that it was definitely a possibility to be explored.

"Yes," Mark had said, "worth investigating. Definitely."

They'd talked then about her father's will, Caroline's inheritance of Ashenden Manor and now her unexpected estate responsibilities. It changed things. "Maybe we should give up our plans for the house in Ballsbridge," Mark had said, "and live at Ashenden Manor." As for Scott—

In Mark's arms she'd felt a surge of bitterness toward her dead father and love and loyalty to Scott. "Poor Scott!"

"Oh, I expect Scott will be all right without a bequest," Mark had said comfortingly. "He seems to be in funds."

At that, Caroline had gone quiet. Mark, too, seemed to have no more to say. He turned out the light and took Caroline in his arms.

Now on the west lawn, in the old chinchilla coat, Caroline said, "Mark, you look like an angel in that striped tie. Here's Scott." Scott was coming out through the terrace. He wore a long, black soft leather coat. A wide-banded watch glittered on one wrist. He was carrying something under his arm, hitching along; grass was difficult for him. He reached the rhododendrons. "Morning, Ma. And"—he raised his brows at Mark—"and Pa."

"What's *that*?" Caroline asked. It was a shagreen box, old looking, the edges worn.

"Delivery. The Chinese chess set. I'm taking it to Padraic Collins. His booty, right?"

Caroline said, "Scott, have you had breakfast? You look so, so peaked. You don't eat enough."

Scott smiled at her. "Who, me? I'm omnivorous. Ma, I'm leaving it to you to gather up the trinkets, those little bequests that the good Dr. Ashenden left to his former medical colleagues. Cuff links, tiepin, and so on." He gave his mother and Mark a half salute, emerald on a ring finger. "I'm off to Dublin."

"Scott? A minute."

He halted. "Yes, Ma?"

But she couldn't say it: *My father, that bastard, how could he have? Leaving you nothing. Nothing.* She said, "At least have a decent lunch in Dublin. Fish is full of something awfully good."

"Yes, Ma."

The watch, or it might be a bracelet, glittered as he went hitching off across the grass.

27

Sergeant Bryson looked more closely at the inside of the pot. It was aluminum and supposed to be new. But the inside looked stained, as though tea or the like had been boiled in it more than a few times. Two pounds six, he'd paid. The gypsy had said it was new. Spangled earrings, flashing white teeth, neck needed washing.

The police station door opened, then closed with its definite click. "Afternoon, Sergeant. What's that?"

At Inspector O'Hare's tone, Byron knew the inspector was on the sharp. "Afternoon, Inspector. A pot. It's a pot. For cooking. I bought it. Two pounds six. Aluminum. So I guess that's cheap."

"It might be, if it has a purpose."

Inspector O'Hare leaned down and patted Nelson who was lying over near the Coke machine, nosing his old rag doll, relic of his puppyhood; Nelson looked up and wagged his tail.

"I thought maybe if we'd want to boil an egg?"

"Two pounds six? It's got a dent."

"Oh . . . Oh, yes. I didn't at first see. . . ." Sergeant Bryson fingered the dent.

"That wooden handle'll burn in no time, Bryson. Two pounds six of Gardai money out the window."

"I paid her for it personally, Inspector, not through the office. My own money."

"Paid whom personally? Got plucked by whom? A pot with a dent!"

"The gypsy. Same one as last year, the Romanian. She's got a caravan and a pony in the woods by those old oaks at Castle Moore. Not one of the tinkers, but same as them."

Inspector O'Hare was already at his desk, picking up his phone, his face concentrated. His color was high, and his eyes had that squinty look as though he were looking into the sun, Inspector O'Hare was definitely on the scent. "Inspector O'Hare," he said into the phone when he reached his party. "Six days since the murder. About time! Right. Wickham and Slocum?" Inspector O'Hare was making notes on his yellow pad. "Who? Definitely. I'll expect the fax."

Bryson looked enviously at O'Hare's cherry-red cheeks and fox-gleaming eyes. Someday, he too, Sergeant Bryson, would be heading a murder investigation. Not like his usual day, this morning's piddling troubles and grievances: the Blodgetts' fence, the Walshes' straying chickens, the Nolans' kitchen garden despoiled by the Hickey twins, those little bastards.

O'Hare said, "Dr. Ashenden's will, Jimmy. Always a revelation, a murdered person's will. Wills and insurance policies account for ninety percent of family murders."

"Ninety percent, Inspector!"

"Or similar figures, Jimmy. And believe me, Dr. Ashenden's murder is strictly family."

28

At Collins Court, Padraic Collins carefully replaced each ivory chessman in the faded leather box. He was in his favorite worn old suede chair at the gateleg table in the drawing room. He breathed in the sandalwood smell of the lining of the shagreen box. How many evenings in the library at Ashenden Manor, sitting opposite Gerald Ashenden, had he moved those exquisite chess pieces: that queen, that king, that knight, that pawn? And now, to his surprise, Gerald had left the set to him.

He closed the box. Peaceful evenings through the years, soft light from the bronze-based old Tiffany lamps. Afterward, cigars and a finger of Hennessey. It had never occurred to him that Gerald would die before him. Gerald was in such splendid shape. He kept himself fit, young, *passionately* young, you might say. Handsome and vigorous, with his crisp hair still thick, though gray.

"Not like me!" He himself, so pear-shaped and pudgy. His own fault! Self-indulgent, knowing better, but unable to resist the pleasures of the table. Why *not* indulge himself, he would think mutinously, the juices running in his mouth at sight of the crackling skin of the roast duck, the baby lamb chops with the charred delicious fat and the meat barely pink. And what of the veritable basin of trifle that sagged beneath its burden of thick cream and strawberries? Why not baby himself, what with his asthma, slight though it was, and his tendency to catch cold in the smallest draft? Hard-bodied Gerald, and pudgy Padraic. He'd never been jealous of Gerald on that account, never resented it. Through the years, the closest of friends.

But sex was private. They never exchanged sexual confidences. His secret shame, each time he gave in to his torment and got in the Honda and drove fast to Cork, sometimes with the fire burning so inside him that it was like a blast furnace, and him half choking with his need. He'd had to go. Ah, he *had* to! But never revealed.

Nor did Ashenden ever confide a sexual relationship to him. Neither through the years had there been rumors of illicit love affairs in Ashenden's social life in Dublin. Ashenden preferred an active life at Ashenden Manor: schooling his horses, teaching Rowena to ride and to swim and taking her hiking through the mountains of western Wicklow. No young girl ever had such a solicitous grandfather. Padraic suddenly covered his face with his hands and moved his head from side to side.

A deep breath finally steadied him. He'd better get going. He had a full schedule; the damp weather was affecting more children than usual, and they needed seeing to. This evening after dinner he'd set up the chessmen, get out his chess books and study a few moves.

"Doctor?" Helen Lavery was in the study doorway, an anxious frown creasing her brow. "Doctor, she's hanging about again. The gypsy. Near the hedge, this side of the gates. Makes me nervous."

"Oh? Back again is she?" Padraic gave Helen a reassuring smile. "Don't worry. Gypsies! Known to be full of lies, as well as thievery. Persistent, yes. But not dangerous. Don't fret that she's dangerous." He looked at his watch. "I'm going now. I've got to look in on the Robbins boy. I'll send her away."

In the old Honda, he rattled down the drive. Nearing the

hedge, he saw the woman and stopped the car. Mass of dark hair to her shoulders, half a dozen rings on her dirty fingers, teeth flashing. "Go away!" he called out, trying to sound fierce, "Go away!"

In the evening, the weather turned wild. Branches of trees thrashed about in gusts of wind; young maples bent level with the ground. Sergeant Bryson, starting for home, stood a moment outside the police station. His rubber raincoat whipped about his legs. Farther down the street, Nolan's Bed-and-Breakfast sign swung, creaking; shop windows rattled. Bryson knew that loose stones from the old bridge at the end of Butler Street would go clattering down into the stream. In the woods, foxes, squirrels, rabbits would be hiding in old fallen oaks; on the mountainsides, sheep would be huddled and border collies would be alert for orders. And now here came the rain, smacking Bryson in the face. "Ooooff!" He shook his head, and drops of rain trickled down his nose. The rain would be sweeping in sheets down the village streets, on the hills, and across the broad lawns of Castle Moore, of Collins Court, and of Ashenden Manor. At dinner tables, the lights would flicker and go out, then go on again, then out . . . and on.

In the dining room at Ashenden Manor, the lights flickered for the third time.

"Where the devil are some matches?" Scott put down his soup spoon. "Candles, but no matches. Oh, sweet Jesus! Since everybody stopped smoking, you can't find a match. Not even, as the butler said about cucumbers in that Oscar Wilde play, 'Not even for ready money.' "

Rowena laughed. Mark Temple grinned and took a folder of matches, from his pocket. Caroline watched him, smiling as he lit the flat, little brass round of candles on the table. It was funny, in a way, how Mark had been champing at the bit to move into the new house they were building in

Ballsbridge and then in the last week or so had changed. It was as if by some strange alchemy, at her father's death, Mark had become lord of the manor, born to it. She'd even had to laugh at the new clothes he'd bought. "So country squire!" And he had laughed along with her, looking embarrassed.

As for Scott . . . With a constriction of the heart, Caroline looked at Scott who sat across the dinner table from Mark. Always, Scott's cynical game, his light tone, a disguise put on as though it could conceal his pitifully wasted-looking leg. Besides, she knew him for a secret smoker. She knew too that he had a little gold lighter, a present from one of his friends in Dublin. The thought pained her. And as for Rowena . . .

Caroline saw that Rowena hadn't eaten the spinach soup. She looked tired; her eyelids were tinged pink, her hair, usually such a gleaming red, looking dull. She was not attending her vet classes at University College in Dublin. Caroline could guess why: She imagined curious looks from Rowena's classmates, covert whispers, *The papers say she did it . . . her grandfather . . . gathering evidence . . . they'll find out why . . . Bet you five pounds she'll get away with it.* Not that Rowena moped. She exercised her bay mare and Winifred Moore's two horses at the castle. She rushed to help whenever a Ballynagh villager called with an animal in trouble and Liam Gogarty was busy elsewhere. Other than that, she walked the woods with Torrey Tunet. There was something . . . *waiting* about her.

Rowena had gotten up and was at the window. "The rain's stopping. I'm going to Castle Moore. I want to take a look at Winifred's horses. This kind of storm spooks them." Caroline worriedly watched her go, walking so heavily.

Caroline for an instant closed her eyes. The terrible thing was that everyone near and dear to her seemed to have cause to hate her father. But of course not enough to murder him. No, no! The murderer was someone from away, from outside Ballynagh, a madman of a patient. Surely. It had to be.

"Ma?" Scott was looking at her. "Those keepsakes that grandfather left in his will, want me to drop them off at Wickham and Slocum when I'm in Dublin tomorrow? Let the lawyers do the honors."

"I suppose that's best. I haven't gathered them up yet. I'll do it in the morning." At a passing thought, she frowned. "Why d'you suppose my father had his will out on the desk? Doesn't it seem, well, odd?"

"Ma, your father *was* odd."

"Really, Scott!" She looked over at Mark, smiling in fond exasperation at her son's words. Mark, her dear, loving Mark smiled sympathetically back at her.

29

Back and back. It goes back and back. Torrey couldn't get it out of her head. She smelled the musty stable and saw Rowena crying, her face pressed against the horse's flank. Goes back to what? And what did Rowena mean by "it?" Murder snaking back and back to the "it"?

On Butler Street, Torrey waited while Willy, the grocer's older son, put the groceries in the basket of her bicycle. Capers, heavy cream, butter, oranges. The "it." A quarrel? A fight? A death? Back to Rowena's mother? Or back even before Caroline? Related somehow, at least in Rowena's mind, to the murder of Gerald Ashenden, a murder that was only now ten days old? Rowena crying, dust motes in the horse's stall.

"Sorry about the black grapes. Next week, though."

"Thanks, Willy." She put Jasper's grocery list in the pocket of her corduroys. Butler Street was all cobblestones, so she walked her bicycle back along the narrow sidewalk. She passed Grogan's Needlework Shop. Above the shop, the swanshaped sign, Nolan's Bed-and-Breakfast, swayed in the wind. Tonight, Jasper, skilled chef and lover, was making a *turban de filets de sole* followed by *bavarois a l'orange*, whatever that was. He hadn't yet decided on the wine.

Back and back, such despair in Rowena's voice. "How's it going with Rowena?" Jasper had asked her last night. It was close to midnight, and she was in bed, drowsily watching him put on his clothes. His bike was outside; he'd be back at Nolan's before they locked up. She still smelled him on her skin and in her bed. At his question, she felt her skin tighten with a kind of secrecy, because there wasn't a way to tell Jasper any of it without revealing Rowena's pregnancy. So she answered, "She's keeping so quiet, I hardly know."

Back and back. Crying.

Wheeling her bicycle past the glass-fronted Ballynagh police station, she glanced in. Sergeant Bryson was there alone, sitting at a corner desk bent over paperwork. Jimmy Bryson, who half the time blushed over God knows what. Nelson, the black Lab, was lying inside the glass-fronted door. He lifted his head and wagged his tail as Torrey went past.

A cold wind swept a swirl of leaves up the street and sent an icy chill down Torrey's back. She shivered. She should have worn her windbreaker, or at least a heavier sweater. It was getting on to four o'clock. The mountains above the village were sharp-edged autumnal cutouts against a graying sky.

"Ho, there! Ms. Tunet!"

Winifred Moore crossed over from the other side of the road. She looked like a sturdy mountaineer in breeches, laced boots, a dark-green parka, and brimmed leather hat. "Need a lift? I can stick your bicycle in the back of my Jeep."

"Thanks. But right now I need a cup of hot tea." Ahead was Amelia's Tea Shop. "Join me?"

"Tea? Not likely! I could do with a Guinness, though. O'Malley's can give you a pot of tea while I have a beer."

O'Malleys pub was uncrowded. Torrey had never been here before. So this was the place where, gossip in Ballynagh said, Rowena had come in that afternoon, face enraged and green eyes wild, and ("You can ask Sean O'Malley!") had gotten crazy drunk. "That bastard! That inhuman bastard! He belongs in hell!" Sean had eyes and ears and never

89

missed. "And whom else could the girl have meant, seeing what she did in the meadow an hour after?" But *why* "inhuman bastard"? Torrey could not even begin to conjecture.

Warmth, blessed warmth. Smell of hops. Smell of hickory smoke from the fire. Wall sconces shed a yellow light on dark, polished wood walls that had framed posters. One showed a turn-of-the-century railroad train traveling through mountainous countryside. In another, a Spanish couple danced, the man in a sombrero, the woman's flamenco skirt twirling.

A handful of men in workmen's clothes and three or four others in country tweeds were talking at the bar, served by a curly-haired young bartender in shirtsleeves and a green vest. There was occasional laughter. Only two tables were occupied. At one, a middle-aged couple sat quietly over their beer. At the other, an elderly man with tousled white hair was reading a newspaper.

They settled at a small table close to the fire. Bliss, the warmth of the fire. Torrey's cold hands cupped a wonderfully hot cup of tea. She was unexpectedly hungry and ate a surprisingly tasty slice of sponge cake that came in a cellophane wrapper. Never mind that Jasper would have made a disgusted face.

"So," Winifred said, over her pint, "what's this I hear? Dr. Ashenden's will being read at the manor last night." At Torrey's look of surprise, she explained, "Telephone communication, once referred to as backstairs gossip."

"Oh."

"My underground informant tells me that Scott Keegan got left in the cloakroom. Skunked."

"Hmmm?" This morning, working on the kids' language book, she'd found herself frowning off into space, eyes narrowed. Dr. Ashenden had cut Scott off with only a handful of pence. Why? Because of course it was all one narrative. *It goes back and back*. Back to what?

"I'll have another pint," Winifred said to the waitress. And to Torrey, "You're remarkably mum about your friends."

"Well, I don't exactly... I'm working on this language book, it's for kids, I'm up to here in—"

Winifred Moore gave a hoot of a laugh. "I wish Sheila were as circumspect about my personal business as you are about Rowena and that Ashenden affair." To the waitress who set down her pint, "Bring my friend another pot of tea. This one's gotten cold."

A shadow, someone was looming over the table. "Ms. Moore!" It was the man with the tousled white hair, a tall old fellow, maybe in his seventies, newspaper now under his arm, face alight with recognition. "Ms. Winifred Moore, is it?"

"It is," Winifred pushed out a chair with her booted foot. "Sit down. Buy you a drink? Can't say I remember you."

The man sat down. Tousled white hair. Keen eyes in a weathered face. Worn old tweeds, navy flannel shirt. "Didn't say I knew you. Except for photographs in the paper the time you won the Irish Women's Poetry Prize. Knew your cousin Desmond, though."

"Did you? Desmond? Would've been hanged if someone hadn't sliced him up first. This is my friend, Ms. Tunet."

"Your tea, ma'am." The waitress set down the pot and a fresh cup.

"And a pint for me," the old man told the waitress. He had a tenor voice, something lyrical about it. He sat at ease. "I'm Michael McIntyre. Wicklow born, world educated. I've hung my hat from the Antilles to Togo but always a finger on the old pulse. Ballynagh. Now back for good." A gnarled hand went up and ruffled his disordered hair. "Don't miss much. Know every newborn cat and dog on Butler Street. Know how much Mrs. Mc-this and Mrs. O-that owes O'Curry's Meats. Know what's in folks' closets and who's in their beds. Seen this young lady"—he grinned at Torrey— "seen you help Rowena Keegan doctor a sick cow in Sweeney's barn. Seen the pair of you hiking the hills with the Ashenden dogs."

"Pity you didn't also see what they're now calling 'The

Bridle Path Murder,' " Winifred said. "Could've saved a lot of newspaper print."

"Now there's a fancy murder for you! Dr. Ashenden, done in with a knitting needle in a horse's rump! That's a lady's touch." McIntyre ruffled his white hair, gave a laugh and a belch, and moved his glass in a circle on the table. "Know that Ashenden family, though, from way back. Knew Gerald Ashenden's wife. Kathleen, her name was. A waitress here in O'Malley's back then. A young fawn. Been here in Ballynagh two weeks when I first saw her. Eighteen years old and not knowing a pint from a quart. Come from Galway to live with her spinster aunt, tragic accident. Brady family in Galway drowned on a birthday outing to the Aran Islands, their own miserable little boat, should've known better. Story was, Kathleen was afraid of the sea so she'd hid in the barn. Saved by fate, right?

"I'd sit down at my regular table, by the wall there, and Kathleen'd bring me my pint. Dark green barmaid's apron, shamrocks on it. Canny old O'Malley thought that up for the tourists. Shamrocks! Kathleen Brady was her name. Tell me a name once, I'll know it forever."

"You're a poem, Mr. McIntyre, a poem." Winifred got up and pulled on her parka. "A pity I've got to leave. I'll get the bill, Torrey. Sheila's waiting for me. Put your bike in the Jeep."

"Never mind, you go ahead."

Gnarled hand swiping through ruffled white hair, another dark, foam-topped, then another, McIntyre's head tipped up to drink, down the gullet, gulping, Adam's apple going up and down, oddly lyrical voice. Torrey was like a shadow, listening. "That girl, Kathleen. I'd been away back then, was in the islands. Tahiti. You know that painter? Pictures of girls naked above the waist, flower tucked behind an ear, arms holding ripe melons." A long, thoughtful pause, then a shake of the head. "Kathleen Brady. Lush as a tropical plant, but oh, an innocent! A combination to take your breath away. Made my hand tremble round my glass."

Torrey said not a word. Her tea grew cold, and there was no other sound for her than the old man's voice lingering over memories. Kathleen Brady took shape before her: black-haired, slender and small-boned, with a breathtaking curve of bosom and hip, long slender legs and narrow ankles. Eyes so intensely blue that your own eyes smarted for an instant when you looked into them. "Yes, smarted and teared! Her eyelids were always heavy, as though she were sleepy, which she was: the girl was anemic and often tired. Her idea of heaven was a midday nap. But that was out of the question. At closing time, she'd be yawning and often stumbling."

McIntyre's photographic eye, projected back in time, brought pictures, and Torrey saw Kathleen in the shamrock apron over moss-green cotton dresses, all the same style, products of the spinster aunt's needle. Short sleeves for convenience in serving. Kathleen's cardigan, a rusty red, did for autumn weather, a duffle coat and boots from a jumble sale did for winter. She lived above the needlework shop with the aunt. Two rooms, a bathroom down the hall shared with another tenant.

"She had friends?" Torrey's first words in a half hour.

"No, no girls her age nearby. Boys? Boys hung about, but inept. Country boys. She was shy of them."

Then one late afternoon in June, Gerald Ashenden, having just passed his final medical exams, dropped in at O'Malley's Pub. Gerald Ashenden, tall, fair-haired, with dark eyes under thick, blond brows. Gerald Ashenden. Not a boy. A man.

Out on the street it was dusk. She had left Michael McIntyre in the pub. He'd stood up with unsteady courtesy, then accompanied her as far as the bar for a chat with friends. "I'll buy you a brew next time, lass. And Winifred

Moore, poet. Six hundred years of Irish poetry and not three women poets among them. Not till now. But washed a lot of clothes, poor lasses."

Dusk, shops closed, no one about. A dim night light showed from Amelia's Tea Shop. Above Grogan's Needlework, three narrow casement windows were lighted. For a long moment, Torrey gazed at those windows, wondering if one of them might have been that of the young Kathleen who'd been afraid of the sea and come from Galway. A dog barked, and Torrey looked farther down Butler Street where bright light spilled across the road from the police station. So small a village, so narrow this deserted, cobbled street. It was like being in a ravine, the village at the bottom of a cleft in the hills, and all around were the mountains she could not see.

She got on her bike. So late, so dark. But her groceries were in her bicycle basket, safe, untouched. She thought how there was so very little theft in Ballynagh. And almost no crime.

30

By eight o'clock the next morning, the morning Torrey later thought of as "the morning of the gypsy," she had breakfasted and was at her desk, working on the three-language book. The publisher's contract called for forty-four pages, one third of each page for three-color illustrations.

At eleven o'clock, she stretched and got up to get a glass of water. At the window above the kitchen sink she disgustedly surveyed the last of the tomatoes on the withered, sticklike stalks. Tomatoes, for God's sake! Why had she tried to grow tomatoes? She'd planted them way too late, and a frost would come any day now and ruin what was left. She'd planted tomatoes just to show off. As though anyone in Ballynagh would be impressed and think admiringly, "The American woman in the cottage is growing tomatoes." All summer she could've bought better tomatoes in Coyle's on Butler Street.

Purple among the tomato vines. Purple? She leaned closer to the window. Purple skirt, ragged-looking tan sweater. A woman leaning down, picking up a tomato from the ground, putting it in her skirt pocket. Fine. Good riddance, Torrey thought.

But then the woman straightened and pulled a ripe tomato from a vine. Then another. Oh, no, my dear woman, not my last good ones! You go too far.

Torrey put down her glass of water and went outside to stop the depredation. *Depredation*, from the Latin: "to plunder." She loved that word: *plunder*. So rich, so . . . velvety soft? The woman was plundering her tomatoes.

"There's plenty more, and it's still hot."

The gypsy nodded. Torrey poured more tea into her cup. They sat at the kitchen table.

Torrey cut two more slices from the soda bread on the wooden board. She'd baked the bread herself. Jasper wouldn't eat it, but he'd complimented her on making a good start. She bravely ate it in front of him with lots of butter, saying how good it was. He was in Dunlavin today, having read in the *Independent* about an estate sale, entire contents of a house. Might even be a windfall of books for him.

"More bread and butter?"

The gypsy shook her head. "No, Missus." She was about forty or so, thin, with a mass of dusty dark hair and gold earrings.

Torrey, walking toward the woman among the tomato vines, had known at once, at the woman's "Good day, Missus," that she was from Romania. She'd likely be one of the Romanian gypsies who'd arrived in Ireland in the last few years, traveling across France, bringing with them their few possessions and their own gypsy language mingled with Romanian.

Gypsy or not, a Romanian. Aside from her own father, Vlad Tunet, Torrey hadn't known half a dozen Romanians. So now, four shiny aluminum pots, at two pounds ten pence each, rested on the side table under the window, and the gypsy sat drinking her third cup of tea. Admittedly, not an appealing lady. Something grasping about her, the greedy way her glance slid about the cottage as she commented, "Pretty things." The copper bowls on the sideboard, the hand-knitted afghan on the back of the rocking chair, the enamel three-legged clock on the mantel. Drying on the wooden clothes rack was Torrey's nightgown, the white with yellow daisies, her favorite. "In Dublin I'll get me a pretty nightgown like that, all daisies on it," staring at the nightgown.

"Yes, well, I'd better get back to work." Torrey looked toward her computer on the card table in the corner; the computer screen had gone reproachfully blank.

In the doorway, as the gypsy left, Torrey said, "Take as many tomatoes as you want. There's a frost coming, they'll only get mushy. Come any time."

The gypsy gone, Torrey went slowly to the card table that held her work. If she missed the deadline, she'd have killed the golden goose. She had to stop torturing herself about Rowena being suspected of murdering her grandfather and about an illegal abortionist's possibly unsanitary operating room. Pay attention to her own affairs. Sit down. Get back to work.

She stood looking down at the computer for a long minute. Then at the kitchen table she picked up the soda bread, threw it into the garbage, and went out and got on her bike.

Tousle-haired old McIntyre grinned when he looked up and saw Torrey standing there. He was at his usual table in O'Malley's. "You're in pursuit of me, I wouldn't doubt." He put down his newspaper. "Could be that I'm your true love."

"Close, very close." When he had reminisced in his lyrical tenor voice, she'd felt there were things almost within her grasp. She saw Columbus sailing toward a shore that might, after all, be a mirage, but then again, what was that, glimpsed low at the horizon? Shadow of a cloud? Or substance?

She sat down. "So then? They fell in love?"

McIntyre had ordered O'Malley's special noontime lunch with his pint. Two sausages, fried potatoes, cabbage, pot of

tea. Torrey did the same. Not a word about it would Mc-
Intyre say until he'd cut into the first sausage and chewed
it about. "More than adequate." Then, sometimes resting
fork and knife against the edge of his plate, he talked.
"Love? Do you know the word *spoor*?" At her nod, McIntyre
too nodded. "Spoor! Some would call it that. Some would
say desire. When young Ashenden came into the pub and
saw Kathleen, it was like a terrible desire, take my word.
Something he had to get out of his system, like some eva-
nescent childhood illness — chicken pox, measles, whooping
cough — something to go through on the way to become an
adult. I imagine it so.

"But the young man found himself trapped in the illness.
He had been careful, but grievously he'd not been careful
enough. And she? At his touch, she had flowered. She was
bewildered, but happy, and in love." McIntyre speared a
sausage. "They used to call it 'with child.' When I was a boy
I'd imagine the woman's breasts becoming tender, mysteri-
ous things happening so that her skin became more flushed,
her eye brighter, her mouth fuller. With one like Kathleen
Brady, I saw it happen, that flowering."

McIntyre's own eyes were brighter. "Ah, what a flowering!"

"And him? Ashenden?"

A gulp of Guinness. "What would you say? A Catholic
girl, uneducated, and him recovering from that disease, desire. Spoor evaporated. That blinding crystal fell from his
eyes. He saw again. Saw that in a year, he'd have his medical
license, an office in Dublin, a wealthy practice, a social life,
beautiful, educated, marriageable young women."

"But he married her, Mr. McIntyre. He did the only decent thing, he married Kathleen Brady."

"Decent? My dear Ms. Tunet, I would not necessarily say
decent. I would possibly say *cornered*."

"How, cornered?"

"I ruminated back then, Ms. Tunet, over *why*. I do not

know. I can guess. His parents? You'd have thought the Ashendens would have found a way to obstruct such a marriage, when they discovered—and by chance they discovered it, they were not told—that Kathleen Brady was pregnant by their son."

"Yes. I would have thought—not being cynical, only realistic about how people, influenced by society—"

"Hogwash. There are people and there are extraordinary people. Gerald Ashenden's parents were extraordinary. Not religious people. I think they bundled it all together: Catholic or Protestant, Old Testament or New, Buddism, Judaism, Confucianism, the like. Polite, didn't talk about it.

"Ethical, that was it. Old Miles Ashenden had a maxim, 'Don't do that which, if everybody did, it would destroy society.' Can you top that one, Ms. Tunet?"

"Not even if hard-pressed, Mr. McIntyre."

"Indeed! Indeed! I can see it, the elderly old father, white-mustached, he was, in the library with young Ashenden, 'Who do you think you are, Gerald? That immoral Tolstoy who'd go strolling on his estate and push any passing peasant girl into the bushes and use her? Then dry himself on her clothing and stroll on? You'll marry this pregnant Catholic girl, Gerald. Or you're no longer my son.' "

McIntyre's color was high, his keen eyes sparkled. "What a scene it must've been in that library! For Gerald Ashenden, it would be good-bye to the money to open his office on Merrion Street in Dublin, good-bye to the Ashenden estate and its five hundred acres. Even good-bye to his mother. The doors of Ashenden Manor closed against him. Disowned. Cast out! Cast out like . . . like somebody in the Bible. Can't remember. Some fellow. Who was it, Ms. Tunet?"

"Isaac? Jacob? I don't remember either, Mr. McIntyre."

By half past twelve, it had gotten noisy in O'Malley's, and several people, beer glasses in hand, had come up to their table to say hello to McIntyre and things like, "Back from Australia, McIntyre? Seen any kangaroos? Waltzing Matildas?" But by one o'clock it was quiet again, customers gone back to work. An occasional clash of dishes from the kitchen; Sean O'Malley at the bar, washing glasses and watching a rugby game on the television, keeping the sound low. He had put more logs on the fire: the warmth enveloped McIntyre's table. Replete, McIntyre mused, "It wasn't any wonder that Kathleen Brady Ashenden came often to O'Malley's. 'Twas the only warm place in her life. Coldness at home can turn a person to drink. Coldness and misery." The once-beautiful Kathleen became not so radiant. "More on the thick side. Gray in her hair, hair that had been black satin. The blue eyes not so blue, the electricity diminished. They were wavering eyes, pleading eyes. Bewildered. It wasn't Gerald Ashenden got trapped, but Kathleen Brady. Poor little hen!"

Torrey gazed at the fire, which flared up suddenly. "She died so young. A brushfire, wasn't it? Rowena once told me about it. She was only about . . . ?"

"She was thirty-one. Had that little girl, Caroline, eleven or so, at the time."

A silence. Something about the silence made Torrey turn from the fire and look at McIntyre. He was watching her, an assessing look. Somewhere in the past she'd seen that look, doubtful, not quite sure, saying silently: Does she qualify, can I tell her? Torrey looked steadily back into the keen old eyes. "Tell me."

McIntyre tipped up his pint and drank, a long drink. He put it down and wiped his mouth. He gave Torrey a nod. "She was here in the pub that night, before the brushfire started. The last night of her life. She sat where you're sitting. She started to talk, low and halting. 'When I was little, I would worry so. I would say to my mother, "When I grow up, who will marry me?" I thought no one would ever want to marry me. And my mother would laugh and say. "Don't worry. Someday a knight will come along on a white horse and marry you.' " McIntyre shook his head. "Blue eyes awash with drunken tears, yet tears to break the heart. 'I thought Gerald was the knight.' She raised her glass of beer to drink, and her hand shook so that half the beer spilled over the table and onto her skirt. I said, 'Here, now,' and tried to hand her a paper napkin to blot it, but she pushed my hand away and looked down at her skirt, 'It's done for, same as me. Done for.' She left then. I didn't think twice about anything deeper. But when I went to light my pipe, my folder of matches was gone."

On the cobbled street outside O'Malley's, Torrey stood in the bright sunlight beside her bike that she'd left leaning against the brick wall. Brilliant blue sky, white clouds, a fresh breeze. But she felt heavy with McIntyre's story about Kathleen Brady. It seemed somehow to cast a shadow over the sunlit village street.

Pensively, she ran a finger down the side of her nose. Next door to O'Malley's, a woman with two small children was shopping for vegetables at Coyle's stand. A farm truck went past. The driver, a girl, honked a greeting to Coyle's boy, who waved back. Farther down the street, a few people went in and out of shops. A bell jangled as someone entered Grogan's Needlework Shop across the street. Beside the needlework shop entrance was another door, a wide, handsome door with a curved top and a fresh, lace curtain across the glass. Nolan's Bed-and-Breakfast. *She came from Galway to live with her spinster aunt above the needlework shop.*

It was like being drawn on a string. How could she not? Torrey crossed the street.

The stairs were wide and carpeted in dark green, the bannister was polished mahogany, the walls were rose-patterned. Pristine.

A buzzer sounded as she entered a small parlor with the

same rose-figured wallpaper. A fresh-faced, dark-haired woman, possibly in her midforties, hair in a bun, navy cardigan over a blue dress, came through a doorway, smiling. "Good afternoon. I'm Sara Hobbs. Mrs. Greer, isn't it? The room's ready, Number six, double bed, that you asked for. Mr. Greer will be bringing up your baggage? Or I can send my boy down."

No, Torrey explained, she was not Mrs. Greer. She was a friend of . . . of Caroline Keegan Temple, who'd been Caroline Ashenden. "Caroline's mother, Kathleen Brady Ashenden, had an aunt who lived here years ago, I don't know her name." She felt a fool, what was she doing here? "Way before your time, of course, Mrs. Hobbs. It isn't likely you'd have even been—"

"Alice Coggins! My heavens! Of *course*! Of course I remember! A good thirty-five or forty years ago. My mother was the proprietor then. Good heavens, yes! Dr. Ashenden's wife. Kathleen. She'd often come to visit her aunt, an unmarried lady. She sometimes brought her little girl, Caroline. We were the same age, and we'd play together. Alice Coggins made us each a rag doll out of sewing scraps; mine had a blue dress, and Caroline's was pink. We'd play tea party. I still have my doll. I'm sentimental—I loved my childhood. I keep the doll on my bedroom shelf with my old dolls' tea set. Brian, my husband, laughs about it." Sara Hobbs, marveling at the past, grew misty-eyed.

"Alice Coggins died about a year after Kathleen Ashenden was killed in a brushfire. I was too ashamed to send Alice's poor things to them at Ashenden Manor, bits of material, sewing things and such: It would've been an embarrassment to her. I was betwixt and between, you might say. But I couldn't throw them out. As I told you, I'm sentimental. Her box must still be in the attic."

"Mrs. Hobbs? I'm Mrs. Greer." A ruddy-faced woman in a plaid cape was coming in, panting a little from the stairs.

"My husband's on the the way up. The roads! Crowded! We'd have thought to get here earlier. Is it possible to have tea when we're settled in?"

On the way out, Torrey looked back and mouthed "Thank you" to Sara Hobbs, who smiled in response.

31

It was past four o'clock when Torrey pedaled back home along the narrow access road between the hedges that were higher than her head. Behind the hedges, unseen, would be an occasional cottage, a farm, a field with cows, she could only guess at the hidden landscape. At Nolan's Bed-and-Breakfast, listening to Sara Hobbs talk of Kathleen Brady, she'd had that same feeling of a hidden landscape.

A wind had sprung up, the sky had turned a cold gray. Overcast. Traitorous weather, a promise betrayed. There'd be sneezing and runny noses tonight in Ballynagh and in cottages in this mountainous corner of Wicklow. People would be opening storage chests and digging about for the warm clothes they'd put away last spring.

Luckily, Torrey had left her sleeveless padded vest in her bicycle basket. She stopped, planted a foot on the road on each side of the bike to hold it steady, put on the vest, and zipped it up. And at least it was less windy on the access road; the high hedges were good protection from the wind. And it wasn't far now to the cottage.

A half mile farther up, she reached the break in the hedge. She got off the bike and wheeled it through the opening and past the marshy little pond. Because of the woods, it was darker around the cottage than on the road. Except for the little vegetable garden in the patch that the sun could reach, there were tall trees all around, and at this season the green grass was mottled with brown.

A light in the cottage. Ah, so Jasper was there. The thought warmed her. They'd get a fire going and have a late tea with some of Jasper's delicious biscuits, the ones with currants. There were three left; she'd heat them up. And there was bread and canned salmon. He'd tell her about his trip to Dunlavin.

She leaned her bike against the cottage and opened the door.

"Hello, Missus!"

The gypsy stood beside the kitchen table. Purple skirt, ragged tan sweater, the mass of dark hair. One of Jasper's bottles of Bordeaux was open on the table and half empty.

"Hello, Missus!" The gypsy's teeth flashed a smile. Gold bracelets clinked as she waved a wineglass, one of Torrey's two Waterford wineglasses, then brought the glass waveringly to her lips and sipped, her head tipped down, her dark eyes on Torrey over the rim of the glass.

"What are you doing here? What do you want?" Somehow, the gypsy being a Romanian made it worse. And now she saw that the woman was tipsy, no, not tipsy, she was drunk, drunk on Jasper's precious wine.

"Ah, Missus!" It was unpleasant, a snigger. "Your kindness brought me back. You'll be glad you gave me that bit of tea! And that you're a Romanian, besides *Tunet*, thunder, Missus. And *fulger*, lightning. And *furtuna*, ah! *Furtuna*, a storm!"

"What are you talking about?" Torrey said impatiently. She was tired, she was hungry, and where was Jasper? She wanted to clean up the table and put on a fresh tablecloth and change her clothes, and —

"Something evil." The gypsy sniggered. "Yes, Missus, evil. I saw something. Something evil. But a gypsy's words, they might be smoke. A lady like you is different, could make something of it. A reward, is there?" The gypsy swayed and reached for the bottle of wine. "You'll give me half, and I'll buy a pretty nightgown like yours, all yellow daisies." She lurched against the table. The bottle fell and rolled on the floor. The gypsy stared at it until it rolled against a chair leg and stopped. Then she shook herself and went to the door. *"Tunet, fulger, furtuna.* You think, Missus. You think about it. I'll come back."

32

Jackpot! Out of the blue!"

"Take it easy," Jasper said. "You're assuming—"

"Come *on*, Jasper. She's got a caravan or wagon or something in the woods; everybody knows that. She saw something evil, and she's going to tell me. All because I—"

"Gave her a cup of tea and some soda bread? And tomatoes? Torrey—"

"And because I'm Romanian. And she wants a reward. She's already got the taste of money on her tongue. I could tell. You know what this means, Jasper? It means *she knows who killed Gerald Ashenden.*"

For dinner Jasper made a *poulet en cocotte*, the chicken browned to a golden color in the casserole. With it, they had a bottle of the Bordeaux. Torrey could hardly eat for excitement. Who? She'd know soon who'd murdered Ashenden. Strange, unbelievable. But so.

After dinner, Jasper turned on the radio to RTE for the political news and was instantly absorbed. But Torrey walked around in circles, saying "because of tomatoes!" and "freakish chance!" and "a windfall, right in my lap!" Rowena, Rowena would be the first she'd tell. Though rightly she should go first to Inspector Egan O'Hare, bringing the gypsy with her. Her eyewitness. An eyewitness who had seen the killer shoot the knitting needle into Ashenden's horse.

She looked at Jasper, her dark-haired love, so comfortably heavy, chin in hand, unaware that his eyes were narrowed and his long face intent, and that a muscle twitched in his jaw. He was fiercely outraged at the so-called real IRA bombings. He was, he'd once mentioned, originally from Cork, with a Catholic background. Seeing his narrow-eyed intensity, she'd wondered at first if he was more than a bystander, somehow politically involved. But when she'd asked, he'd laughed away the notion. "I'm a man of inaction, love, a sit-by-the-fire idealist. Books are my passion, not politics." It seemed to her a lot of protest to her simple question. But why pry?

At nine-thirty they did the dishes, then settled on the couch. Jasper said the estate library in Dunlavin was a bust. "Popular hardback trash." He'd bought nothing. But in a poor cottage, he'd found a copy of Steinbeck's *Winter of Our Discontent.* "A paperback not worth ten pence, but I paid a pound for it — I'm in the mood for Steinbeck." He poked up the fire and read a chapter aloud. He had a rich baritone that brought the scenes alive, "In the doorway stood . . ." and so on. Torrey heard nothing beyond the first sentence.

At ten-thirty they were in bed, making love; at eleven-thirty Jasper was off to Nolan's on his bike. Before he left, he stood beside the bed looking down on her. "The gypsy. Said she'd be back, all right. But when?"

"She didn't say. I just assumed tomorrow. If she doesn't come by afternoon, I'll go crazy! I'll look for her in the woods; I'll ask in Ballynagh where her wagon is. Someone'll know." She shivered with excitement. "She *knows!* My God, she *knows!*"

"Don't go looking for her." Jasper was frowning down at her. "I know enough about gypsies to know it would be a mistake. She'll come when she's ready."

"Well, if I can stand it."

"Torrey, another thing. You're making an assumption." Heavy, serious, Jasper's baritone voice.

"Yes? What?"

"You're assuming that whoever shot that knitting needle into Ashenden's horse wasn't Rowena Keegan."

Torrey said, "Rowena? If the world stops spinning tomorrow, I'll believe it was Rowena."

33

Elated. Thrilled. In the morning, Torrey, working at the computer, turned her head a half dozen times toward the door. Any minute the woman would appear, the gypsy in her purple skirt with her secret to tell. Torrey shivered with anticipation. Already she saw herself finding Rowena in the stables at Ashenden Manor or at Castle Moore and smilingly telling her, "I have a witness to your grandfather's murder." Or maybe she'd say, "You're safe, now, Rowena. The most amazing thing happened." And she'd tell Rowena who had shot the knitting needle into Thor. And there'd be inexpressible relief on Rowena's face, so drawn now, the green eyes with the lids lately so tinged with pink.

She worked to one o'clock, concentrating on a basic simple vocabulary, thinking of French children who by the time they were six would be trilingual, speaking English and Spanish as well as their mother tongue, moving with ease from one language to another. She hoped, she hoped! The second book would be American kids speaking, let's see . . . Never mind! Finish working out this one first. When it came to the illustrations, she'd have to tie her hands behind her back and put tape over her mouth to keep from meddling.

At one o'clock she stopped for a lunch of leftover curried carrot soup that Jasper had made. It was a sunny day and warm enough for her to take the bowl of soup outside and sit in the sun on the old wooden bench beside the door. From there she could see anyone coming. Wind made the leaves rustle, a bird trilled, but among the trees and near the hedge was no touch of purple. *A reward, is there? I saw something evil.*

Back in the cottage she worked until four. Then just sat, biting the inside of her lip. Could the gypsy's *I'll be back* mean not today, but tomorrow? Frustrating and exasperating, not to know.

At five o'clock the low sun glimmered gold through the trees. Torrey put on her heavy shawl-necked sweater against the evening chill. She'd walk up the access road a bit. Just a bit. A few steps. Maybe the gypsy had missed the break in the hedge? That was perfectly possible, wasn't it?

She wrote a note for Jasper. He was going to make dinner. She never knew where he was during the day. Riding around the countryside on his bike, he'd told her, looking for old books. "You never know what rare books you might find in these villages. I've a friend who found a first edition of Homer's *Odyssey*, with the N. C. Wyeth illustrations, in a cottage in County Kerry. He bought it for two pounds, worth maybe, in your American money, two thousand dollars." But now that she thought of it, Jasper had never shown her any of his lucky finds. Not once. That Steinbeck book, *Winter of Our Discontent*, that he'd brought to the cottage didn't count. She'd even seen one like it on the second-hand shelf in the little variety store in Ballynagh.

She went through the opening in the hedge and started up the access road. The bus from Dublin came up behind her and went past, south toward Cork. A group of teenage boys in their home soccer jackets bicycled north. She heard a car behind her slow down.

"Ms. Tunet! Torrey!" The car came abreast. It was Caroline Temple. "Can I give you a lift?"

Torrey halted. The road ahead was empty, nobody in clinking bracelets and a voice with a Romanian gypsy accent to tell her the wished-for revelation of the murderer. She might as well go back to the cottage.

"Torrey?"

"Thanks, Caroline. I was getting chilled." She got in the car.

The car was at least a dozen years old, but luxurious, a Mercedes with worn, dove-colored upholstery. "I was at Fogerty's farm, getting asparagus. They don't sell to grocers." Caroline's voice was falsely bright and chatty as she drove on. "You have to go yourself." Her pale face was strained, her hands on the steering wheel trembled. She was wearing an old chinchilla coat that looked definitely moth-eaten. "Asparagus," she repeated. She put up a hand and rubbed her forehead. "I'm a bit distracted lately. I went to see Inspector O'Hare. He was polite and sympathetic. But I saw *at once* that he's convinced Rowena killed my father. *Convinced!*"

Caroline gave a little whimper. She tipped her head down and momentarily closed her eyes.

A boy and a girl were walking on the road toward them, laughing, the boy's arm around the girl. The road was narrow, but the Mercedes didn't slow down or start to swing around the couple. The girl's eyes widened in fright; the car was headed straight toward them.

"Oh, *God!*" Caroline screamed and wrenched the steering wheel and the car drove into the hedge. The boy and the girl went hurriedly up the road.

Caroline put her elbows on the steering wheel and dropped her head in her hands. "Dear God!"

Torrey, mouth dry, gazed at the nose of the Mercedes buried in the hedge.

"Dear God! Dear God! They have men guards in prisons. They do what they want to the women prisoners! Rape! *Anything!* I saw a report on television! It was horrible." The words came out muffled; Caroline's face was still buried in her hands. She shook her head back and forth.

"They won't," Torrey said. "They won't put Rowena in prison."

"Oh, yes! Inspector O'Hare. He'll find miserable little bits and pieces enough to make it look as if Rowena killed my father. Dublin Castle reprimanded him. He's got to prove he was right to jail her in the first place. He'll do *anything* to prove it." Pale face, fair hair in disarray, eyes awash with tears.

"You folks all right?" A kindly red face, bushy white eyebrows, a bald pate; a farm truck behind him. "Get yourself out of the hedge, can you?"

Torrey answered for Caroline. "Yes, thanks. We can manage."

And then, as Torrey was later to realize, that was when she made her mistake.

The farmer gone, Torrey put a compassionate hand on Caroline's shoulder. "Listen, something's come up. I think someone was near the bridle path, may have seen what happened. She saw—"

"A witness? Someone saw . . . ?"

"I *think*. I only *think* that *maybe* someone saw. I'm not saying for sure. But it's a possibility. Only a possibility. I'm waiting to find out."

"You mean there's a chance that—Find out? When?"

"I don't know. Maybe tonight. Or tomorrow. I'm not . . . not positive." She was suddenly overwhelmingly weary. She wanted to say, *But it may come to nothing*. Yet she could not. She looked at Caroline's hopeful face framed in the collar of the old coat. No, she could not. Instead she said, "That's the softest fur, that fur you're wearing! Chinchilla, isn't it?"

"Yes."

34

As Winifred Moore said near midnight that Tuesday, when she and Sheila got back to Castle Moore, "It was like an underground trickle, a whisper here, a whisper there, and who knew who was tapping into it? The source, of course, was Torrey Tunet. Her telling Caroline in the first place. A pity. So, trickle, trickle, reaching the ears of a murderer."

Sheila said, "I guess. I wish I hadn't been there. It was so *gruesome*."

All that Tuesday it had poured. When Torrey got up, the first thing she thought was, *The gypsy won't come today.* By late afternoon, looking out the window at the rain pounding down on the trees and at the overflowing pond, she was unhappily sure of it. "Maybe the gypsy was just so drunk on the Bordeaux that she didn't know what she —"

"She'll turn up tomorrow," Jasper said, "This rain's enough to drown in. Don't worry. She hears the clink of gold." He was lying on the couch by the fire, reading her copy of Dickson's *The Official Rules*. "How about this one: 'The Umbrella Law. You will need three umbrellas: one to leave at the office, one to leave at home, and one to leave on the train.'" He put down the book and swung his legs off the couch. "Stop thinking about the gypsy. I won't make dinner. I'm taking you to the movies. *The Governess* is playing in Dunlavin. We can take the bus, see the early show, have a bite afterward in the village, at O'Malley's. The best sausages and mashed in Wicklow County."

"All right." She smiled at him.

They were at the bus stop on the access road, both under her umbrella, when she said, "I didn't lock the door. Did you?"

"Hmmm? No. There's the bus."

35

At half past nine they were in O'Malley's pub eating hot mashed potatoes and sausages with Winifred Moore and Sheila Flaxton, who'd been at the movie and given them a lift back to Ballynagh. The rain had stopped.

"I liked the *concept* of the movie," Sheila Flaxton said, delicately forking up a marble-sized bit of mashed, "but I didn't actually like the *plot*."

"Good evening." Dr. Collins, passing their table, paused, smiling. Brown corduroy jacket over his woolen vest, and as usual wearing his old tweed cap. "Having a good dinner?"

"Dr. Collins!" Winifred said. "Hello! Join us? We've barely started."

Dr. Collins shook his head. "Just came by to check on Sean O'Malley's youngest. Hives." He smiled at Torrey. "Take care in Ballynagh's variable weather, Ms. Tunet. Don't want another touch of the flu." He nodded good-bye and went off.

"Really, a bitch of a night," Winifred said. And to Torrey, "We'll drive you home,"

"Right," Jasper said. "And at the cottage I'll give you and Sheila a nightcap, a cognac that brings tears of joy to a connoisseur's eye."

———

Winifred parked the Jeep by the side of the road. The wet hedges glistened in the headlights. Jasper led the way with the torch that Winifred kept in the car. They single-filed through the break in the hedge and past the pond.

The flashlight picked out the bulk of Jasper's bike covered with its black plastic, leaning against the cottage wall. A wind tore at the plastic, making it billow. "Lead me to that cognac!" Winifred said.

Inside, Torrey turned on lamps in the kitchen and Jasper lit the fire. Torrey took down the globular cognac glasses. She loved the cottage like this, cozy, with friends, her lover, firelight. Jasper would warm the cognac with a candle flame; and they all would have a companionable nightcap. First she'd change her shoes. They weren't exactly damp, but Dr. Collins was right about being careful, the flu.

In the bedroom, she turned on the bedside light. She glanced at the bed, and stood stunned. A chill of horror crawled down her back and along her arms. She put a hand to her throat, staring down, trying not to believe what she was seeing.

The gypsy, in Torrey's nightgown with the yellow daisies, lay in her bed. The woman's mass of dark hair was tumbled on the pillow. And her hands with the many rings lay still. The gypsy's eyes did not flash. They stared, open, sightless. Her tongue protruded through clenched teeth.

36

Torrey sat beside the kitchen table, gazing down at the floor, police shoes going past, the police photographer's flash reflecting repeatedly through the open door of the bedroom. She lifted her head when the Gardai wheeled the gurney with the sheeted body past her on the way out and she saw the van's blue light beyond the hedge turning the hedge blue each time it revolved. She became aware that Jasper was leaning against the kitchen sink and that Winifred Moore was pacing the room from stove to fireplace.

"Whoever smothered that poor woman," Winifred said, "meant to kill Torrey."

At that, Torrey lifted her head. "I'm not sure. Was it in the dark? How much could the killer see?"

"What do you mean?"

"Simply," Torrey said, "that the gypsy told me she'd seen 'something evil' happen on the bridle path: She wanted a reward for telling. It had to be that she saw who shot the knitting needle into the horse as Dr. Ashenden rode by. She was going to come back and tell me. She was —"

"A witness?" Winifred, hands on hips, leaned toward Torrey. "Did you mention it to anybody?"

"Only to Caroline Temple."

"Hellfire!" Winifred said. "Caroline would've likely told Mark. And Scott. Encouraging them, getting their hopes up for Rowena." She smacked a fist into her palm. "God knows who else Mark or Scott might've told."

"Well, now!" Inspector O'Hare came from the bedroom, notebook in hand, flipping a page. His police cap was set firmly on his graying head; his color was high. He glanced around the kitchen, taking it all in at a glance; he was good at that and knew it. Had, in fact, in his early years, come out first in a voluntary police observation test. He turned to Torrey. "So, now. The gypsy woman. Smothered with a pillow. Dead approximately three hours. Smelling of drink. Succinctly"—Inspector O'Hare lingered over the word, it was one of his favorite words—"succinctly, must've been drunk. How drunk? The crime lab's report will tell us. So: Her clothes lying on the floor. Wearing only a nightgown with yellow daisies. A nightgown of yours, Ms. Tunet?" The inspector's ballpoint pen hovered over the notebook. And at Torrey's nod, "Any idea, Ms. Tunet, how the gypsy came to be here in your house, in your bed, wearing your nightgown?"

Torrey shook her head. "The door was unlocked. I knew she was coming here to see me, but I didn't know it might be tonight. I was at the movies. She must have come in. That's all I know. Except that she liked that nightgown."

"Coming here to see you? Why?"

Torrey hesitated, then shrugged. Tell him. Nothing to lose. She'd already told Winifred. "Well . . ."

Inspector O'Hare listened, studying the ceiling, nodding, whistling under his breath. "And you believed that nonsense? My dear Ms. Tunet! You didn't suspect what that gypsy was up to? Telling you a dozen lies to sell you a kitchenful of pots and pans? Dented, at that. And to drink your whiskey and be off on her way!"

"Yes, I believed her."

Inspector O'Hare shook his head in pity. "The Gardai is familiar with gypsy habits. Likely she returned here, found your door open, and instead of stealing, which would have been more usual, fell drunkenly into bed in one of your nightgowns. Didn't you say that when you went into the bedroom, you turned on the light?"

"Yes."

"Have you considered, Ms. Tunet, that in the dark, some-one entered your bedroom and smothered the gypsy think-ing it was you?" O'Hare looked hard at Torrey. "Your life, Ms. Tunet, is in danger." Inspector O'Hare paused. "Why would that be, Ms. Tunet?"

"I don't know." But suddenly a thought washed over her: The killer could have entered a *lighted* bedroom, and leaving it, could have turned out the light. In that case, the killer knew very well who his victim was—which would mean that indeed the gypsy had witnessed something on the bridle path. And someone had killed her because of it.

"No idea at all, Ms. Tunet? No idea who might've . . . ?"

"None." Torrey shook her head. "No idea." But who? Knitting needle. Knitting needle. Her heart beat faster. Get on with it. *Tunet, fulger, furtuna*. Thunder. Lightning. Storm.

When Inspector O'Hare and the last of the technical crew from Dublin were gone, Winifred said, "If ever we needed a life-enhancing elixir, Jasper O'Mara, the time is now." Jasper opened the precious bottle and poured the dark gold cognac into the balloon glasses.

They sipped. Winifred blew out an appreciative breath, Jasper rolled his tongue around in his mouth, Sheila deli-cately licked her lips, and Torrey let the cognac rest on her tongue, her mouth a little open.

"Whoosh!" Winifred said.

When Winifred and Sheila left, Torrey stood beside Jas-per, watching from the doorway. The wet leaves of the sur-rounding trees glistened in the moonlight.

"Stay out of it," Jasper said, one arm around her shoul-ders, "I smell danger." He gave her earlobe a little tug. "I'm not in the mood to lose you. The idea makes me fretful."

But Torrey hardly heard him. She was seeing Butler Street: across from O'Malley's, those two adjacent doorways. She had entered one doorway and climbed the staircase with the rose-patterned wallpaper. She had come that far. It was related, she knew it. *It goes back and back!* Rowena crying.

As for that other doorway, the one with the jangling bell: Tomorrow.

37

Torrey stood beside Coyle's vegetable stand eating an apple. She couldn't remember when she'd gotten into the habit of eating something before attacking a problem. As to why she felt that need, she wondered if it gave her a hiatus, a special bit of thinking time, as a diver poised on the edge of a diving board might pause, gathering a final impetus.

Butler Street. Ten-thirty, sunny, women shopping, cobbles fresh washed by last night's driving rain. At the corner, beyond O'Malley's, a couple of men in overalls tinkered with a motorcycle. An empty school bus rattled past.

Torrey nibbled around the apple core and tossed it into Coyle's trash bin. Across the street, the bell above Grogan's Needlework Shop jangled each time a customer went in or out. Grogan's was one of the busiest shops in the village, what with needlework and knitting supplies, notions, dress patterns, and even a small selection of yard goods.

Torrey crossed the street. Two steps up. The bell jangled as she opened the door. A gray-haired woman clerk in rimless glasses was measuring out grosgrain ribbon for a customer, a young girl clerk was ringing up a sale, and another woman customer waiting. The narrow shop smelled of fresh dry goods and of cloves from a basketful of potpourri on the glass countertop. On shelves behind the counter were hanks of embroidery floss and knitting yarn and balls of mercerized cotton. A rack on the counter held tatting shut-tles, crochet needles, and knitting needles in various gauges. The police report had said ten-gauge, so —

"Ma'am? May I help you, ma'am?" The young girl clerk, freckled, had a light, childish voice.

Torrey said, "I'd like a pair of knitting needles. Ten-gauge is the one I want."

The clerk ran a finger along the cards of knitting needles and detached a card with a set of the narrowest needles. "This one. Ten-gauge. It's that newer material, so light. Everybody's using it."

Torrey held the card. The pair of knitting needles was not the wooden kind she remembered, and it wasn't plastic ei-ther. It was a fine-pointed, lightweight, pink-tinged alumi-num. Ah, yes, *The Devil take the blue-tailed fly*. The gypsy had seen too much.

"People do like these knitting needles the best," the clerk said, "the way the stitches slide off so smoothly."

"Yes. I'll take it."

It was one pound fifty pence. The girl clerk wrapped the card of needles in green tissue, then twisted each end, so that it made a pretty little package. Torrey, paying, thought of Caroline's knitting bag hanging on the arm of a chair in the sitting room at Ashenden Manor and how easy it would be for someone to slide a pair of knitting needles from the bag: People were in and out, Scott, Padraic Collins, Mark Temple, other visitors. Now she herself would drop in at Ashenden Manor and somehow find a chance to slide a hand into that knitting bag and see if by chance one of a pair of ten-gauge knitting needles was missing. It would be a be-ginning, a small step, but a step.

"Mrs. Tunet, isn't it?" The gray-haired clerk in the rimless glasses was leaning over the counter toward her, "Oh, my dear! I'm Mary Grogan. I heard! In your cottage last night, that poor gypsy woman!"

"Oh, yes. I—"

"So terrible! The poor woman." Mary Grogan put a hand to her black dress in the vicinity of her heart. "Oh, I can see it! That gypsy wandering drunk—she was often so—into your cottage in the storm, someone likely following her. There are other gypsies about; it could have been one of them, sneaky, dangerous. Oh, my dear! Mrs. Bryson—that's Jimmy Bryson's mother, he's Sergeant Jimmy Bryson, with the police—Mrs. Bryson was in this morning talking about it. So upsetting!"

"Yes." Torrey, feeling something was wanted, added, "I was at the movies. It was certainly—"

"Just two days ago, she came into the shop! Not Mrs. Bryson. The gypsy. The gypsy woman! I can tell you, I was a bit surprised. Though of course why shouldn't a gypsy knit?"

Torrey wet her lips. "What did she buy?"

"Well, it was a funny thing." Mary Grogan shook her head. "She wanted a pair of knitting needles. Not any particular size. 'The cheapest,' she told me, and she laughed; she had very white teeth. Well, everybody in the village buys these newer knitting needles now. So I was getting rid of the old wooden ones. I was selling off the big ten-millimeter for a pittance; nobody was going to buy them. I told her fifty pence. Good enough to knit with, they are. But it made no sense, her buying any size, as long as it's cheap. No sense at all! I told her so, but she just flashed her teeth at me and said, 'They'll make me rich!' And she gave me the fifty pence and I wrapped them in the twist of green and off she went."

38

Torrey came into the cool hall at Ashenden Manor. All the way since she'd left Grogan's Needlework Shop and bicycled along the road, she kept seeing Caroline Temple's knitting bag that hung on the arm of the Italian easy chair in the sitting room. The image nagged her. No reason except that, well, the knitting bag was so accessible. To anyone. Torrey felt it then: that little tingle between her shoulder blades, that signal of excitement, of daring. No longer a thief, but in this case some necessary . . . exploration? Like entering a different country, foreign, unknown —

"Ms. Tunet? Oh, Ms. Tunet! Good morning!" Jennie O'Shea, pulling a vacuum cleaner across the hall floor, stopped short. "Terrible! That gypsy! Smothered with a pillow! Ooooh! Only hours ago! Right in your cottage!" Jennie's eyes were wide. "A pillow! Oh, dear! Every day of my life, from this day forth, making up the beds, shaking out the pillows, I'll . . . Ooooh!"

"Yes, Jennie. Who's about?"

"They're in the sitting room, Ms. Caroline and Dr. Temple and Scott. All like on tiptoe, like with 'bated breath' as they say in books. 'Bated breath' about something. But *what*, I don't know — Except for Ms. Rowena who's up in her bedroom studying, what with her vet exams coming up next week. Doesn't even take time to put on lipstick. Not that she really needs — "

"Yes, Jennie. Thanks."

Torrey came into the sitting room.

"Torrey!" Caroline gave a little cry and let her knitting drop into her lap. "Torrey! What an awful thing. Dreadful for you, coming home to the cottage last night. And that poor gypsy! What happened?" Compassion and bewilderment in her low, husky voice.

Scott, lying on the sofa, lazily turned his handsome head and smiled at Torrey. "Better to've found a grandmother wolf in your bed."

Mark Temple, in new-looking country tweeds, stopped pacing the room. "A shock to Inspector O'Hare, no doubt."

Yes, Torrey agreed, of course a shock ... yes, the police were ... yes, yes, she was all right, except she was buying a new bed, she couldn't quite —

"Of course," Caroline said. But her white-lidded hazel eyes were wide, riveted on Torrey; her face was questioning, asking something more. She seemed almost to hold her breath, waiting.

Torrey became aware of that same waiting in Scott, his transparent-looking eyes expectant, and in the alert gaze of Dr. Mark Temple. For a moment after she stopped speaking, it was quiet in the sitting room, only the ticking of a wall clock.

Then Caroline said, "What about, you know, what you told me when I picked you up on the access road? About Rowena. That *maybe* you knew of ... of someone who'd been near the bridle path when my father was killed, someone who may have seen — "

"A witness," Scott broke in. "You told my mother that, possibly ..." He waited, eyebrows raised questioningly, one hand sporadically clenching and unclenching.

Mark Temple said, "You told Caroline you might have a witness to my father-in-law's murder."

Torrey looked blankly from Mark Temple to Scott, then to Caroline, Caroline's eyes blazing with hope. Caroline said, "You said you might know more today."

The slow realization came as Torrey looked from one face to the other. They didn't know. She bit her lip. But she had no choice. "The gypsy. The gypsy was my witness," she said, and heard a stricken moan from Caroline.

39

Torrey, in pity, looked away from the devastation in Caroline's face. Mark Temple said abruptly to Caroline, "I'm taking you for a walk. Good for your circulation. Better than sitting there and knitting—it only exercises your fingers." It was his afternoon half day.

Scott sat up, then hoisted himself from the sofa, using his cane. "I'm off, too. On my nefarious pursuits."

Torrey dragged her gaze from Caroline's knitting bag hanging on the arm of the Italian chair. It was a maroon linen bag with two big circles of bamboo as handles, so the bag could be opened wide.

"I'll just run up and see Rowena," she said. Caroline nodded, pale, wordless. Torrey watched them leave. Then she stood at the sitting room window until she saw Scott get into his Miata and zoom off down the drive.

She turned to the knitting bag. Heavier than she expected. Balls of wool, crochet needles, pain pills, a curved, tortoiseshell comb. Five pairs of knitting needles, all different gauges. A fruitless search. She felt chagrined; she'd been so hopeful of finding a lead.

She sat thinking. Rowena crying. *Back and back! It goes back and back!* Back to something in the Ashenden family? Something back to when? To what?—this murder of Dr. Ashenden.

From the kitchen, she heard the sound of a television show, a comedy, canned laughter. Everyone gone; only Rowena deep in her vet studies in the west wing. Only the eyes in the Ashenden portraits on the hall staircase to look down and see her.

40

In the library, dead quiet. The smell of old books, of leather, of wood smoke from last night's fire in the grate. Scattering of chairs, leather sofa. At the far end, the fireplace with a high-backed upholstered chair and fat footstool drawn cozily close. Under the tall windows was an English kneehole desk. Morning sunlight struck one corner of it.

The desk. She drew closer, hands clasped behind her, and looked down at the desk. On the left was a silver-framed photograph of a teenage Rowena on horseback. Velvet riding cap, red hair hidden. Stock and jodhpurs. The desktop also held a crystal tray of pens and pencils and a plastic ruby-colored magnetic shaker of paper clips. Weighed down by an egg-shaped piece of polished marble were a half dozen copies of the British medical publication *The Lancet*.

Torrey pulled open a drawer. There might, there just might be something. The drawer slid open easily at her touch. Monogrammed stationery, maps of the Wicklow countryside, stamps. Other drawers held clippings of sheep-growing publications, more stationery, magnifying glass, ruler. And in the bottom left-hand drawer a blue folder: *The Last Will and Testament of Gerald Ashenden*.

Torrey drew it out. Same as the copy of the will, made out two years ago, that Rowena had given her. She flipped through it. Same.

But—

On the cover, a different date. Four years ago. Torrey skimmed the will. So simple, only a couple of pages. Everything the same as that later will.

But—

Not quite the same. "To my grandson, Scott Keegan, a trust, to be administered by his mother, Caroline Keegan, providing him an income of ten thousand pounds annually."

What? Scott disinherited two years ago. Torrey looked down again at the will. Had Dr. Ashenden found out something about Scott that . . . what? Enraged him? Disgusted him? Were Scott's sexual preferences the cause? Or perhaps his extravagance? Scott had a taste for luxury. His jackets were enviable, the finest cashmere; his watch was melted gold on his wrist, his shoes handmade. He must have a good income from somewhere. Possibly through his late father?

Whatever the reason, his grandfather's punishment had crashed down on Scott. A legacy of ten pence.

Torrey put the will back and closed the drawer. Had Scott known that he'd been disinherited? Or, at his grandfather's death, had he expected a sizable inheritance?

She barely knew Scott. She'd been in Ballynagh only three months and friends with Rowena not that long. And Scott seemed to be always off to Dublin. What went on in his handsome head? Bitterness, for one thing: it showed in the downward little twist at a corner of his mouth. Cheated. He'd been cheated. His crippled leg. As a child, had he cried at night about it? Did he even now think, wretchedly, *Why me?*

Standing beside the desk, Torrey hesitated. So quiet, this manor house. But of course there were servants in the kitchen, Jennie O'Shea and the other girl, Mary. Possibly already preparing dinner? The upstairs work done?

Scott gone off somewhere. Caroline and Mark Temple out walking. Rowena studying.

Two wills, two years apart. And Rowena in Inspector O'Hare's sights. Torrey drew a breath and left the library.

Upstairs at the west end of the hall, the arched walnut door she knew was Scott's room. She turned the knob.

Simple, even chaste, this bedroom with its high, vaulted ceiling and arched fireplace. There was a single bed with a plump, white down comforter. The walls were papered, once red, but now faded to pink. There was a chest of drawers of polished tiger maple. On it was a photograph of a rock group with a young woman. Torrey approached and saw that the fair-haired young woman with a circlet around her brow was Caroline, who must then have been Caroline Ashenden. The man beside her, holding a trumpet in the air in a gesture of triumph must have been Tom Keegan, Scott's father.

She glanced into a tiled bathroom, then went through a dressing room to a comfortable sitting room with a table holding a scattering of magazines. There was an upright piano and piano bench on an oval rug and a rack piled with sheet music. Beyond was another door. Opening it, she saw it led into the back hall, a staircase going down.

What am I doing here? She didn't exactly know. But stubbornly, back again in the bedroom she poked impatiently through the dresser drawers hoping to find . . . what? In any case, she found nothing.

Enough! In the sitting room, she stopped abruptly beside the piano. Leave it. *Go!* You're not helping Rowena by snooping around Scott's rooms. You're reaching for something more ephemeral than a spider's web. In exasperation she thought: *There is nothing here to help!* Then on impulse, lifted the top of the piano bench.

Letters. She knelt on the floor. Two bundles of letters. She shuffled through them. Square, creamy, expensive envelopes addressed in an elegant script to Dr. Gerald Ashenden. Danish postmarks. Old. Years old. Picking up one of the letters, she saw underneath a small red leather notebook. She opened it. It was a list of checks received from Dr. Gerald Ashenden. Amounts in thousands of pounds. Checks made out to Scott Keegan, their dates going back from two weeks ago to two years ago.

Torrey sank back, staring at the list of checks. So that's where Scott's money came from! Blackmailing his grandfather. He must have found these letters two years ago. That's when he had suddenly become rich. Blackmail. Scott's secret river of gold. But *why*? Why risk his inheritance? She itched to read the letters. She picked up one of the square envelopes and began to slide out the letter — and heard, beyond the dressing room, the door to the bedroom open. Then Scott's voice, "Put it down there, by the door. Easy, now, easy! It's breakable, and one of a kind. Careful! *Careful*, for Christ's sake!"

She dropped the envelope back into the piano bench. In a minute she was through the sitting room door and down the back stairs, wishing she had dared steal at least one of the letters.

41

In the Jeep, coming back with Sheila from an Irish Women Poets Society reading in Dublin, Winifred had to slow down to go around the delivery truck parked by the side of the road. *Bellinger's Bedding*, the truck read, *Instant Delivery and Pickup.* Two delivery men in heavy tan sweatshirts were coming from the break in the hedgerow that led to the groundsman's cottage. They were carrying a bed whose rails were flecked with rust and peeling paint.

"A bit *too* finicky," Sheila said, as they drove on. "For instance, at Castle Moore, *generations* have died in the same family beds."

"But not assisted by a pillow mashed down on their face," Winifred said. "It rather changes things when you get under the blanket and turn out the light."

"She's a darling-*looking* young woman," Sheila said. "Torrey. Those gray eyes and that swag of dark hair that keeps falling over her forehead. I quite see how Jasper O'Mara can be taken with her, but—"

"And she with him. He's a fine piece of meat, that Jasper O'Mara. And a mind that sings." Then, thoughtfully, "But why it's singing in Ballynagh wonders me."

Sheila, though, was off on another tack. "Winifred? Awful as it is, maybe Rowena Keegan *did* kill her grandfather. Torrey Tunet would never believe it. Torrey will likely be claiming that the *real* murderer of Dr. Ashenden meant to smother *her*, Torrey, not the gypsy, because she's getting on to him."

"Or her," Winifred said automatically. She stepped harder on the gas. She wasn't going to tell Sheila of her dismaying suspicion, having these last few days from her study window seen Rowena walk Gravy Train back to the stable, that heavy walk that somehow . . . Yes, thinking back and back about Rowena and her grandfather. Obsessed with the child. It could be. A tragic poem she'd never write.

She hoped Inspector Egan O'Hare had no inkling.

At the Ballynagh police station, at four in the afternoon, Inspector Egan O'Hare absentmindedly watched Sergeant Bryson squeeze a little plastic envelope of mustard onto a corned beef sandwich, Bryson's idea of a teatime collation. He himself was having a mug of tea and a scone.

"Two murders in ten days." Chief Superintendent O'Reilly's voice on the phone from Dublin an hour ago had been silky smooth. "Any connection, Egan? Between the two murders? An eminent surgeon and a gypsy! What's going on there?"

What was going on was that he had let a murderess out of jail, and a drunken gypsy had got herself killed by being in the wrong bed. The bed of the meddlesome Ms. Tunet who might have been murdered if she hadn't been off at the movies and then rounding off her evening at O'Malley's.

If only he had the one missing piece! That tantalizingly missing piece: the *why* of Rowena Keegan's murdering her grandfather.

Tantalizing. It couldn't have been money. Dr. Ashenden would have given that girl the moon. O'Hare, exasperated, blew out a breath and shook his head. Evenings at home, staring at the television screen while Noreen was doing the dishes with Marcy's help — Marcy at eighteen was still at home, but the boys already off on their own—he'd kept trying to get at it. The *why* of the girl's murderous action. If he had that, the rest would be easy.

In the police station, the smell of mustard reached him. He looked over at Sergeant Bryson. "You've got that list, Jimmy?"

"Right here, Inspector."

Sergeant Bryson tossed the empty packet of mustard into the wastebasket and brought the list from the file.

Inspector O'Hare only glanced at it, after all. He knew it by heart. Not an alibi in the lot. Interrogation after interrogation. Wasting his time, reading it for the thousandth time, *Just walking about, Inspector . . . No, Inspector, can't say I did run into anybody . . . Lured out by the foliage, Inspector. Didn't see a soul, though.* One after another. Winifred Moore, Sheila Flaxton, Scott Keegan, Mark Temple, and the others.

Inspector O'Hare threw down the list. "Who's that writer fellow said, 'No man is an island'? Donne. John Donne. Well, Mr. Donne, each possible suspect in Dr. Ashenden's murder is an island."

"And what about the gypsy's murder, Inspector?" Sergeant Bryson asked.

O'Hare didn't even hear. He was thinking of Rowena Keegan. He was seeing again the fax of the water-stained notebook from the gully lying on his desk, seeing Rowena beside the desk in an old pair of stained jodhpurs, holding a can of diet Coke. Rowena lying to him, beads of perspiration on her forehead darkening the red-gold ringlets that fell across her brow. And something else. Something different, that creamy softness, an indefinable fullness, a heaviness like his wife Noreen when—

O'Hare caught his breath.

42

So—" Jasper was refilling his glass with the dark beer; the firelight reflected on the glass. "So your shameless snooping in Scott's rooms indicates exactly what? That he's absolutely not the murderer because killing his grandfather would've dried up the stream of his blackmailing riches? So that lets him out?"

Torrey nodded. Her mouth was full. Jasper had made braised lamb and an Irish dish called colcannon, a mixture of hot mashed potato, cabbage, butter, and milk, with a touch of nutmeg. Tonight's wine wasn't a wine but the dark beer. Guinness.

Jasper said, "Aren't you missing something, Torrey? Scott did himself out of his inheritance by blackmailing his grandfather. A mite shortsighted."

Torrey shrugged. "Maybe he turned to blackmail because he hungered for money *now*, not fifteen or twenty years from now. His grandfather was hale and hearty and could've lived a long time. Besides, maybe Scott felt his grandfather didn't think much of him—limping around on his skinny leg, and gay—so mightn't leave him much of anything." She sipped beer. "*I* don't know. I'm just a worker in the fields."

"All right," Jasper said. "So what have we here? One blackmailing. Two killings. Quite a shocker in this village where in O'Malley's pub the talk is of soccer and weather, with a bit of politics. And the wooded lands are like a poster, 'Come visit this corner of Ireland, bosky dells and sweet—' "

"Bosky dells, yes. But death in these woods has happened before. Rowena once told me of a heavy rain one spring. It made a bit of a landslide the other side of Castle Moore. A child caught in it was lost. And Kathleen Brady, Gerald Ashenden's wife, died in a fire in the woods."

"I didn't know."

"And another death, one that gave me shivers, Rowena said that when she was young, she'd heard tell how years before, one night at a dinner party at Ashenden Manor, a guest from Dublin got so drunk he wandered off and fell facedown in a bog. Too drunk to get up. He suffocated. There's a death for you!"

"Thanks, no. Glad I wasn't the one to find him. Never had a strong stomach." Jasper squinted at his glass of beer. It was a twenty-ounce draft glass, a pub glass. He'd bought two of them from Sean O'Malley.

"Dr. Collins found him," Torrey said. "He'd worried and gone looking. But too late. He got Ashenden to help him carry the fellow's body back to the manor. Padraic Collins didn't have the strength. He's small, too. And maybe pudgy back then, besides. Rowena says he likes his dinner too much."

Jasper raised a brow and helped himself to more colcannon. His comfortably overweight body in a black corduroy shirt and loose pants was relaxed. But after a few mouthfuls, he put down his fork, got up, and went to the fireplace. "These logs are damp; the dew went right through the canvas." With the poker he shifted the logs. The fire flared, then steadied. Jasper stood watching the licking flames, his back to Torrey. Then he turned. His long-jawed face was serious. "You've snared yourself in Rowena Keegan's troubles, Torrey. Stop it. You could make things worse for her, antagonizing Inspector O'Hare. And you're wearing yourself out." He shoved his hands into his pockets. "I come in at four o'clock this afternoon and find you sleeping with your head on the computer. Not good."

Torrey said, "But —"

"And what's on your computer? None of your work. Just one word on the computer: *brev*. A few dozen times. *Brev, brev, brev*. What's *brev*?"

"*Brev?* Danish. It means 'letter.' That batch of letters I told you about? In Scott's piano bench? I must've been thinking about that." She narrowed her eyes, concentrating. "There's something I almost remember about Denmark, something recent, but I can't quite . . ." She gave up, shrugged, and shook her head. "The sort of thing that can drive you crazy. Trying to remember something that's always just escaping you. Denmark. *Denmark*, damn it! *Denmark*." She blew out a breath. "Oh, well . . . This colcannon is strictly heaven. Why's it called colcannon?"

"Gaelic. Irish Gaelic, *cál ceannan*, white-headed cabbage. It also . . ."

But Torrey no longer heard. *Brev*. Danish. Of course! She suddenly felt almost breathlessly on track. Dr. Ashenden's will. Denmark. Bequests. "Well, well . . . !"

"*Now* what?" Jasper's black brows were drawn. He was studying her sharply. Torrey smiled at him. It warmed her, Jasper's concern for her. Lucky she was, that Jasper had come into her life, come by chance, come out of the blue. Caring, loving. As for tomorrow —

She shivered with anticipation, impatient for tomorrow. Meanwhile —

She forked up a mouthful of the wonderful, Irish dish. "Delicious, this colcannon. I think it's the nutmeg."

43

Cold, brisk October morning air. At nine-thirty, Torrey in duffle coat, woolen cap, jeans, and brogues pedaled fast up the oak-lined drive of Ashenden Manor.

"Oh, no, it isn't too early! I'm always up at six," Caroline Temple had told her when she'd phoned a half hour earlier, "Come right over! Scott calls them trinkets, those bequests. Would mementos be a better word? Or keepsakes? Can I give you breakfast? No? Well, anyway, yes. Now's fine. I'm alone, Rowena's already doing the horses at Castle Moore, and Scott's off somewhere. Mark just left for his office."

The "trinkets" lay on the sideboard in the dining room. Caroline had taken them from an envelope and lined them up. Torrey, still in her duffle coat, gazed down at them.

Her father's will in hand, Caroline said, "I should've already gotten them off to Wickham and Slocum—they're the lawyers. But anyway, I didn't." With a finger, she poked at a pair of cuff links, cameos set in filigreed silver. "These to"—she looked at her father's will—"to Dr. Leon Seuret, in Montreal. And this"—she pushed at a gold tie clip shaped like a fish with a sapphire for its eye—"this clip to Dr. Clive Mahoney, in Galway." Next, "The stopwatch—marvelous, isn't it?—to Dr. Campbell in Edinburgh. And the gold ring with the silver inlay to Dr. Steensen in Copenhagen. My father did have an eye! All beautiful things. Which he wore."

"Hmmm?" Torrey picked up the ring. It was a wide gold ring, inset with intertwining leaves in silver. She could see that there was an inscription inside. She held the ring up to the light and scanned the inscription. It was in Danish.

Caroline said, "I must ask Scott or Mark to drop these off at Wickham and Slocum tomorrow. If I remember. Honestly, sometimes I think I'm losing my —"

"Caroline? Could I possibly borrow this?" She was holding the heavy gold ring. "Until tomorrow or so? I'd like to show it to Jasper. He's so keen on Danish craftsmanship, he'd be fascinated." She almost bit her tongue on the lie.

Ten minutes later, the Danish ring wrapped in a napkin in her pocket, she pedalled as fast as possible back up the drive between the rows of ancient oaks.

"A message for you, Mr. O'Mara."

Sara Hobbs, at the reception desk at Nolan's Bed-and-Breakfast, slid the bit of blue paper from the cubbyhole. She blushed when she handed it to Mr. O'Mara. The note seemed so breezily intimate, so free and open, not caring who was looking or what might be forbidden. More like with a bit of laughter. She'd taken the message over the telephone, writing it down in her careful penmanship. The message was even somehow romantic: *Jasper — Skip today. Am on a hunt. How about a steak-and-kidney pie tomorrow night? And some kind of Irish tart? Besides this American one, ha ha. Love and kisses.*

The note was signed, simply, "T." But of course she knew it was Torrey Tunet who'd rented the old groundsman's cottage. Ms. Tunet, who'd stopped in at Nolan's a week ago, asking about Kathleen Brady from Galway. Sweet, bewildered Kathleen Brady who'd become Mrs. Gerald Ashenden and had visited her spinster aunt, bringing the thin-boned little Caroline. Ms. Tunet's visit had called up her own dear childhood memories and made her eyes misty.

Anyway, Ms. Tunet. Something slantingly lovely about that young woman, though why she'd thought *slantingly,* Sara couldn't really say. For some reason, Sara straightened and pulled up from a comfortable slouch. Shameful the way she was letting herself go.

"Thanks, Mrs. Hobbs." Jasper slipped the note into his corduroy pants pocket, smiled at her, and took himself off down the carpeted stairs.

Sara Hobbs settled down at the desk and went back to working on the accounts. Mr. O'Mara had the best room, the one with its own bath. And a telephone besides. He made only a few telephone calls. Most of them to other countries. Spain, Italy, France. But lately only to Portugal. She carefully billed the calls to his account.

44

It was windy at Kastrup Airport outside of Copenhagen and about fifty degrees, though the morning was sunny. Torrey felt smugly pleased that she had thought to wear her heavy jacket. She took her knitted woolen cap from her shoulder bag and put it on: it was shaped like a casque and snugly covered her ears. She looked at her watch. Ten minutes past two. The eleven o'clock morning flight from Dublin airport had taken two hours. But there was the hour's time change. She felt a familiar sense of excitement, something exhilarating that made her feel alert, as though her blood ran faster. *I've got the wind up,* she thought. The gold-and-silver ring with its Danish inscription was in an envelope in her shoulder bag.

Dr. Steensen. The address was in Nyhavn. That would be the old harbor area. Torrey remembered it from two years before when she'd been in Copenhagen on an EU inter-preting job. Nyhavn was an old part of the city, hundreds of years old, and the one-time notorious hangout of sailors, roving and drunk. But in recent years Nyhavn had become an elegant quarter of Copenhagen. The conference at which Torrey had interpreted had been held at the eighteenth-century Hotel D'Angleterre in Nyhavn, the most expensive hotel in Copenhagen. The roistering harbor was now fash-ionable apartments and elegant private houses.

Dr. Steensen's address was on a narrow street that was

quiet and spotless. It was one of a row of low, cream-colored buildings.

"Ms. Tunet? Dr. Steensen is expecting you." The girl who opened the door spoke in English. She was not much more than a schoolgirl, with short-cut blonde hair, and wearing corduroy jeans and a round-necked sweater. She was pulling on a puffy red windbreaker, one arm already in a sleeve. "I'm on my way out. Dr. Steensen's in there," she added as she jerked her head back, grabbed up a shoulder bag from a chair, and was out the door. It closed behind her with a solid click.

Torrey pulled off her knitted cap and combed her fingers through her hair. It was so quiet, so *richly* quiet. The hall had ivory walls and a rainbow-patterned rug on the bleached oak floor. A V-shaped translucent wall sconce sent soft light upward. Nothing else but a small green chair beside the door and an antlered coat stand of pale, polished wood. Torrey blew out a sigh of sensuous pleasure. Then she took off her jacket, hung it on an antler, and walked down the hall.

The room she entered struck her as dazzling yet comfortable. To her left was a brushed steel spiral staircase. In the center of the room, two brilliant red couches faced each other across an African woolen rug. Between the couches was a low black coffee table that held a few tattered magazines, a dish of cookies, and a Danish silver tea service that Torrey recognized as Jensen. Beyond, a scattering of rattan chairs faced a half-moon fireplace in which a small fire burned. The room smelled of hickory smoke.

But Dr. Steensen? The room was empty. Prickles of anxiety slid down Torrey's spine. Could Dr. Steensen have decided against seeing her? Would an efficient secretary appear with an excuse? *I'm sorry, Dr. Steensen has been taken ill.* Or maybe, *Dr. Steensen was unexpectedly called away.* Some excuse. Any excuse, having had a change of heart.

Too apprehensive to sit down, Torrey picked up one of the tattered magazines from the coffee table and flipped the pages. A bit of blue paper marked a page. Torrey read, "Dr. Steensen invariably looks as though she has just returned from Africa or the Far East, having dispensed vitally needed medicines and information on pedriatics. That often is true. Primarily in—"

But she was interrupted by quick, sure footsteps and a contralto voice, "So sorry! A phone call!"

Dr. Ingeborg Steensen, tall, straight-backed, came toward her. She wore a lavender silk-knitted sweater and gray flannel skirt. Her long fair hair was drawn back from her forehead and worn in a bun at her nape. The hand she held out, and that Torrey clasped, was warm and strong.

Torrey gazed at Dr. Steensen. She thought that a Scandinavian princess of a thousand years ago might have had that perfect face. Dr. Steensen must now be in her midseventies. There were fine wrinkles around her brown eyes and on her oval, tanned face. There were silvery streaks in the flaxen hair.

And just now, a scrutinizing, unsmiling look in Dr. Steensen's brown eyes as she met Torrey's gaze. "Please sit down, Ms. Tunet." As they sat down opposite each other on the red couches, Dr. Steensen said, "I see you've been trapped by one of the magazines my grandchildren insist on keeping." But it was a mechanical phrase, and Torrey was aware of a waiting tension in Dr. Steensen's straight back. How to start?

"Tea?" Dr. Steensen asked. "This is African; I think you'll like it. Very popular in Ireland, I remember." Dr. Steensen's contralto voice faltered over the word *Ireland*. She poured tea and held put the plate of cookies, "These are—" But abruptly she put down the plate, her hand so unsteady that the cookies slid off the plate onto the table. She looked squarely at Torrey.

"When you called me from Ballynagh, you said, 'about Dr. Gerald Ashenden.' I knew he was dead. Murdered. It was on the RTE news from Ireland. I don't know who you are. You said you wanted to bring me something. You said that it might help reveal who . . . who—"

"Yes. Reveal who murdered Dr. Ashenden."

"But," Dr. Steensen looked puzzled. "But according to the reports, the Gardai already have reason to believe they know who killed him. It was his granddaughter, Rowena Keegan."

"So they suspect," Torrey said. "But I don't. She wouldn't. Not Rowena! She's my friend. I know her."

Dr. Steensen sat back against the red cushions and folded her arms. The thin lavender sweater clung softly against her neck and shoulders; her brown eyes gazed at Torrey. She sighed and shook her head, and the light shone on her silvery hair. "And in what magical way do you think I can help solve this mystery? And save your friend Rowena?"

Torrey reached down to where she had rested her shoulder bag against the red couch. She slid in a hand and withdrew the envelope and handed it across the table to Dr. Steensen. "There's this."

Watching Dr. Steensen open the envelope, her heart began to beat more rapidly. All the way on the plane from Dublin, she had thought of that gold ring with its chaste design in silver. It was a man's wedding ring with the inscription in Danish: *To Gerald, my love, to our union. October 1940. Ingeborg.*

But Gerald Ashenden had married Kathleen Brady in August of that same year.

"Where did you get this ring?" Dr. Steensen's voice was husky. She slipped the ring onto her middle finger, where it hung loosely. *"Where?"*

"I borrowed it. Dr. Ashenden left it to you in his will. I

have to return it so that it can be sent you properly, through the lawyers."

"I see. And this is your magic? To bring me this ring! As though I could know something that might help save your friend? Your friend Rowena, who murdered her grandfather? Ah, no, Ms. Tunet! Ah, no!"

"But she didn't! She didn't kill him! When I read the inscription in the wedding ring, I thought, *Go to Dr. Steensen! Maybe she knows something that would help me.* Help Rowena, I mean." She was gabbling, she knew, but she couldn't stop. "I thought at least you could . . . could give me a lead. Or, oh, I don't know!" Abruptly she felt ridiculous, a fool. What in God's name was she doing in Copenhagen in this apartment with its satiny steel spiral staircase and red couches, looking across a Jensen teapot at this beautiful Scandinavian woman named Ingeborg Steensen who after all had not married the young Dr. Gerald Ashenden. Fool, *fool!* And what, anyway, had it to do with Rowena? Was she losing her mind? A wasted trip.

"I'm sorry." She rubbed her temples. She would have to ask for the wedding ring back, then leave. She looked at Dr. Ingeborg Steensen, who gave no smile in return, nothing but a steady regard from her brown eyes.

"You see," Torrey burst out impulsively, defensively, "Rowena is pregnant!" And then she thought, *But what has that to do with it?*

Dr. Steensen's brown eyes widened. "Ahhh!" It was almost a groan. Then, softly, "I pity her."

"Pity her? Why? What do you mean?"

Dr. Steensen said quietly, "Because now I know that I truly cannot tell you anything that will help her."

They sat staring at each other. "What?" Torrey managed at last. "What is it?"

Dr. Steensen turned the ring around and around in her fingers. She looked down at it. "I was a medical student in

Dublin. I was in love with Gerald Ashenden. We were going to marry. Then something terrible happened. I learned of it only by chance from a drunken X-ray technician. When I learned of it, I was filled with horror. I packed my clothes and student books and fled home to Denmark." Dr. Steensen drew a breath, "Yet" — she shook her head in disbelief — "yet years later I fell to answering Gerald's letters. Even though, in my mind, I rehearsed over and over what he had done and why I fled from him. An endless round, round, and round. Strange. I had long since married. I had children, I have grandchildren."

A silence. Torrey waited. She was seeing Ingeborg Steensen, a flaxen-haired young medical student, brown eyes wide with horror, stuffing clothes and books into a traveling bag with brass clasps. Yet, years later, letters . . .

"So, Ms. Tunet, I will tell you why I fled. Can it help Rowena Keegan? Alas, no. I can only tell you that, were I Rowena, I might have tried to kill him too." Dr. Steensen put the Danish ring down on the coffee table and slid it slowly toward Torrey. "It is not a tale you will enjoy hearing, Ms. Tunet." She looked at her wristwatch, then sat back against the red cushions. "We have time."

45

W inifred?"

"Sheila, you're interrupting me. When I wear my cap on backward, it means the Muse is with me. Which you very well know."

"Yes, but—" Sheila came farther into Winifred's workroom in the old tower section of the castle. It was midafternoon, but dull. A green-shaded lamp glowed on Winifred's heavy old oak desk with a blotter set in an old-fashioned blotter holder with leather edges. There was a glass filled with a miscellany of pens and pencils and a dish of paper clips and rubber bands. Right now, but not usually, a bottle of ink rested on a corner of the blotter. On a nearby table was a computer, temporarily shrouded with a kitchen towel.

"But what?"

"I've been to see Inspector O'Hare. To confess about Rowena Keegan. My conscience! Torture! Sleepless nights! Tossing and turning."

Winifred carefully put down the feather pen on which she'd been working on a rondel. A rondel was not a computer poem, but a feather pen poem. It made a difference. "Sheila, I want no clichés in this room. No 'tossing and turning.' No 'sleepless nights.' It sticks to the walls." But the look she turned on Sheila was serious. "You've been to Inspector O'Hare to confess what about Rowena Keegan?"

"That day on the bridle path? When Dr. Ashenden was killed? The hot water heater went off and I wanted to wash my hair and have a bath. I couldn't find Meecham's address under plumbing, and neither could Rose, and it turned out you'd gone off racewalking. So I went looking for you. I went past the bridle path just five minutes before that awful — just before Dr. Ashenden came galloping, cantering, whichever. Anyway, I saw Rowena Keegan *right there*. Looking very sneaky, somehow. Up to something. I could tell."

Winifred regarded Sheila. "What did Inspector O'Hare say to that?"

"Say? He asked me to repeat it and told Sergeant Bryson to type up what I said."

"And then you signed it? What Sergeant Bryson typed?"

"Yes. But now I'm *worried* about it. It doesn't actually prove anything against Rowena. And I like her. She's one of my favorite — but finally I had no choice, it was a matter of my conscience. At night I kept tossing and — "

"Sheila, *please*!"

46

"Got you!" Inspector O'Hare said aloud. He was alone in the station and pacing fast, Coke machine to toilet door and back. He was on a coffee high. One eight-ounce morning cup was usual, but he'd had two. It was a jubilant occasion, after all. "Got you!"

Stunned. Exactly how he'd realized Rowena Keegan was pregnant, he couldn't say. That creamy look under her chin? No, not that. Nothing different in her figure, either. But he had only to think of Noreen to know.

Lying in bed last night beside Noreen, he'd thought, *Pregnant by whom?* Strange that Rowena Keegan had never brought a young man or two to Ashenden Manor. It would've been common knowledge if she had. Old Mrs. Brennan would have known, would have gossiped about it, would have ferreted out the possible suitor's age, religion, business, family background, social position, likely inheritance, height, education, drinking habits, and whether he was country or city bred. All of Ballynagh would have known. Besides, Jennie O'Shea at Ashenden Manor was a magpie on the phone to Rose at Castle Moore and would have mentioned this or that prospective suitor, and Rose's younger sister Hannah kept company with Jimmy Bryson, not that if Hannah had mentioned to Jimmy . . .

Indeed. Because this was Ballynagh, where a cat's spawn

in a barn was known within minutes, as well as O'Malley's daughter's having taken ten pounds from the till to go larking in Dublin.

In bed, Noreen's soft breathing. O'Hare, staring into the dark, was remembering having years ago seen a newspaper photograph of the pretty little Rowena when only eight being held astride a mettlesome young horse by her grandfather, as though the three of them had become one, something sexual in it. He was remembering and remembering; other scenes through later years floated across his vision.

So now, was it *possible*? His heart beat hard. All those years, the girl a victim? And now, finding herself pregnant. Yes! Her repressed rage bursting forth. Revenge! That elusive *why* of Rowena's attack on her grandfather in the meadow! And, finally, the murder of her grandfather on the bridle path.

Now, pacing the police station, O'Hare told himself, *Sit down*, but instead he gave a laugh and a shudder and kept pacing. He'd have to work out his procedure. But now that he had the link, the nexus, however tenuous, he'd forge ahead, get proof. He was sharp and had proved himself in the past. He thought of the confession he'd ultimately get from Rowena Keegan. He thought of delivering his final successful, startling, sensational conclusion of the Ashenden case to Chief Superintendent O'Reilly at Dublin Castle. Those damned eyebrows above the chief superintendent's cold blue eyes would —

"Morning, Inspector." Sergeant Jimmy Bryson, a half hour late — it was already nine o'clock. He was taking something from a paper bag. "I got this for Nelson." A fake bone, meat-flavored. Nelson was standing up and going to Bryson, wagging his tail and nosing into Bryson's hand. He always knew.

"Very nice."

"The forensic report about the gypsy, Inspector. It came in by fax last night. I put it in the green folder."

At his desk, O'Hare flipped open the folder. The forensic crime report was short. Death: eight-fifteen P.M. Alcohol level in the woman's body: point three three. So, very drunk when smothered with the pillow. No blood. No fingerprints. A cigarette butt in the grass beside the lintel.

Sergeant Bryson said, "I'd lay a thousand pounds, Inspector, that they'll just file it away. Unsolved. It isn't upper-class society. Not even drug-related. Or bloody and sexy."

O'Hare nodded. The gypsy's wagon had proved unrevealing: A stack of pots and pans. A dishpan full of cheap earrings, bracelets, necklaces. A kneesock contained thirty-four pounds and some pence. The gypsy's sad-eyed, shaggy little pony was now in the Castle Moore stables, courtesy of Ms. Winifred Moore.

O'Hare closed the green folder. It was to the shame of Ireland, as he'd said more than once to Sergeant Bryson, that those itinerants—gypsies, tinkers, and "travelers" as those folks in their caravans were called—were scorned as lesser citizens.

And meanwhile! Meanwhile, look at the shenanigans of the rich landowners in such stately homes as Ashenden Manor!

"Inspector?" Jimmy Bryson was looking out onto Butler Street. "Them, again, isn't it?"

Inspector O'Hare followed Bryson's gaze. Two people going past. He recognized them. They'd been in Ballynagh on a previous case. That skinny photographer in his black turtleneck and duffle and camera bags was from the scandal sheet *Scoop*. The fat girl with the shaggy bangs and big behind was his assistant. The sharks were closing in.

47

On the plane from Copenhagen heading southwest toward Dublin, Torrey ate the last half of the chocolate bar with almonds she'd bought at the Copenhagen airport; she'd had no time for lunch. Against the dark windowpane, she saw Ingeborg Steensen's face and heard her voice: *I can only tell you that, were I Rowena, I might have tried to kill him too.*

Torrey rubbed her temples. Devastating to hear, but — something off, something missing. Two things: Rowena, because she *was* Rowena, would never have committed anything premeditated like the bridle path murder. Never! Not Rowena.

The second thing was the perplexing question: Why, up to the very day that Rowena tried to ride down her grandfather in the meadow, had she and her grandfather been such close, loving friends? Up to that very day. Up to that very afternoon.

That very afternoon.

In Dublin it was raining. The plane touched down at the Dublin Airport in Collinstown eight miles north of the city center. The temperature had fallen. Outside the airport it was cold, with gusts of rain. In minutes, Torrey's heavy woolen jacket and knitted cap were damp. Shivering, she looked around for the 41A bus to Dublin. The bus would be chilly, clammy, smelling of damp newspapers and rubber. In Dublin, she'd have to get the local bus south and finally get off the bus on the access road to Ballynagh. She couldn't afford the luxury of a taxi even to Dublin; the taxi fare was about fifteen pounds, and then the tip. The shockingly expensive air fare to Copenhagen and back had knocked out her budget for the next month. In her shoulder purse right now she had two pounds and a handful of twenty and tenpence coins, enough for the regular bus fare to Dublin, which was a pound thirty pence and would take until doomsday to reach the city in this miserable wet weather. People were hurrying past her, wet mackintoshes and umbrellas on all sides.

She looked at her watch. Five-forty-five, and having had no lunch, she was hungry. She pictured a bowl of Jasper's delicious corn soup with the dash of hot red pepper, followed by one of his heartwarming and body-warming dinners while a fire glowed in the fireplace —

A shove made her stagger, and a grating voice said, "Get on there, miss, if you're going!" A man in a greasy cap and shapeless overcoat pushed roughly past her, hurrying toward the 41A bus.

She followed, pulling her jacket collar closer, only to feel its cold dampness against her neck. To her left she noticed a sleek, dark blue Jaguar, parked but with its motor running. She thought longingly of the luxury of its soft leather cushions, the quiet purr of the expensive motor, the warmth of the air within, the —

"Torrey! *Torrey!*" The driver-side window of the Jaguar had slid down, and someone in the driver's seat was calling her name. Or was she imagining —

"Torrey!"

The rain was coming down harder; it blurred her vision. A gust of wind yanked at her hair. A taxi whizzed past and a sheet of water splashed up and soaked her legs and shoes. Damn!

"Torrey! Over here!" That familiar, resonant voice. A parka-clad arm beckoned from the Jaguar.

In the driver's seat, Jasper O'Mara.

Smooth mahogany dashboard, a silver-edged clock. The warm air was delicious, cozy, relaxing. Torrey toed off her wet shoes and and sank back against the soft leather. She wouldn't ask. Not yet. In minutes, the car was purring along the road to Dublin as though gliding on silk, the landscape sliding past. Outside, rain spattered on the Jaguar's blue hood.

"Try this." A leather-covered thermos. "Hot raspberry tea with lemon and a shot of rum."

She drank from the little cup. Her stomach glowed. Heaven. It was several minutes more before she said carefully, wondering too many things, "How'd you know I'd gone to Copenhagen? I'd told no one."

"A book dealer wouldn't have known." Amusement in Jasper's voice. "But easy enough for an investigative journalist to find out."

She ran a finger reflectively around the rim of the thermos. "So that's what you are? I was never really sure you were a book dealer. I thought maybe a chef."

"A chef would've been my second choice. But I like puzzles even more. Less money, though. This Jag's ten years old, but I baby it." He shrugged. "Fine with me."

"Exactly what else you told me was the truth?"

"Well . . ." A fog was coming in and he was squinting at the road ahead. "Dún Laoghaire to Clifden was the truth. I was only passing through Ballynagh, planning just bed-and-breakfast for the night. But there you were on the road, like a dying swan in jeans. Next morning, when I politely came by to check that you'd survived, I thought, *Ms. Tunet needs feeding up. Looks like Ophelia just dredged out of the lake. Potato and mushroom soup with a bit of fresh tarragon. Chicken dipped in the finest of bread crumbs, then sautéed. Green beans barely par-boiled, crunchy to the bite.* So I thought I'd stay a night or two longer in Ballynagh. And then—"

"Then you stayed on. And seduced me with gastronomy."

"Well, yes."

"What about those rare books you were always bicycling off after? Rare books. Eureka! A Yeats first edition found in a thatch-covered hut. Or maybe finding a volume of a James Stephens in a cow barn, propping up a chair leg. A lie, right?"

"Well, rare books sounded romantic. I thought that would intrigue you, you love books. The fact is, I've a sideline. I was gathering recipes for a weekly column I write. So I—"

"You're not JASPER! *That* Jasper? In the *Gaelic Guide*?"

"It relaxes me. With my kind of investigative reporting, I need it."

Torrey looked at his solid, comfortable body. He wore old tweed pants and a gray-green sweater. "What's your real name?"

"Shaw. Jasper Shaw."

She recognized the name. Political, the *Irish Times*. Standing with Gerry Adams. She'd read his piece attacking the violence of the "real IRA" that was responsible for the shameful explosions in Northern Ireland. Photos of mangled bodies, dead children. "But why call yourself Jasper O'Mara?"

"Why? Because nobody's ever heard of Jasper O'Mara. He doesn't exist. But Jasper Shaw? At every bed-and-breakfast, the proprietor recognizes the name and gets a wild look in his eye, or *her* eye, and I've no peace over my breakfast while they're tipping me off to an investigation I'm missing, such as who really shot crime reporter Veronica Guerin of the *Sunday Independent*, but they'll give me a lead, the *inside story*. What's more, they're going to give it to me *right now*, over my sausages and eggs. Same thing in pubs.

Wherever. From whomever. Why didn't I tell you? I was always about to. But, I don't know. We had something I didn't want to jostle."

Torrey said, "I see. Sort of." But for now she had too much else to think about. "How'd you know to meet my flight tonight?"

"Easy. There's only one afternoon return flight from Denmark that would've given you any time in Copenhagen." She felt his glance. "*Brev:* Danish for 'letters.' Denmark. It was about Rowena?"

She felt suddenly exhausted and hopeless beyond belief. "Yes, Rowena." She clasped the leather-covered thermos and helplessly began to talk. She never thought, can I trust Jasper O'Mara who is really Jasper Shaw? She knew only that in this warm blue Jaguar she couldn't keep from confiding everything to him. To Jasper: dissembler, investigative journalist, marvelous cook, and lover.

Gazing through the windshield at the rainswept road, she told it all. At the end, exhausted, she said, "Rowena didn't kill him. Somebody else did. Who?" And tiredly she leaned her head against Jasper's shoulder and fell asleep.

A hand. A strong, tanned hand on the steering wheel. She woke to the luxurious purr of the car, aware of a clear dark sky, of stars, of the mountains of Wicklow. Lights of an occasional oncoming car swept up and vanished.

But the hand. He was left-handed, guiding the car negligently. His hand, then the wrist, and between the hand and the sleeve of his gray-green sweater, on his wrist, the watch. The watch he'd lost in the woods that fatal afternoon of the knitting needle death of Dr. Ashenden.

Torrey stirred and lifted her head from his shoulder. Her neck was stiff. She rubbed it. "I see you found your watch."

"Awake, are you? My watch? I never lost it."

"But, remember —"

"A lie. I couldn't trust you then. I couldn't trust anybody.

I said I'd lost my watch, an excuse so I could secretly meet Rowena in the gully. The gully where she lost the notebook the Gardai found that next day."

"*You?* Meet with *Rowena*?" She turned to stare at him. Her head began to ache.

Jasper said, "I couldn't tell you before. It goes like this: I've a good friend, Flann. He's gotten involved in a political — a bit of trouble. In certain confidential quarters it's known that he's also involved with Rowena. He — "

"With *Rowena*? Rowena *Keegan*?"

"They're lovers. Planning to marry. After this political . . . uh, situation is over. Once he gets clear and can safely return."

It was too stunning to take in. Rowena's lover. Rowena had a lover. Flann. Flann something.

"What's he like, this Flann?"

"Trinity College. With ideals, but not a firebrand. His heaven is more a small manor house, a loving wife who was formerly Rowena Keegan, a pack of kids, and running a local liberal paper. Plus a horse or two."

"Sounds . . . a gem." Did this gem, Flann, know that Rowena was pregnant? And planning an abortion?

Moreover, if he was a gem, why was he in hiding from the law? And what did Jasper mean by "can safely return"?

"So, this Flann, return from where? How are *you* involved?"

"We keep in touch, Flann and I. When he learned I was going through Ballynagh, he asked me to let Rowena know he was still safe, and where, and when he'd return. But we're known in those same certain quarters to be friends, Flann and I. A phone conversation wasn't safe; it could be bugged. So we met in the gully."

Ahead, to the left, the lights of the Duggans' farmhouse, it was seven-thirty and full dark. In a few minutes they'd reach the break in the hedge; the groundsman's cottage was only a few yards the other side of the hedge. "Leek and garlic soup," Jasper said. "Mashed sweet potatoes, mint peas, and sausages. All on the stove, only needing heating. I'll park the Jag in Ballynagh. Back in twenty minutes."

"About Flann, return from where?" She felt obstinate.

"The price of petrol is going up," Jasper said, "and wasn't that ever the way of the world?" He kissed her on the nose and reached across her and unlatched the door. "Out. Out."

48

Torrey wormed the Danish ring from the tight front pocket of her jeans. "Here. And thanks so much, Caroline."

Caroline took the ring and looked up at Torrey who hadn't even sat down but stood beside the breakfast table at Ashenden Manor looking so . . . well, so in*tense*. Her black-fringed gray eyes were strained, as though she hadn't slept. For another thing, Torrey's rust-colored sweater was on inside out, all the seams showing, as though she'd dressed inattentively, her mind elsewhere. And on her dark hair she wore, like a headband, a kerchief, orange and turquoise, with a design of blue peacocks. A Chinese-looking thing. Incongruous. But then, there were quite a few things that Ms. Torrey Tunet didn't care a fig about.

Caroline pensively turned the Danish ring over and over. Lovely, intricate design. "What did he think of it? The craftsmanship."

"What? Who?"

"Jasper. Your friend, Jasper O'Mara. You thought he'd be interested in the Danish craftsmanship." She waited.

"Jasper. Oh, yes. Admirable, he thought, remarkably . . . Caroline, I want to ask you something." And now Torrey did sit down.

Caroline said, "Do. And have some tea. You look a bit

chilled." She poured a cup of tea. "And the toast's still warm."

"Thanks. Think back, will you, Caroline?" Torrey's face was serious. "The night before Rowena ran down —*accidentally* ran down — her grandfather in the meadow, were they friendly?"

"Of course! As always. And of course it was an accident. It couldn't have been otherwise."

"Yes, certainly. I just —"

"The night before, they had a whiskey nightcap before bed, in the library. They always did that. Just the two of them, Rowena and my father. Scott didn't get on with his grandfather; neither did Mark. I went to bed after dinner, as usual, to read for a couple of hours or knit and watch television. Why? Does that answer your —"

"And the next morning? Rowena and her grandfather? Still . . . friends?"

"Torrey, really! Of course! Why ever not?"

"I *mean*, what I'm trying to get at, Caroline — were they still friends right up to the time your father left for Dublin that morning? That's what I'm asking."

Caroline sighed. How was this helping Rowena? Impossible. She gazed at Torrey in the inside-out sweater. "Yes, friends. Right up to the time he left for Dublin. I was going out to the kitchen garden behind the stable, and I heard them talking horses. Chatting, laughing. On my way back, I saw Rowena kiss him good-bye. As always." She waited, then said triumphantly, "So you see! No enmity at all!"

But Torrey persisted. "That would've been about what time?"

"About . . ." Caroline thought. "It was a Friday. My father's short day, end of the week. Not medical. Business. Accounts and such. Lunch at the Shelbourne or Merrion. He left here about ten that morning as usual. He was always back by three." She waited, looking at Torrey, feeling helpless. She seemed to see not Torrey Tunet but her Rowena growing smaller and smaller in the distance, a dwindling, lost figure.

Torrey stood up. To Caroline's surprise, she now looked remarkably wide awake. Her eyes were bright, and there was a flush of color on her cheeks.

"I'm off." She gave Caroline something that was rather like a military salute, and was out the door.

49

Jennie O'Shea was deadheading the geraniums in the big concrete pot beside the stable door. The pot of geraniums had been Ms. Rowena's idea, to dress up the stables. End of October, cold weather, this would be the last of the geraniums. Jennie liked deadheading: bend and snap, bend and snap, breaking off right at that knobby part, no twisting or tearing, and not having to bring scissors or a knife from the kitchen. Only thing, that bastard stallion, Thor, always lunging off to the side and taking a bite out of the geraniums. But no more. Dead as a doornail, knitting needle in his behind. Now there was only Sweet William, the bay, Ms. Rowena's three-year-old. His coat was like brown satin — she wouldn't mind having hair like that, gleaming like brown satin, not like her own black dull hair, though at least curly, curlier than Rose's over at Castle Moore.

Jennie straightened, holding the plastic dish with the withered geraniums to be got rid of, and said "Oh!" for there was Ms. Tunet not five feet away, and Jennie hadn't heard a thing.

"Sorry, Jennie, did I startle you?" Ms. Tunet said. She was wearing some fancy-looking scarf tied around her head, pretty colors, mostly turquoise.

"Oh, that's all right, I was just —" Jennie shook the plastic dish.

"I was looking for you," Ms. Tunet said. "I wanted to ask you. You know Ms. Rowena and I are friends, so I'm sort of trying to, well, *figure* out some things. Maybe in some minor way, to help her. So there won't be any, uh, miscarriage of justice. You see?"

"Oh, yes! I do!" She liked Ms. Rowena so much. It was all so scary. She and Rose were on the telephone every morning with each bit of news; it looked worse and worse for Ms. Rowena.

"I was wondering, Jennie," Ms. Tunet said. "That Friday. The Friday that Ms. Rowena rode the stallion into the meadow? And accidentally might've killed Dr. Ashenden? That morning. Were you here, Jennie?"

"Oh, yes. *Tuesday's* my day off, Ms. Tunet."

"Well, let's see." Ms. Tunet smiled at her. "That Friday morning. Have I got it straight, that Dr. Ashenden left about ten o'clock that morning for Dublin?"

Jennie could smell the sharp, acrid aroma of dead geraniums in the plastic bowl. "Yes, he always did, Fridays." A waste of petrol, spending such a short day in Dublin, but Dr. Ashenden was rich; he could spend his money any old way he liked.

"Uh-huh," Ms. Tunet said, "What happened then?"

Jennie was puzzled. "Nothing *happened*, that I can exactly — well, Ms. Rowena went up to her bedroom to study. I made them soup and sandwiches for lunch. They eat dinner at night."

"Them?" Ms. Tunet said. She looked very intense, her eyes almost squinting.

"I mean Ms. Rowena and her brother Scott and her mother. Of course Dr. Temple was at his office in Dublin, it being a weekday. After lunch, Ms. Temple went to lie down; her neck or back was out. Sometimes she doesn't come down until maybe three o'clock. Even later. Reading and such. Napping."

"So . . . let's see," Ms. Tunet said. "So after lunch, well, what I'm asking is, just before Ms. Rowena left the house and went down to O'Malley's and got drunk, and then *supposedly* tried to ride down her grandfather in the meadow . . . well, what I'm saying is, did anything happen to upset Ms. Rowena? that you know of?"

Jennie started to get that creepy-crawly feeling she'd had when she'd told Rose on the telephone about it. But it wasn't exactly related, so she'd thought better not get involved, what with her holiday coming up and all.

"Anything particular?" Ms. Tunet asked.

"Particular? Not particular, I wouldn't say particular." She felt funny, because now that she was thinking of it again, it began to swell up, seemed to get bigger and bigger. It was like she was beginning to see it through a magnifying glass. "Not particular." In her hands the bowl trembled.

"What?" Ms. Tunet said. Then again, louder, "*What*, Jennie?"

"Oh, Ms. Tunet! Nothing much." But maybe it wasn't nothing much. Uneasy guilt rode her shoulder. "Just . . . it was after lunch, maybe half past one o'clock." Now that she'd started, it wasn't so bad. "I'd cleared the dishes and all. I heard Jimmy Hogan — he's the postman — ring his bicycle bell, and I went out through the hall and got the post. I came back in and I was walking past the library. It was all so peaceful. I could hear Ms. Rowena and Scott talking in the library, having a chat, I guess. Then all of a sudden, I heard Ms. Rowena give an awful . . . like a scream. Then she came out of the library. She was walking like a sleep-walker, her eyes staring like they were painted on her face. She went right past me, out the front door.

"Scott went hitching after her. He almost fell down the front steps, calling after her. But she paid no attention." Jennie stopped. She felt breathless.

"And?" Ms. Tunet said.

"And? They said later she went down to the village to O'Malley's and got drunk."

"Did he follow her? Scott?" Ms. Tunet asked.

"No, he just sat down on the bottom step. It must've been cold, those granite stones. He sat there rubbing his face. But after a minute he got up and he almost fell over on account of his leg. His little car was in front. He got in and went off. I could see down past the main gate. He went left, toward Dublin."

Well, now she'd told it, she was relieved. Not that it amounted to anything. And the rest didn't count. She was getting cold; it was nippy and she had only her cardigan. She could do with a hot cup of tea. She hesitated. She looked off, like checking on the sheep up there on the mountainside. She knew her face was getting red and that Ms. Tunet was seeing her face get red. She had a feeling that Ms. Tunet, having seen it, was going to keep her here until Doomsday until she knew top to bottom about that Friday. Though for her part, she couldn't see how the rest was related to anything, but separate.

"So then, there you were, standing in the hall, holding the mail," Ms. Tunet said, like giving her a hard little shove.

"Yes, holding the post, the mail. And I turned around and Dr. Collins was coming from the library. I said 'Oooff!' I was a bit startled. Dr. Collins has the run of the house, though. He likes to drop in and maybe spend a few minutes in the sitting room with Mrs. Temple, such a sunny room. She likes to knit in there. Or he goes to sit in the library before the fire in that big wing chair and snoozes, so cozy, so hidden. You'd never know he was there!

"Anyway, there he was, he looked like, well, his *face*. It was all blotchy, and then he just stood, like a store dummy, so still, I got frightened, you hear about heart attacks and strokes and such. I said, 'Are you all right, Dr. Collins?' But he just looked at me for a whole minute, like in a trance.

Then he said, 'A little flutter of the heart, Jennie. But I'm fine. I'll just sit here for a bit.' And he sat down on a side chair, and I went into the dining room to sort out the letters. That's all, Ms. Tunet."

Jennie felt funny, then, the way Ms. Tunet was staring at her as though she'd been struck by a blow. Been hit by something. But all she said was, "Thank you, Jennie. I'm going back inside with you. I want to use the phone." They went together back to the house, Jennie not saying anything more, except, "You've got your sweater on inside out, Ms. Tunet," and Ms. Tunet looked down at her sweater, surprised.

Sorting the mail in the dining room, Jennie could hear Ms. Tunet on the hall telephone. It was the strangest thing, Ms. Tunet calling Collins Court and saying to Helen Lavery, Dr. Collins's housekeeper — Helen always took the calls at Collins Court — that there was an emergency, a boy in a tractor accident at the McGinnis farm, and was Dr. Collins there? And then telling Helen Lavery, well, tell Dr. Collins to please come immediately, the boy had crushed his leg. Then there was silence in the hall, and Jennie knew that Ms. Tunet had gone.

50

Helen Lavery was frightened, shaking, crying in her sleep and awakening bewildered, her gray hair long enough to be damp with tears, the way she rolled her head around in bed, must have done, and the bedclothes all tangled up. For days now.

She kept seeing that late Friday afternoon when Dr. Collins had bandaged up Dr. Ashenden's shoulder. It had been so peaceful at Collins Court, the afternoon sunlight reflected on the glass-fronted bookcase in the library. She'd been vacuuming the rug that Dr. Collins's great-great-grandfather had brought from India, when she saw Dr. Collins reflected in the glass-fronted bookcase.

Helen shut off the vacuum and turned around. Dr. Collins looked terrible, all white and shaken, and the makeup he used around his eyes that he thought nobody knew he wore, it was all runny. He took the decanter of whiskey from the tray that had come down from his great-aunt Agnes, who'd had the Victorian house in Bray and that Helen used the special silver polish on, the best polish, to Helen's mind, though it always left a bit of dried pink in the embossed edging. Dr. Collins splashed whiskey into one of the cut-glass tumblers that Helen kept sparkling clean. Dr. Collins never drank except the one whiskey before dinner, and on the evenings he played chess with Dr. Ashenden, when he'd sometimes come home feeling good if he'd won. Then he'd have a small one. Tiny.

But that afternoon of the meadow! "She rode him down, Helen! Sergeant Bryson saw it! Such a dreadful—" and he started to cry, which made the makeup run even worse. Helen had never seen him cry, not in all those twenty-two years.

And then with the whiskey glass trembling in his hand and the tears smearing his makeup, he'd begun babbling such awful, frightening things about back then in the woods, something that had happened. At first she couldn't make it out. But seeing his misery, she understood in some round-about way that she loved Dr. Collins and suffered when he suffered. A revelation.

And now, with Dr. Ashenden gone, Dr. Collins at least had her, Helen Lavery. She knew that she would always care for him and protect him. She always had done.

Anyway, now, except for nighttimes with the frightening dreams, Helen felt pretty much in charge of herself. Answering the phone as usual, cooking the meals, shopping for the foods Dr. Collins liked, and taking messages. Right now, from the kitchen window, she could see that a rabbit had gotten into the kitchen garden and was hopping down toward the carrots. She shook out a handful of dried kidney beans from the glass jar. She'd get rid of Mr. Rabbit in two shakes, as usual. But the doorbell was ringing. She'd answer it first.

She went unhurriedly through the great hall to answer the door. Right now Dr. Collins was out, off on an emergency: a boy in a tractor accident at the McGinnis farm. The boy had a crushed leg, the excited caller had said.

Helen opened the door. She recognized the young woman standing there. The American young woman who'd rented the old groundsman's cottage that belonged to Castle Moore. Ms. Torrey Tunet.

Ms. Tunet smiled at her, a friendly smile. But for some reason Helen felt a tension at the back of her neck and along her shoulders.

51

At lunchtime, the bar on Parliament Street was jammed and noisy. Scott Keegan, at a table in the narrow room, said to the waiter at his elbow, "Here she is," and shot up a hand to signal to Rowena who'd just come in and was looking around. He added, "Two lagers, Aiden." Rowena liked a lager.

His sister came over. "If I'm late, I'll think of a reason in a minute." She put her clutch of vet books on the floor, hung her windbreaker on the back of the chair, and sat down. He was glad of the books, glad she'd gone back to classes, the hell with the gossipy whispers of her classmates.

But the way she looked! He was less glad about that. Rowena was hardly the fresh-faced, glowing young beauty of weeks ago. Puffy lids over her green eyes, pale face. Pregnancy alone? Or fear and anguish? She wore a midcalf navy skirt and one of those androgynous tunic tops.

"Did you talk to him?" Rowena's eyes were anxious.

Scott nodded. "I just came from seeing him. Our current best friend. 'Dr. Sunshine,' as he calls himself. Maybe he has a sense of humor. Here's the menu. I ordered us a lager."

Rowena took the menu but didn't look at it. Scott saw that she'd been biting her nails again, as she'd done when she was ten or so. "What did he say?" She was leaning forward, her eyes anxious, "You told him *why* I'm so worried? because I swear I can actually *feel*..." Her voice faltered, her face went even paler.

"Yes, I told him. About feeling it move. The good Dr. Sunshine says that's nonsense; it's way too early. But all right, he'll move it ahead to this coming Wednesday. Says he's unusually booked up, so it'll be ten percent extra. He gets the whole thing up front. Cash. No checks. No credit cards. I gave him the money."

"Then it's all set? For Wednesday?" When Scott nodded, Rowena gave a near-hysterical laugh. At that, he leaned forward and covered her nail-bitten hand with his own carefully manicured hand. "Hang on, Rowena. Just hang on. By this time next week, It'll all be over."

"Yes."

"As though none of it ever happened."

"Yes."

All over, courtesy of Dr. Sunshine.

Then all Rowena would have left to worry about would be the possibility of being found guilty of murdering their grandfather.

52

Lamb," Jasper said to Dennis O'Curry in O'Curry's Meats. It was two o'clock Friday afternoon. O'Curry had finished wrapping Mrs. Leary's package of beef kidneys and made her change. "Lamb chops, Mr. O'Curry. Four of them."

"Ah," Dennis O'Curry said, "going to make that Chinese dish again, Mr. O'Mara? With the candied ginger? Liked it, did she? Ms. Tunet? With the vermouth in it, and all?" He was jocular, in no hurry; there were no other customers,

"Smacked her lips," Jasper said. "Used up eight paper napkins. You've got to use paper. And your hands. Like you do with asparagus, which we also had and are having again."

Mr. O'Curry said, "Lamb's in the cold room." He went into the cold room, which had a window into the shop.

Waiting, Jasper stood jingling the change in his pocket and gazing out at Butler Street. Yesterday at the Dublin airport, seeing Torrey's rain-battered figure and white, exhausted face, he'd felt an unaccustomed emotion. Falling in love was hardly his style. It interfered. He frowned.

"The best of Wicklow." Dennis O'Curry heaved the side of ribs onto the block. "Small and sweetly marbled." With an artist's love of his work, he sliced carefully, then put the chops on shiny butcher's paper and held them out for Jasper's inspection. "There you are. What's that buzz?"

"My cell phone. Wrap them up, please. Be with you in a minute."

Outside, he stood in the lane that ran between O'Curry's and the vegetable stand, the phone to his ear. A buzzing, a crackling, a woman's voice in Portuguese. The call would be coming from Portimão on the southern coast. "Hello, hello! Flann?"

Then, "Jasper!" Flann's voice, angry, outraged, even in that single word.

"Flann! Been trying to —"

"Damn you for a devil! Why didn't you tell me? I just saw it on Portuguese television! The RTV News. Rowena accused of murdering her grandfather." Fury, rage, betrayal. Flann's voice was choked. "And I can't get there! What the *hell* is going on?"

"I've been trying to reach —"

"Christ! Rowena wouldn't hurt a black widow spider! What do they take her for? Can't they see?" Flann's voice broke. The brilliant young news correspondent was going to pieces. "How is she? Still feeling weak? And sick? The pregnancy's been giving her such a bad time. I've been worrying. We don't want —"

"She's fine, Flann. She's —"

"We don't want to lose the baby! It would break her heart! And mine! Jasper, for Christ's sake! I'm —"

"Flann —"

"I'm going crazy! I can be there tonight, there's a TAP plane to Heathrow, then I can —"

"What about Rory?"

A silence. Waiting, Jasper could see Flann's anguished face, the responsible son caught in his father's political mess. In the dark of night Flann had bundled the old man, if you could call wrong-headed Rory Fallon, age fifty-five, an old man, onto the thirty-five-foot *Dancing Waters* and in the dark had put-putted quietly out of Crosshaven at Cork Harbor. What good were Rory Fallon's regrets now? Penitent, yes,

174

and sickened, and covering his head with ashes, rethinking the break with Sinn Fein and his joining the renegade group and their setting off of the explosion. Oh, yes, Rory was rethinking now, but too late. And was he yet safely away?

"I'll figure out something about Rory. But Rowena! She must be half out of her — "

"For God's sake, Flann, don't come! It would only make fodder for the gossip sheets, raw meat for the vultures. The good news is that I've a smart friend here. She's onto something that'll whisk Rowena out of the line of fire." It was a lie, full of assurance, of comfort.

Twelve minutes later Jasper, shirt soaked with sweat, clicked off his phone, sure of having convinced Flann Fallon to stay on his father's case in Portugal.

Back up the lane again, in O'Curry's. "Four punts six," O'Curry told him, handing over the wrapped chops.

"Thanks." His voice was thick, his mouth dry. He felt he'd run a marathon and, chest bursting, had collapsed across the tape.

The dark, polished bar at O'Malley's had four white plates with little squares of cheese on toothpicks and the like, all for free, "Sean O'Malley being no fool," the old fellow with the wild white hair said to Jasper. Sharp, shrewd eyes, lyrical voice. Talk and laughter, a scattering of toothpicks on the bar, a burst of laughter at some fellow's low-toned joke. Sean's second son, bartender in a green apron, topped off the twenty-ounce glass of Guinness for Jasper. The package with the lamb chops and the bag of asparagus lay on the bar. He desperately needed this short respite at O'Malley's, then he'd be off. His sweat-dampened shirt felt clammy under his jacket.

The white-haired man put his sweater-clad arm on the edge of the bar, and with a hand clasped around his glass turned toward Jasper. "You the fellow buys elephant garlic at Coyle's? And wanting those pea-sized Greek black olives

175

and the like? Boiling and bubbling potions to enchant the lass in the groundsman's cottage?"

Jasper's nostrils twitched, repressing laughter. He felt his tension begin to disappear, soothed away by the lyrical voice and the long, cool draft of beer sliding down his throat. "That I am."

"McIntyre, here. The American lass all involved, a white knight out to rescue the Ashenden Manor maiden. Rowena. Old English name, Rowena. I've heard the grandfather named her himself. Old English. Rowena. Ivanhoe, Knights Templars. One hears things."

A little drunk, McIntyre, at four in the afternoon, stabbing squares of cheese, smiling to himself; a man with secrets. Jasper found him soothing, but not for long.

"Rowena. That knitting needle murder." A shake of the head. "The first death in these Ballynagh woods near Ashenden Manor, not since Cromwell—"

"The first death? I heard tell of a child lost in a landslide in the woods, a heavy rain one spring." Jasper speared a square of cheese. Then recalling more of what Torrey had told him, "And didn't Gerald Ashenden's wife die in a fire in the woods?"

McIntyre looked into his glass of beer. He said softly, "So she did. Kathleen her name was."

Jasper said, "And in the woods, another—something about a guest at a dinner party at Ashenden Manor. Wandered off drunk and fell facedown in a bog and suffocated."

McIntyre's thickets of white eyebrows rose. "By God, that's so! I was in Ballynagh then, just back from New Zealand, the Polynesian Islands. Right you are, sir! A friend of Ashenden's, an X-ray technician in Dublin, fellow with a crooked eye. Suffocated in the bog. There'd been a rain, bog like thick oatmeal. Can't remember his—Slattery! Donal Slattery! That's it. I've a cousin, Donald Slattery in Dingle, so it stuck in my mind. New Zealand, now, the native Maoris are wide as barns and strong as oxen. . . ."

53

Incest. The newspapers and a couple of Dublin's scandal sheets lay on Inspector O'Hare's desk. Nothing flat out. But underlying hints of incest in the gossip columns about "The Knitting Needle Murder" that involved Dr. Ashenden's granddaughter, who was something of a looker. Obvious hints.

Inspector O'Hare gazed in frustrated anger at a gaggle of photographs splashed across the front page of the scandal sheet *Scoop*: eight socialite photos of the handsome Dr. Gerald Ashenden with his pretty little granddaughter, Rowena, from the time she was six years old. Horse show photos, she at ten, at twelve, at fourteen, astride her grandfather's winning horses; she and her grandfather waltzing together at her eighteenth birthday party: lunching tête-a-tête at the Merrion, snapped having tea at the Shelbourne; the pair of them visiting a dog shelter in New Ross. "A *close* relationship?" inquired the scandal sheet, "or a significantly *loving* relationship?"

And where, *Scoop* inquired maliciously, were the Gardai getting in their investigation of this titillating Knitting Needle Murder case?

"God *damn* it!" O'Hare's shoulders ached with tension. Chief Superintendent O'Reilly's rage would be monumental if a news reporter scooped the Gardai, making the Gardai look like the flapping tail on a kite. "God *damn* it!"

"But, Sir! It's only what-d'you-call-it? — supposition." Sergeant Jimmy Bryson, at his corner desk, pushed away the copy of *Scoop* he'd been reading. He'd blushed as he read the column with its smarmy hints about little girls and the writer's recollection of a family murder by a forty-year-old woman who'd been molested as a child. "I got even," she'd said. No actual finger-pointing, not related to the Ashenden case, of course.

"Those gossipmongers are too damn close," Inspector O'Hare said bitterly. *Scoop*'s rhetorical question about the Gardai had instantly dried up the saliva in his mouth. He looked down at his lunch from Finney's: hot, crisply fried cod that Jimmy Bryson had put down on his desk only minutes before. He pushed it away and got up.

Pacing, frustrated, he hated *Scoop*, his job, Ballynagh, Ms. Torrey Tunet, the weather, this damned murder case, and Chief Superintendent O'Reilly of the ice-blue eyes.

Then abruptly he stopped pacing, struck with a sudden wonderful realization: Of course! Of *course*! He was way ahead of those gossipmongers! Miles ahead! He knew something they didn't know.

He knew that Rowena Keegan was pregnant.

Ah, yes, indeed. Wonderful! Couldn't be better. Pregnant, Rowena Keegan would be visiting a doctor, likely in Dublin.

O'Hare sat down at his desk, picked up the phone, and got through to the Crime Investigation Department at Dublin Castle.

When O'Hare put down the phone, he stood up and stretched, smiling. It was all in place: The Crime Investigation Department would put a trail on Rowena Keegan. She'd likely be using a false name. But once they had the doctor, he'd confirm that the young woman was pregnant. Then she wouldn't be able to hold out. They'd have her confession.

So! It would be the Gardai and not those smarmy rags

who'd uncover the truth. It'd be the Gardai who'd open up the whole rotten fruit. Not that he didn't feel sorry for Rowena Keegan. She must've been through quite enough horror.

He looked over at Sergeant Bryson. "You heard?" and at Jimmy Bryson's nod, "Keep mum. Not a word even to Hannah." Hannah was Bryson's girlfriend. "And you might see to the Dolans' fuss about their chickens and the Sullivans' dog."

Jimmy Bryson gone to the Dolans, O'Hare had only time to give himself a thumbs-up sign when the door opened. He looked over.

Ms. Torrey Tunet.

54

It startled O'Hare, the look of Ms. Tunet. An excitement that was almost electric emanated from her. Nelson rose lazily to greet her, his tail wagging, and she wrinkled her nose and said, "Phew! You stink, you darling!" and she leaned down and scrambled her fingers along his neck, and Nelson gave her his moony look.

O'Hare regarded this nemesis of his, this liar, this obstruction to the truth. Ms. Tunet approached his desk. Her face was blazing with suppressed excitement. "God! I'm glad you're here, Inspector! I've something to—" Her glance fell on the fish sandwich he'd pushed away. "You going to eat that? I haven't had lunch. I'm starved." O'Hare nudged the sandwich, cold now, toward her. He watched the blissful way she gulped it down. She was wearing some kind of many-colored bandanna on her dark hair. One end had come free and hung down along her neck. Her sweater was on inside out. While she ate, her gray eyes promised him something. Not that he needed anything Ms. Tunet could deliver. Ms. Tunet who was his adversary, his barrier to the truth, his antagonist, his nemesis, his . . . He ran out of bitter analogies. Besides, likely in days he'd have the pregnant Rowena Keegan's confession and the case wrapped up.

The sandwich finished, Torrey said, "Thanks." She sat down on the varnished chair beside his desk, pulled it closer, and began to talk.

55

W inifred?"

"If it's about the manure, tell him we manufacture our own. After all, we've got two horses. And we hardly need the garden, what with being in London." Winifred was at the dining room table laboriously sewing up a rip in the pocket of her brown corduroys.

"That's not it," Sheila said. It seemed to her that she was always standing in one doorway or another asking or telling Winifred something important that was invariably viewed by Winifred as nonsense. "Sergeant Bryson called. Inspector O'Hare wants me to be at the Ballynagh police station to-morrow morning. For an informal inquiry."

"What time does he want us?"

"Not *us*, Winifred. Just me. Only those involved. Because I saw Rowena near the bridle path."

"Just you? Oh, no! Not without me! Just let Inspector O'Hare try to throw me out!" Winifred jabbed the needle hard through the corduroys and Sheila shuddered for Inspector O'Hare.

Mark Temple stood looking down the hill from the rise above Ashenden Manor. In the late afternoon sunlight that was fading to a pale gold with a lavender tinge, the manor and the stone outbuildings reminded him of paintings he'd seen in the British Museum. So. Ashenden Manor. It was

181

his now. His and Caroline's. The snake was gone from Paradise.

Caroline was down there by the stables, a small figure, waving to him. He waved back and made his way down. When he got to her, he saw that her face was pale, and his heart constricted. He kissed her. "Are you all right?"

"Oh, yes. Only" — she drew a wavering breath — "only that we've had a call from Sergeant Bryson. Ten o'clock tomorrow. An informal inquiry. Have you seen Rowena about?"

Rowena was washing Scott's red Miata just outside the stables. She was in a sweatshirt, old jodhpurs, and rubber boots. She was hosing off splashes of mud because Scott had driven through the rain from Dublin late last night. Scott was leaning against the fence, looking chilled, though he was wearing the motheaten old chinchilla coat that he'd found hanging in the back hall. He said soberly, "The inspector is fishing, that's his modus operandi, getting passions flaring, enmities clashing. Raw flesh. We'll keep our cool, won't we, Rowena? No matter what entrails are exposed."

Rowena put down the hose. She dipped the sponge in the pail of water and squeezed it, dripping water on the hood of the car. "It's all phony. He'll be skittering around trying to dig out why I tried to kill Gerald."

"Don't refer to the old bastard as Gerald at the inquiry. Call him 'my grandfather.' "

"What if O'Hare finds out I'm pregnant? Pregnant! *That* would put the cap on it. I can imagine him rubbing his hands."

"Just hope he won't find out. Keep wearing that tight rubber thing under your jodhpurs. And Dr. Sunshine is right around the corner."

"But Torrey guessed."

"Torrey knows you intimately. And she has a special antenna. I can almost see it growing out of that satiny thatch of hair. I've known you all my life, but I wouldn't've known if you hadn't told me—"

"When I threw up in the stable."

"Yes. But—"

"You're my darling little brother. I wanted you to know."

". . . and New Zealand doesn't have any snakes. Not a *single* snake in those islands! Ever hear of the kea? They have keas. A kea's a parrot that can fly."

"That so?" But Jasper hardly heard. *Slattery, who'd suffocated in the bog.* Jasper put down his half-finished beer. "Been a pleasure," he said to the rampant-haired Michael McIntyre, and two minutes later he was out of O'Malley's and across the road to Nolan's Bed-and-Breakfast.

In his room he put the bag with the lamb chops and fresh asparagus on the bureau, sat down on the bed, picked up the bedside phone, and called Torrey. No luck. Where was she? He was onto something — or might be. He left a message on her machine: "If my phone's busy, try again."

He picked up the Dublin phone book from the bedside table, leafed through it, and found the listing: Slattery. Slatterys, plentiful as confetti. Adelaide Road, Burlington, Clyde, Elgin, Oxmantown Road, Sandymount, Howth. Dozens of them. Slattery, Donal. Several. A son named for his father, if he was lucky. Even a grandson? But what if not in Dublin any longer but in a village or town in Meath or Armagh or Mayo, or Roscommon, or Country Clare or God knows where. Jesus!

"Cup of tea, Mr. O'Mara?" Sara Hobbs, smiling in the doorway, Chinese tray in hand, teapot and cookies.

Jasper had just crossed off another Slattery, his ninth fruitless call. From the sheen in Mrs. Hobbs's eyes, he saw that she'd had her five o'clock sherry, not tea, and he inwardly groaned; the sherry always made her chatty and sentimental. Sara Hobbs was very taken with Torrey. She'd told Jasper three different times how Ms. Tunet, his American friend, had come up the stairs of Nolan's Bed-and-Breakfast a week ago, and how they'd had a lovely chat, all about Nolan's early days and Sara's childhood, and how back then Kathleen Brady who'd married Dr. Gerald Ashenden would come to Nolan's to visit her old spinster aunt, Alice Coggins, and would bring her little girl, Caroline, "a year younger than me," Sara Hobbs would say, "and we'd play jacks and all." Sara Hobbs, eyes brightened by the sherry and often tears, would add, "Lost under the sea, the whole Brady family, and she, Kathleen, poor lass, left all alone but for her aunt. So tragic!"

Jasper managed a smile, declined tea, and wished Mrs. Hobbs would disappear in a puff of smoke. He knew the story by heart, Mrs. Hobbs's five o'clock sherry story. He looked at his penciled check marks in the phone book and rubbed his forehead. So damn many Slatterys!

Some time during the next hour he looked up and noticed that Sara Hobbs was gone but had left tea and cookies. He ate a cookie and drank cold tea. His eyes ached. But he couldn't let go. He dialed again, a wrong number as it turned out, and had a conversation with a Patrick O'Toole, age eight, who said, "You want me da, but he's still at the shop and anyway his name's Liam."

It was getting on toward six when he called a Donal Slattery and a teenager's voice answered, "Donal Slattery? Yeah, that's me. My da? Him, too. *Doctor* Donal Slattery? You've got the wrong number. Not on your — ooops! I guess you'd be wanting my grandpa?"

"Right." Grandpa. *The Donal Slattery, dead in a bog?* "I'd like to get in touch with him. Do you have his number?"

"Not likely! Never met the old man. Died before I was born. Had a crooked eye, my pa said. Would that be the one?"

He held his breath. Then, "What about your gran? Is she —"

"Grandma Nora? She's Mrs. Patrick McLaughlin now. Lives in Kilkenny. You want the number?"

He'd done it. For an instant he couldn't believe it. Now, if only, if only!

When he hung up he made two more phone calls. The first was to Kilkenny, where he talked for some minutes. The second was to Torrey, leaving a message on her machine saying that he had an appointment, couldn't make it for dinner tonight, and would call her in the morning.

Downstairs, on the way out he stopped by the reception desk where Sara Hobbs was reading a copy of *Queen*. He handed her the bag with the lamb chops and asparagus. "These'd be good for your tonight's dinner or even tomorrow's if you put them in the refrigerator. Have you tried a bit of mustard on lamb chops? Grilled with rosemary?"

"Mustard? Oh, dear! I'm not sure my Tom would — but thank you so much, Mr. O'Mara. From O'Curry's, are they? And asparagus! In October!"

South on the N81, then onto N9 through to Carlow. Thank God he kept the Jaguar in Ballynagh now instead of garaged at his apartment in Dublin. No secrets now from Torrey. Or at least only a few.

The sun was setting. This was gentler country, not the mountains of the western part of Wicklow. Here were hills and plains and small farms, a more placid countryside. Dirt lanes branching off from the highway looked red-gold in the evening sun.

Onto the N10, broad highway, Kilkenny ahead, "Branch to the left," she'd said, a Dublin accent, "quarter mile beyond the third Kilkenny sign." Already a rose-tinged, lavender dusk. The road to the left no longer touched by sun, a wide lane, clipped grass edging the gravel. People who cared. Fogarty Lane.

The house was well kept, a brick house, set back, with a fenced bit of lawn. Two black Lab puppies, tails wagging, nipped at his heels as he went up the walk. It was almost eight o'clock when he rang the bell at 34 Fogarty Lane.

57

On Butler Street, McIntyre bit into a Finney's hot-sausage-on-a-bun. Ah, yes, he knew the seas from Antartica to the Indian Ocean, and in the West Indies he'd drunk exotic hallucinations from a coconut shell. North of Reykjavik, he'd seen green-black ice floes like jewels. And in Madagascar hadn't he frolicked with ladies of unimaginable skills?

But nothing better than standing on Butler Street in Ballynagh at half past nine of a flag-bright Saturday morning biting into a Finney's hot-sausage-on-a-bun. Not to mention having a bit of a laugh, watching widow Bryson's boy, Jimmy — *Sergeant* Jimmy Bryson now — carry those folding chairs from Grogan's Needlework Shop across the street to the police station. Three trips the lad had to make. Every time Inspector O'Hare had more than six people at a meeting in the Ballynagh police station, Jimmy Bryson had to go borrowing the Grogan sisters' chairs.

A few of the morning regulars drifted out of Finney's, warming their hands around containers of steaming tea or coffee. "What's it all about, McIntyre?" a newcomer wanted to know.

"About probing the deviousness of man," McIntyre said, "which is a bottomless pit." He took a bite of the sausage-on-a-bun. He had a sweater over his navy shirt, and over that, his worn old tweed jacket, a bit raveled at the cuffs but good enough. The breeze was knocking his hair about, but his cap was in some bureau drawer or other, so never mind. He watched the scene with a feeling of waiting. Had an eye out for that American young woman, his friend from O'Malley's. She was in the thick of it, he'd be a fool not to know it.

And here came the handsome, crippled gay boy, Ashenden, arriving in a gleaming little red convertible, his sister beside him. Rowena. The lass that gave fodder to the scandal sheets. Possible murderess. And if she did it, he, McIntyre, was all for it. Provided the girl had a good reason, of course. Ashenden had been a seeming gent if you didn't look too close into his eyes, but he, McIntyre, had once looked close and didn't care for what he saw. The girl wore gray pants and a navy pea coat with the collar up, her face down in the collar, just the top of her red hair showing.

Ah, the poet! Winifred Moore. Drawing up in a Jeep and parking it skillfully. And with her, her "companion" they called it nowadays, the skinny, wispy English woman with a bit of a fringe on her forehead. At McIntyre's shoulder, a stranger, likely a tourist, said admiringly, "The big one, in the plaid cape. A fine-looking woman!" To which McIntyre said drily, "Not on the market, mister."

Next, on foot, having parked their car farther down in front of Coyle's market, here came the Temples. Passing McIntyre, the fair-haired Caroline, mother of the possible murderess, turned her head, and her great beautiful hazel eyes looked at him. Slender woman in a long black coat. He always had an eye out for a glimpse of her in the village. She had a cocky jaw, a bit of mischief there, but this morning somewhat in absentia because of the circumstances. Her new husband, Dr. Temple, manipulator of folks' bones, wore country squire clothes. He had short, rusty hair, and his body had the thickness of a wrestler.

Butler Street was empty now except for the tea and coffee container drinkers. McIntyre took the last bite of the sausage bun. Where was the darling young woman, the American? Listened like a shadow on the wall, listened like a moth at the edge—

Here came Dr. Collins. Padraic Collins in his father's old tweed cap. Family-proud Anglo-Irish, generations of it. Collins Court. At Dr. Collins's elbow was his housekeeper, stocky Helen Lavery, in a rump-sprung wool skirt and buttoned jacket that strained across her bosom. Dyed hair, must've dyed it herself, a waste of dye. But known to be a kind woman and hardworking. Took care of Dr. Collins's needs except for sex, which McIntyre'd heard the good doctor found elsewhere . . . though Helen Lavery likely was pining away with love of him, housekeepers always were. Or governesses. Jane Eyre types abounded. What a—

Ah, *there*! Riding up on a bike, the American young woman, Torrey her name was. Lovely looking thing even in the navy pants and red sweater. A gray-eyed, satin-haired young woman with a mouth like a flower. Parked the bike, and going past him into the police station, gave him a bit of a nod and a wink. Sassy. High color in her cheeks, back straight as a soldier's.

"Well, then, McIntyre, what's it about?" Someone behind him gave a laugh and jogged his elbow. "You always know."

"About modern life," McIntyre said, "and civilization, or the lack thereof, from the time of the Ice Age." One of that lot, now inside the police station, was a murderer. Or maybe two of them were killers—there'd been the gypsy mixed up in it too.

Good luck to you, Inspector Egan O'Hare.

58

Inspector Egan O'Hare, half sitting on the edge of his desk, looked at his watch. Five minutes to ten. There was low talk and rustling. They'd all arrived.

Yesterday afternoon when Torrey Tunet had burst into the police station, he'd listened skeptically to her startling tale. He'd even smiled. After all, he already had the Ashenden murder case well in hand.

Yet . . . yet. Such an incredible tale! And, strangely, unwilling as he was to think so, *possible*. And he'd thought, *Best to cover myself*, because what if in fact there was something valid in Torrey Tuner's astonishing tale? If he ignored it, he risked ending up having bet the wrong horse. A thousand-to-one chance. Still . . . So "an informal meeting," he'd told Sergeant Bryson.

Now here they all were.

The clock on top of the Coke machine gave its tinny chimes. Ten o'clock. The low talk and rustling subsided. Winifred Moore, glaring, crushed out her cigarette in the paper plate that Sergeant Bryson held out while he shook his head and mouthed, "No smoking."

O'Hare cleared his throat. He remained half sitting on the front edge of his desk, swinging one leg. Informal, that was the ticket. He smiled at the attentive faces. Nine people.

"It may seem odd, this informal inquiry. But in earlier cases, I've found that bringing together those concerned invariably elicits remarkably helpful information that—" Smiling, smiling, on he blathered, knowing that he wouldn't get a damned bit of new information from the eight of these nine people he'd questioned in the past weeks. He'd questioned all of them. All but one. Fake it. Go through it. Question the lot. Lull that ninth witness.

"Ms. Sheila Flaxton," he began, "now you stated that . . ."

In the next hour, he questioned one person after another with seeming narrow-eyed intensity. He had never before practiced such trickery.

He carefully did not cast even one glance toward the seated figure at the left who, not yet questioned, was the key to not one murder, but two. At least according to the information from Ms. Torrey Tunet. In any case, he was still having the Gardai in Dublin follow the pregnant Rowena Keegan.

Several times during the questioning, he slid a glance toward Ms. Tunet, who stood against the wall beside the Coke machine. Nelson lay at her feet. Nelson's tail thumped each time Ms. Tunet shifted, which Inspector O'Hare noted was often. Edgy, a high color in her cheeks. She'd brought him such an astonishing revelation, a revelation that, if proved true, would in the next few minutes certainly exonerate Rowena Keegan. Ms. Tunet obviously thought she had placed a sword in his hand. Well, that remained to be seen. No wonder she was edgy, and Nelson sensed it.

But what could be the killer's motivation, if Ms. Tunet was on the right track? Inspector O'Hare felt a chill, not coldness, but a kind of titillation of the nerves. If, in fact, he could in the next few minutes pinpoint *who* had murdered Dr. Ashenden, he still didn't know the *why* of it.

"But *why*?" he had asked, stunned, yesterday afternoon looking back at Torrey Tunet, the peacock bandanna straggling down the back of her neck, her face blazing with what she had just told him. "*Why*, do you suppose?"

He'd been startled to see the blazing excitement in Ms. Tunet's face change to an expression of . . . horror? Her face had gone pale. But she'd said only, "Tomorrow, then?" And he'd nodded. "Yes. Ten o'clock."

Now, creeping up to eleven o'clock. Everyone intent, as though watching a police show on television. Only that cough again, a nervous-sounding little cough-and-whistle from Sheila Flaxton. Nerves? She sat in the folding chair beside Winifred Moore. Such a timid woman, Ms. Flaxton. No wonder Winifred Moore ran the show.

From the other side of the room, a clatter as something fell to the floor and rolled to O'Hare's feet. A silver pencil. Sergeant Bryson picked it up and returned it to Dr. Mark Temple, who whispered, "Sorry," and raised his brows half humorously at O'Hare. The much-divorced chiropractor with a long history of appearing in gossip columns.

O'Hare thought, *Now*, and he cleared his throat and studied his notes, as though to see whom he would question next. Then he looked up. He smiled toward the stocky figure of Dr. Collins's housekeeper. She was seated beside the doctor. "Helen Lavery."

59

At half past ten o'clock Saturday morning, on a narrow country road twenty-two miles north of Kilkenny, Jasper O'Mara wormed his way out from under the Jaguar where he'd been tinkering and sweating for the last thirty-five minutes.

He slapped at the dirt on his pullover and pants and got in the car. Behind the wheel, he took a breath. The sweetest sound he could think of would be that of the engine running. He turned on the ignition. The dashboard lights flickered, steadied. The engine purred.

Jasper turned his head and smiled his relief at the passenger beside him. She smiled back and said, "Lord love us, Mr. O'Mara! You're a genius." Her Dublin accent was from around the Glasnevin area of small lanes, with row houses, mostly working-class people.

"Or more likely a mechanic," he said. Time lost, now he drove fast, north toward Ballynagh. Early this morning, trying again unsuccessfully to reach Torrey at the cottage, he'd called Ashenden Manor. Jennie O'Shea had answered the phone. "Ms. Tunet? No, Mr. O'Mara, she's not here, But later this morning she'll likely be at the Ballynagh police station. Ten o'clock. A sort of inquiry?"

An inquiry, damn it! *Too soon, too soon!* Driving, he was seeing the house on Butler Street with the front casement

194

windows. He was hearing Sara Hobbs's sherry-slurred voice yesterday afternoon telling him her favorite old tale. Sentimental Sara Hobbs, blue eyes misty with sherry. "Another cup of tea, Mr. O'Mara?" Chinese tray tipping in her hands.

He pressed down on the gas. He had to get to Torrey. An inquiry! She might already be in the midst of the horror of it, not guessing what he now suspected. But first —

"You go too fast!" his passenger chided.

"Yes," he answered, but he did not slow down. Because there was more to it. More.

60

Helen Lavery."

It startled her, Inspector O'Hare calling her name. She turned to Dr. Collins, frightened. He looked a little surprised, but he gave her a reassuring smile. It steadied her down. If Inspector O'Hare asked her if she'd seen anyone acting suspicious around the bridle path, she'd remind him that it had been a Friday. That was her church evening, as everyone in Ballynagh knew. So how could she have witnessed anything, the bridle path being in the opposite direction from St. Andrews?

Helen crossed her legs at the ankle, thankful that she was wearing her good brown shoes, what with sitting in the front, over on the side, and Inspector O'Hare only a few feet away, sort of sitting on his desk and swinging one leg, so casual like, and smiling at her. They were even about the same age, she being fifty-four next June, and him being a year younger, which she knew from school. She felt better now. She smiled back at Inspector O'Hare.

"So, Helen," Inspector O'Hare began, but then instead of asking who or what she might have seen regarding Dr. Ashenden killed on the bridle path, he started rambling along about tinkers and gypsies traveling through the countryside. He went on for a whole minute, shaking his head over their thievery and their other unfortunate habits, and saying about himself having bought a dented little pot for two pounds six from from the gypsy woman, that gypsy who'd been murdered right here in Ballynagh. "I believe the unfortunate woman was somewhat of a nettle to some of our Ballynagh farmers. A nettle. And to other folk as well. Been seen hanging around Collins Court, that gypsy. Been a nuisance there too, had she, Helen?" and Inspector O'Hare looked at her expectantly.

Helen nodded. "Oh . . . well, yes. Hanging about. Pots and pans. Scary like, so sudden, there she'd be. And you hear such stories." She stopped. But Inspector O'Hare was waiting for more, smiling at her, that expectant look.

"Scary, Helen? Scary how?"

Helen looked back at Inspector O'Hare. She had a feeling of obligation, that she was owing something, everybody sitting there waiting and looking at her, and she in her good brown shoes, being here. So it was as though she was obliged, she couldn't keep it down.

"Well, last Monday—or maybe it was Tuesday—I'd gone to the village for fish for Dr. Collins's dinner. Cod, it was. When I got back to Collins Court, that gypsy, she'd gotten into the house! She was in Dr. Collins's study. He was shouting to her to get out. 'What's this?' I said. I had the bag of fish and I raised it up like I was going to bash her with it. At that, she made a jabbing motion with her fingers at me but went off past me out the door. Dr. Collins's face had got so white it worried me."

Inspector O'Hare wagged his head, sympathetic. "Brazen, that gypsy. Other people complained too, you're not the only one. And that was the last you saw of her? The gypsy?"

"Well, not the last. Next day she was back. I'd been out where a pesky rabbit was among my vegetables, and I'd left the kitchen door open for a minute. She came right in. Brazen, like you said. The nerve! I had some dried beans in my apron pocket and I'd almost a mind to throw a fistful at her. Dangled a pair of earrings at me, she did. 'A present for you.' " Helen shook her head. "Awful-looking things, cheap earrings, fake rubies—*gypsy* things! Not worth two pence."

Someone coughed, then coughed again. A thin, strangled sound. It was that English friend of Ms. Winifred Moore. She ought to let Dr. Collins have a look at her.

"Earrings?" Inspector O'Hare asked.

Helen nodded. "They do that, the gypsies, to have you on. Presents. 'And here's one for the master,' and she dropped something in a twist of paper on the kitchen table. Just like that!"

Helen looked at Dr. Collins on the folding chair beside her. He was wearing his tweed jacket that she'd given a good brushing, and his vest and all. That pancake makeup around his eyes was all wrong; he didn't know how to put it on. It looked too white. He needed a darker shade, to blend in more.

"So," Inspector O'Hare was asking her in a kindly voice, "What did the gypsy do then?"

"Do? Nothing. She only went off, dirty skirts swirling. I threw the earrings in the garbage." Helen looked around at the listeners. She had again that triumphant feeling, that she'd justified her presence at this whatever it was—informal inquiry—of Egan O'Hare's. And in her good brown shoes.

But Egan O'Hare only kept on. "And the present for Dr. Collins as well?"

Indignation made Helen's voice rise. "I should say not! I don't take it on myself to—the present was for Dr. Collins, and it was to Dr. Collins I gave it. It was for him to throw away if he liked." Generations of service in correctly run households was, Helen hoped, clearly implied in the set of her shoulders.

At that, O'Hare said, "I see." He got off the desk, arched his back, and gave the small of his back a bit of a rub with his knuckles. Helen thought he would glance at Dr. Collins as though to say, You've an excellent housekeeper in Helen Lavery, Dr. Collins.

But instead, Inspector O'Hare slanted a glance over toward Torrey Tunet, who was standing by the Coke machine. Then he looked back at Helen. He smiled at her. "The present for Dr. Collins, was it by any chance in a twist of green paper?"

Helen stared at Inspector O'Hare. She suddenly felt funny. Fooled like. Like she was taking a walk along a safe, sunlit lane that all of sudden had somehow become something different. "Green paper? In a twist of green paper?" She turned her head slowly and looked over at Ms. Tunet. She moved her lips, a kind of nervous flutter that sometimes happened when she got upset.

"Yes, Helen? Ms. Lavery?" Inspector O'Hare's voice was patient.

Helen looked down at her hands in her lap. Her heart had begun to thump so hard she could almost hear it. "Well, like I told Ms. Tunet when she stopped in, but Dr. Collins was out on an emergency. We somehow got to chatting about the gypsy pestering everybody and their tricks and presents and such. And Ms. Tunet asked me the very same thing: Was the present the gypsy gave me for Dr. Collins in a twist of green paper? She said that was the gypsy's most usual way, in green paper."

"And . . . ?"

She felt helpless. "And so it was."

Inspector O'Hare said softly, "Thank you so much, Ms. Lavery." Helen could see that sweat had darkened his shirt collar.

61

Mystified faces. Inspector O'Hare stood a moment, then let out a whistling sigh and rolled his head around to relax tense muscles. There wasn't even the sound of shuffling feet or coughing or nose blowing, only the tinny clock ticking and the hum of refrigeration from the Coke machine. But as Winifred Moore said later to Sheila, "Did you see that look between Torrey Tunet and Inspector O'Hare? As though an electric current zinged between them. If you can imagine such a thing between *that* pair."

But to Dr. Collins, it seemed that Helen Lavery's words were no more significant than a dust mote. He sat gazing abstractedly before him as though his interior thoughts took precedence over whatever was happening in this police station on Butler Street.

Inspector O'Hare said, "Dr. Collins?"

Dr. Collins blinked and looked inquiringly back at Inspector O'Hare. "Yes, Inspector?"

"What was the present the gypsy brought you? In the twist of green paper."

"The present? But how does that—in any case, I didn't bother to look. I threw it away. Some gypsy geegaw, I imagine." Dr. Collins closed his eyes and pinched the bridge of his nose between two fingers.

Inspector O'Hare reached around behind him to his desk

and picked up a slender object wrapped in green tissue. Carefully he removed the tissue. "Then of course, Dr. Collins, you wouldn't recognize these?" He held out the object to Dr. Collins. Necks craned. It was a pair of wooden knitting needles, held together with a rubber band. A thick, heavy pair, the kind used for taking big, loose stitches.

Dr. Collins's balding head gave a sidewise jerk as though struck by a slight buffet of wind. He stared at the knitting needles. He licked dry lips. "So that's my present from the gypsy, is it? Came across it, did you? A bit odd for a present!"

"Odd?" O'Hare tried not to sound ironical. "Not odd, if these needles weren't meant for you to knit with, Dr. Collins, but rather"—he ran his fingers slowly along one of the wooden needles—"to hint that she, this gypsy, knew something that might be of interest to you."

"But what an absurd—! How could—"

"To hint that she had," O'Hare pressed on, "possibly *seen* something of interest to you?"

Dr. Collins gazed back at Inspector O'Hare. Then he gave a sigh and sat up straighter and pulled down his vest so that his round belly no longer bulged. "I have a habit of slumping. But I try to remind myself that even at my age—" Another sigh. "I don't exactly follow, Inspector."

But O'Hare felt a rush of blood, his stepped-up heartbeat. It always happened when he was closing in and the click occurred, the click that boded revelation.

And now he became aware of a bated-breath stillness from the listeners, and not even the creak of anyone shifting in a folding chair. He wet his lips.

"Let's say that the gypsy saw something in the woods, perhaps, where she kept her pony and wagon. Near the bridle path. Saw something happen." O'Hare pulled at his chin, gazing at Dr. Collins.

No answer. The old tweed cap lay in Dr. Collins's lap. He began turning it around and around, his fingers working along the worn edge. Then, as though becoming aware of what he was doing, he looked down and his fingers went still.

O'Hare said softly. "Blackmail, Dr. Collins? The gypsy saw something happen, something so terrible that —"

"No!"

" —that you couldn't let her reveal it."

A heartbeat of time. Then Dr. Collins looked wearily back at Inspector O'Hare. "That gypsy." He shook his head. "That greedy gypsy! I had no choice."

The tinny ticking of the clock. Creak of a folding chair as someone shifted. Indrawn breaths, and from someone a whispered, "My God!"

Cigarette smoke lazed across the room, alerting Sergeant Bryson. Winifred Moore again. So engrossed, so fascinated, as to forget herself. Sergeant Bryson coughed loudly. Ms. Moore looked at him, swore under her breath, then leaned down and ground the cigarette under her heel. From the others, then, a slight stirring. Rowena Keegan, beside her brother, Scott, shook her head, incredulity in her green gaze. Mark Temple sought out his wife's hand. Helen Lavery made a strange, whimpering sound, like a cat in pain. Inspector O'Hare glanced toward Torrey Tunet, whose only reaction was to slip Nelson a cookie.

"So, Dr. Collins?" For some reason he could not understand, Inspector O'Hare spoke gently.

Dr. Collins was again turning the old tweed cap around and around. "I had no plan. I only was looking for her near her wagon by the bridle path. To pay her to go away? To beg her? I didn't know. It kept shifting in my mind, changing, like a tide going in and out.

"It was dusk. I started to follow her." At the groundsman's cottage, the gypsy had pushed open the door. "I looked through the window. She was there alone, drinking. She

202

pulled a nightgown off a drying rack. It was white, with yellow daisies. She took it into the bedroom."

Quietly he'd entered the cottage. "I still didn't know. The bedroom door was open. She was in the nightgown in front of the long mirror, her clothes on the floor.

"She looked at me. She was almost too drunk to stand. But she laughed when she saw me. Her earrings were gold coins. When she laughed, she threw her head back and the gold coins glittered. I pushed her down, and she fell on the bed. A strong woman, but weak from drunkenness." The tweed cap turning and turning in his hands. "I held the pillow over her face."

62

Inspector O'Hare felt compact, organized, in charge, alert, pleased with himself, and triumphant. The police station was a stage; he was the principal actor, the protagonist, as they called it. He was exquisitely aware of his audience on the folding chairs. He straightened his jacket to make sure it was perfectly horizonal across his thighs. He looked down at Dr. Collins, who again sat slumped, belly protruding below his vest like a small, water-filled balloon.

"So," O'Hare said, and now he swept a glance around at the mesmerized faces and spoke to the room at large, "the gypsy was smothered. Murdered. All because on the bridle path she saw Dr. Collins shoot the knitting needle that resulted in the death of Dr. Ashenden." He wanted to add something philosophical but couldn't bring anything to mind.

Dr. Collins jerked his head up. "*What?* Oh no, Inspector! No! No!" The expression on his face was one of astonishment. "I—only because she'd threatened she'd swear to the Gardai that she saw me do such a thing! That murderous attack on Gerald! Oh no, Inspector! I did nothing of the kind!"

63

Stunned, Inspector O'Hare stared at Dr. Collins. What was this he was hearing? Impossible! He was still holding the pair of wooden knitting needles. Impossible.

"My, oh my!" Sheila Flaxton's whisper, followed by her nervous giggle. Then silence.

Dr. Collins, clutching that tweed cap in his lap, gave Inspector O'Hare a shocked, reproving look. "As if I would harm Gerald! Never! My best friend! My dearest friend! All our lives, Gerald and I!" — Dr. Collins's gaze sought out Caroline Temple in the third row. "His daughter can attest to that!"

"Yes! Oh, yes!" Caroline Temple's slender figure leaned forward. "That's so, Inspector! Padraic and my father! Padraic — Dr. Collins — never would have — " Her voice broke. "Never!" she managed, and sank back to the comfort of Mark Temple's encircling arm around her shoulders.

Inspector O'Hare glared at Dr. Collins. He said, between gritted teeth, "Exactly why, Dr. Collins, did you think folks would believe the gypsy if she claimed to've seen you shoot the knitting needle into the stallion? How could you think anybody'd take a gypsy's word for it against yours?" O'Hare half turned and angrily threw the pair of knitting needles down on his desk. Then, jutting his jaw at Dr. Collins, "Ridiculous! On the face of it, ridiculous!"

A silence. A waiting. The refrigeration of the Coke machine started up again. Dr. Collins fussed with his vest, settling and resettling it. Then he said, low, "But you see, the gypsy thought—" He gazed somewhere around the chest button of O'Hare's blue uniform. "You see, the gypsy thought that with those knitting needles she'd frightened me into giving her money. Otherwise, she'd tell that . . . that . . ." He looked down.

"That *what?*" O'Hare said, baffled, exasperated. He saw in amazement Dr. Collins's pale face begin to redden as a blush spread slowly across it.

Oh. Oh. Inspector Egan O'Hare, gazing at the revealing blush, at that instant felt he knew the depth of shame in Dr. Collins. The respected Dr. Collins, family-proud, grave-faced ancestral portraits on the walls of Collins Court. Padraic Collins, that secret frequenter of hookers in Cork and God knew where else. And Inspector O'Hare wondered on which stormy night, with the roads deluged, had Dr. Collins found his way in the woods to the gypsy's wagon.

So that was it. Frightened and ashamed, Dr. Collins, desperate to conceal his unbridled sexual need, had ended by killing the gypsy. Never mind that he had not meant to. He had done it.

"Dr. Collins," O'Hare began, then stopped. He rubbed a hand across his face. Must he force Padraic Collins to reveal to the listeners the sexual weakness that had made him vulnerable to the gypsy's threats? No. Spare Padraic Collins that shame. Later, he'd have Collins's written confession.

O'Hare sighed. Disappointment plunged him down, flattened him. For perhaps four glorious minutes he'd thought he had the killer of Dr. Gerald Ashenden. Surely, Ms. Tunet must have thought so too. A mistake. But, at least, the gypsy. He could thank the exasperating Ms. Tunet for that.

But this informal little inquiry of his was over. No point, just now, in going on. Everybody go home, except for Dr.

Collins. And he thought grimly, *I'll continue my own investigation, Ms. Tunet.*

"Well," he began and swept a glance around the room. A bitter taste of disappointment was in his mouth. The murderer of Dr. Ashenden was in this room. Possibly even laughing at him. His gaze stopped at Scott Keegan. It flickered over Dr. Mark Temple, then over Caroline. It settled on Rowena Keegan. He'd been right all along. "Well, under the—"

But the flutter of something caught his eye. Torrey Tunet was holding up that peacock-strewn turquoise bandanna, waving it at him. A signal? She was shaking her head violently. O'Hare clicked his tongue in annoyance. That exasperating ex-thief, Ms. Torrey Tunet! True, she had delivered one murderer to him. Not that the rich Dr. Padraic Collins would be prosecuted, under the circumstances of a roving, blackmailing, lying gypsy; that was the way of the world. But Torrey Tunet would do anything to protect Rowena Keegan. She was smart. Tricky too. O'Hare reminded himself that she had no regard for law. She'd lied about Rowena's murderous attempt in the meadow, hadn't she? No regard. Not when she'd gotten some conviction in her mind. Still, his curiosity was an itch. Who knew? Whatever she had in mind could be grist for his mill.

That bandanna, waving. O'Hare said to the room at large, "I think a short respite's in order."

64

They'd gone, Winifred Moore striding off toward O'Malley's pub, Sheila hurrying to keep up. Rowena and Scott had accompanied Caroline and Mark Temple across the street to Finney's, likely for a midmorning snack of Finney's specialty of fried soda bread and tea. "We'll continue at half past twelve," Inspector O'Hare had said.

Helen Lavery, however, remained, crouched on one of the folding chairs, wiping her tear-reddened eyes. Aside from Helen Lavery, only Torrey and Dr. Padraic Collins had stayed behind in the police station. Outside, the day had turned gray; dark clouds obscured the sun. With the grayness had come a chill.

Over at his own desk, Sergeant Bryson was laboriously taking down Dr. Collins's statement on the computer. Dr. Collins stood over him, recounting his unhappy tale in broken phrases, then correcting himself. "Did I say yellow daisies? Or dandelions? On the nightgown. *Are* there yellow daisies? Botanically?" Sergeant Bryson sweated.

Inspector O'Hare, standing beside his desk, said to Torrey Tunet, keeping his voice low, "Well, then?" But he was shocked at the way she looked. For a quite lovely young woman, she looked dreadful. Her face had gotten pale. Tension narrowed her eyes, and her brows were drawn together, creating two deep lines between them. Her lips, admittedly quite bewitching lips, were dry. Ms. Torrey Tunet looked as though she would never smile again. Yes. That unhappy. Or tragic. Surprising. Before Dr. Collins's confession, she had not looked this way at all. Quite the opposite. Lively, eager, owning the world, confident about the information she'd put into the inspector's hands. But something had gone off the rails.

Inspector O'Hare, confused, but with a sudden feeling of compassion said, "You're all right, Ms. Tunet? Nothing's the —"

"I'm fine." Torrey Tunet bit her lips. "I'd hoped . . . Inspector, I can still help. There's a road . . . I'd hoped not to have to travel down that particular . . . Will you trust me?"

Trust her? Inspector O'Hare stared. He almost had to laugh. *Trust* Torrey Tunet? He'd never gotten over that she'd been a thief, never mind how young. Moreover, she was given to illegal snooping on private property and among other people's personal possessions. Had she done more of it, her snooping, in this murder of Dr. Ashenden? Undoubtedly. But —

He said, and then stood stunned at his own words, his incredible words of comfort, "Ms. Tunet, I believe that murder because of incest, particularly incest since childhood, has in some cases led the court to be lenient with —"

"Incest?" Torrey Tunet's hand went up and covered her mouth. Her black-fringed gray eyes grew wide. "So *that's* what you think I'm —"

"Pardon me, miss." Sergeant Bryson had come up. Patches of darker blue under his armpits. And to Inspector O'Hare, "We've done, sir. If you want to go over the statement with Dr. Collins, he'll sign it. We'd better get on, sir, it's almost half past twelve. They'll be coming back."

Sergeant Bryson had time to get the broom and dustpan and sweep up the cigarette ashes and the cigarette butt from under the chair where Winifred Moore had sat.

Twenty minutes past twelve.

Torrey Tunet was standing over by the window, looking out at the gray weather, her hands clasped behind her back. She had a straight-backed boy's stance, but right now it was altogether rigid, like stone. Over at his desk, the inspector was finishing reading Dr. Collins's statement.

"Yes . . . yes." The inspector nodded, then looked at Dr. Collins, who stood beside the desk. "You might want to read this over before signing, Dr. Collins."

"No, no, Inspector!" Dr. Collins waved a polite, negative hand. From the breast pocket of his rumpled jacket he took out the tortoiseshell pen with the gold band, the pen that had belonged to his father, the pen with which he'd written up almost all the prescriptions in Ballynagh in the past twenty-two years. He leaned over Inspector O'Hare's desk and with his familiar little flourish signed the document recounting his killing of the gypsy woman.

Helen Lavery, sitting bowed over on a chair, gave a choked, indrawn sob. Sergeant Bryson looked sympathetically at Helen Lavery. Then he glanced curiously over at Torrey Tunet, who was standing by the window. Staring out and biting her lips. Looked miserable, as if she were going to the guillotine or the like. A bit odd, wasn't it? Especially, since Ms. Tunet should be singing and dancing, shouldn't she? Smiling and the like, what with that wooden knitting needle business, so clever, catching the gypsy woman's murderer, after all. And that it should be Dr. Collins!

"Helen." Dr. Collins put his familiar-looking tortoiseshell pen away and looked kindly down at Helen Lavery. "Helen? If you wish to leave my employ now, Helen, I'll send your salary to your brother's in Meath. But if you'd please prepare me a bit of a late lunch? A salad with yesterday's cod will do. And possibly bake a batch of scones? The ones with cranberries?"

"Cranberries," Helen Lavery said, sniffling, eyes red, face

tragic, "and cod. Yes, Doctor." She left unsteadily, bumping against a chair on her way out.

"Well —" Dr. Collins settled the tweed cap on his head. "I ought to look in on old Mrs. O'Gorman. So I might's well —"

"Dr. Collins! Please!" Torrey Tunet was suddenly at Dr. Collins's side. "If you'll just stay, this'll all be over before lunch. Here they all are now." And it was true that Winifred Moore and Sheila Flaxton were already coming in, and on their heels came Rowena, followed by Scott, limping his way along. "I've something . . . there's something you ought to hear."

Dr. Collins hesitated. "Well . . ." He lifted a hand and ran his fingers slowly along an eyebrow, then down to circle slowly under one eye, where he had whitened the darkness. "Yes, well, but I ought —"

"It's about Rowena."

"Oh, well then, of course."

65

In O'Malley's pub, the woman who was drinking a ginger ale at a fireside table said to the friendly old fellow with the wild white hair, "I joined the Temperance when I was thirty. And not a drop since." She had a Dublin accent, gray hair, and a friendly, kind face. She wore a nice-looking dark blue dress.

"Ah," said Michael McIntyre, "and missed a lot of lusty memories and lovers, no doubt." The woman smiled at that, but there were shadows in her eyes, and McIntyre, priding himself on being a sensitive old chap, got off the subject. "That fellow your son? The one with the Jaguar? Staying at Nolan's Bed-and-Breakfast? That fellow who went up? Black-haired?"

"No, just a friend. Had an errand upstairs there, then we'll be off. I'm not one for stairs. My house in Kilkenny's all on one floor."

And here came the black-haired fellow. Same one he'd had a beer with yesterday. But now, face all on fire, cheeks blazing like he had the Holy Grail tucked in his pocket.

In a minute, the pair was gone. McIntrye, going up to the bar for a couple of biscuits from the jar, saw out the window that they were walking up Butler Street. The fellow had left the Jaguar in front of Nolan's. The top was up. Good thing. A wind was beginning to blow and it looked like rain. Ugly weather. McIntyre made a face. Might's well be in the South Pacific.

66

Half past twelve. They were all back. Inspector O'Hare nodded whenever anyone's glance skimmed across his. Everyone had chosen the same seat as earlier. Like ducklings, each one's place imprinted in their brain. Odd, that. Odd for ducklings. Odder even for folks.

Each person, arriving, hesitated, then nodded a polite greeting to Dr. Collins, as though it might be good manners — or out of embarrassment? — to overlook the fact that he was now a confessed murderer. A few minutes before, Dr. Collins had stepped into the toilet, and when he'd returned and sat down, O'Hare had observed that he'd repaired any damage to that overly white makeup he wore around his eyes. O'Hare had the passing thought that Dr. Collins must have begun using cosmetics to appear younger and more attractive to those hookers he'd frequented. Poor lad, thought O'Hare, surprising himself. Besides, Dr. Collins was not a lad.

Torrey Tunet remained standing, leaning against the Coke machine back there. She'd tied that peacock scarf around her head again, and a dark band of satiny hair slanted across her forehead. But even from his desk, O'Hare could see the paleness of Torrey's face. He thought: It's up to her, now. Whatever she had in mind had better be good. Ms. Torrey Tunet: snoop, thief, liar, protector of the murderous Rowena Keegan.

As for himself, O'Hare made a wry face. Curiosity, that tantalizing bitch, had led him to allow Ms. Tunet this . . . this whatever it was. And his owing her for Dr. Collins's signed confession that already lay on his desk and that within the hour he would have Sergeant Jimmy Bryson fax to O'Reilly, chief superintendent of the Murder Squad at Dublin Castle.

A rumble of thunder, then rain spattered hard against the plate-glass window of the police station. Sheila Faxton's thin voice said crossly, "I *told* you, Winifred, you should've put the top up! Now we'll be sitting in puddles!"

But in a matter of seconds, the spattering of rain dwindled, the wind possibly having shifted. And into the silence, Inspector O'Hare said. "I believe, Ms. Tunet, that before I conclude this informal inquiry that has been so productive — I believe, Ms. Tunet — what is it exactly you wished to contribute further?"

And when Torrey Tunet hesitated, O'Hare thought, *Ah! Some tricky business regarding the incest. That's it. But she's losing her nerve, is Ms. Tunet. Doesn't, after all, want to expose that ugly relationship in front of Winifred Moore and the rest. What's she been thinking?*

O'Hare looked over at Rowena Keegan, who sat between her brother Scott and her mother. At his look, Caroline Temple involuntarily reached out a slender white hand and covered Rowena's tanned hands that were clasped in her lap.

"Yes, Ms. Tunet?" O'Hare said patiently.

No answer. Rowena Keegan turned her red head and looked back at Torrey, seemingly puzzled.

Then —

"Thank you, Inspector." Torrey pushed herself away from the Coke machine. She came forward to stand a few feet from Dr. Collins. Her gray eyes, a little wide and very intent, regarded him. She said carefully, clearly: "I think, Dr. Collins, that your friendship with Dr. Ashenden ended the day before he was killed on the bridle path. It ended when you overheard a conversation between Scott Keegan and his sister, Rowena, in the library at Ashenden Manor, a revelation that enraged you beyond reason. Something that made you hate Dr. Ashenden. Hate him enough to—"

"What?" A strangled cry from Scott Keegan. He struggled to his feet, white-faced, unsteady, gripping his cane. He took a step toward Dr. Collins. "You were in the library? You *heard?"* His voice was enraged. He raised his cane. Instantly Sergeant Bryson was beside him, Firmly, Jimmy Bryson took the cane from Scott. Trembling, glaring, Scott sank back onto his chair. Beside him, Rowena sat very still.

67

Dr. Collins had flung up an arm and ducked his head to defend himself. His tweed cap slid off his lap to the floor. He seemed to shrink into himself. O'Hare, closest to him, saw that his small, corpulent body was trembling.

"Here, now!" O'Hare said, narrow-eyed. What was all this? Collins's face had a shattered look, as though Scott's cane had in fact struck him. He bent down and picked up his tweed cap. With shaking hands he began brushing it off, brushing and brushing, as though it demanded intense concentration.

"Padraic!" It was Caroline Temple, in a bewildered voice. "Padraic! Are you all right?" And to her son, reproachfully, "Scott! How *could* you!" And helplessly, "What's going on?"

Dr. Collins's fingers stopped brushing the tweed cap. He looked at Caroline, who was leaning toward him, her hazel eyes anxious. "It's too late, Caroline." His voice was tired, gentle. "No way now to put a stopper on the bottle. I'd thought to spare you this."

Inspector O'Hare glanced over at Torrey Tunet. She looked unhappy but determined. She looked, in fact, like a young officer who had brought unavoidable bad news to the general.

Dr. Collins too looked at Torrey Tunet. "Clever! Clever!"

He shook his head. "But of course, thinking to save your friend . . ."

Dr. Collins's voice was low, but so clear that even Sheila Flaxton, with her poor hearing, did not have to strain forward to hear.

"That day, I'd dropped in for a visit with Caroline, Mrs. Temple, that is. I often did, of a late afternoon. She'd be in the sitting room, reading or knitting. We'd have a chat and a cup of tea. It was one of my favorite—But that day when I arrived, Jennie O'Shea told me Mrs. Temple was shopping in Dublin. I was quite exhausted. It had been a wearing afternoon—a scything accident, then a measles scare. And I thought, *Why not a nap?*"

So in the library at Ashenden Manor he'd settled into his favorite wing chair before the fire. He'd dozed. And then: "I awoke to hear them talking. Rowena and Scott. And I heard—" Dr. Collins's voice faltered. He looked helplessly about. "I can't, I can't—"

"Don't be so sniveling," Scott said furiously. "You can't stop now!" He started to struggle up, but Sergeant Bryson held out a warning hand, palm down.

"No . . . *No!*"

"All right, then, Padraic Collins! I'll tell you what you heard!"

"*No!*"

"You heard that my sister Rowena was pregnant."

Dr. Collins bent his head and stared at the floor. Not a sound in the police station. Scott, looking at Dr. Collins, went on, "You also heard me tell Rowena something I discovered two years ago but kept secret. I had told no one. But now, now that Rowena was pregnant—"

"*No,*" Dr. Collins breathed out, a hopeless, helpless plea.

"Yes, Padraic." Inexorably, Scott went on: "You heard me tell Rowena that our grandfather as a young medical student had used X rays on Kathleen Brady, to kill their unborn baby—"

"*No!*"

"—so he'd be free to marry a Danish girl with whom he was in love. He endangered Kathleen Brady's life. He took that risk."

"Kathleen." Dr. Collins breathed out the name as though it were a melody. "Kathleen."

Scott, his face drawn, went on bitterly, "But Kathleen Brady did not die. Neither did the fetus. The baby was born with weakened bones, damaged by the X ray. A legacy to hand on to future generations."

"Jesus!" Mark Temple put his arm around Caroline's thin shoulders.

Scott abruptly stretched out his crippled leg and yanked up his trouser leg. The metal brace gleamed. "So in the library, I told Rowena, 'Look at me! Look at *me*! And our mother.' I told her that she was lucky to have escaped it *so far*. But she carries the genetic fault to pass on to her child. I told her, 'For God's sake, Rowena, abort the baby! For your baby's sake, abort it!'"

From the listeners, not a sound.

68

Inspector O'Hare heard something like a hum, a drawing in of held breaths, and through it the tinny clicking of the clock. He felt as though he'd been napping, only to awaken to a nightmare of reality. In the village of Ballynagh, this.

O'Hare looked from Scott Keegan's white, impassioned face to Rowena, who sat with a fist to her mouth. Caroline Temple, on Rowena's left, was a stone effigy.

"So, Dr. Collins." Torrey Tunet was standing beside O'Hare's desk, hardly a yard away from Collins. "When you overheard Scott Keegan reveal the X rays to Rowena, what did you do then?"

No answer. Dr. Collins simply sat, gazing down.

Inspector O'Hare, at Torrey Tunet's left, saw her jaw move stubbornly forward. She was standing soldier-straight but with her hands in her pockets; O'Hare could see the bunching of her fists. He felt a flicker of unwilling admiration. A bulldog, Ms. Torrey Tunet was a bulldog, for all her black-fringed gray eyes and the incongrous peacock bandanna on her satiny hair. She'd wanted to protect Rowena Keegan. She'd hated to have to reveal Rowena's secrets. But, no other way, finally, to break open the rotten egg. Pin the tail on the donkey. Murder was murder. O'Hare pulled at his nose and regarded Dr. Collins. So now let's have it, Dr. Collins. No mercy.

Still no answer from Padraic Collins. Torrey leaned toward him. "Dr. Collins? *What did you do then?*"

Rumble of thunder again, then a light scattering of rain against the plate glass. Yet so quiet in the police station, a bated-breath quiet. Sergeant Jimmy Bryson silently moved a step closer to Scott Keegan because who knew, who ever knew? Furious victim, with that skinny leg under the dove-gray trousers. There was always the strength of madness, was there not?

"That Friday afternoon," Dr. Collins said, and he folded his arms across his chest and stared into space, "when Rowena and Scott had gone, I left the library and waited in the hall. Gerald would be arriving home from his office in Dublin. I waited in grief and rage. Kathleen, whom I had loved! And the terrible genetic results to Caroline! And later, to Scott. Only Rowena had seemingly escaped. But I knew she carried within her that terrible legacy. My head was bursting.

"When Gerald came in, I struck him across the face. 'That's for Kathleen, that X ray!' Then I struck him again. 'That's for Caroline. And Scott! And Rowena!' Then I struck him a third time. 'And that's for Donal Slattery!'

"Gerald just stood. He was in shock. Then I saw that he took it in, took in *that I knew*.

"He turned around and walked back out. I stood outside at the top of the steps and looked down and saw him crossing the meadow. He was going toward the woods, stalking away like some sort of automaton. And then I saw Rowena galloping toward him on Thor."

Dr. Collins stopped and gave an enormous, shuddering sigh. Then he began again.

"They brought him in from the meadow. Upstairs, I took care of his sprained shoulder. I looked only once into his eyes. What I saw there made me know that I was done for, just as Donal Slattery had been done for. Because now I had the power to ruin him. I could, if I chose, destroy the reputation of this 'eminent' surgeon. Did he know too that I had loved Kathleen? In any case, I was a danger. A sword of Damocles, hanging over him."

Padraic paused. He looked over at Inspector O'Hare. "Ah, yes, Inspector O'Hare, Donal Slattery, I should explain. Donal Slattery, an X-ray technician. Unfortunately a drunk. Died of a heart attack twenty-something years ago. Fell facedown in that bog near the west woods and suffocated. I'd attested to the heart attack.

"But that wasn't the truth. Slattery had been a dinner guest at Ashenden Manor. I'd left early. Gerald showed up later that night at Collins Court, upset. He told me that Slattery had been drinking and had gone out and must have got lost. He'd been so drunk that he fell facedown in a bog and was too drunk to get up. He'd suffocated. Gerald had found him. It was a wild, windy night in March, I remember. It was known in Dublin that Slattery's drinking was getting out of hand, he was spending all his money on drink, a pity for his wife and children.

"There in the woods, at the bog, Gerald suggested that we cover for Slattery, so as not to shame his family. Why not report that Slattery had died of a heart attack? 'But Slattery and I had a bit of a quarrel,' Gerald told me. 'So best to say that you found him, rather than I.' Of course I agreed."

Another pause. Then the sigh, and Dr. Collins shook his head. "All those years!

"But in the library, when I heard Scott tell Rowena about the X ray to Kathleen, I knew that Slattery hadn't died falling drunk with his face in the bog. Gerald Ashenden had held Slattery's face down in the bog until he suffocated. *Because Slattery knew*. Donal Slattery was an X-ray technician. He'd found out something and wanted money to keep quiet about it. I'd thought it odd that he'd turned up at Ashenden Manor, a bit down at the heels; they'd never been friends."

Padraic stopped. He looked fully at Torrey Tunet and gave her a nod of approbation. He turned back to Inspector O'Hare. "So I knew, Inspector, while I was bandaging up Gerald's sprained shoulder, that now Gerald would have to kill me, too." Dr. Collins drew a deep breath. "So I killed him."

69

The stark confession in Dr. Collins's gentle, well-modulated voice vibrated through the police station. Someone — Sheila Flaxton? — gave a hysterical laugh. As though sensing an oppressive change in the atmosphere, Nelson lifted his head and whined.

"The gypsy saw me," Dr. Collins said, "so then I had to, well . . ." He looked down.

Inspector O'Hare felt like the tail of a kite being whipped around by capricious winds, jerked this way and that. And not understanding by half. He did not look around. He did not want to see the faces. He did not even look at Torrey Tunet, who'd landed this big fish that came floundering up, trailing like seaweed torn from the depths, these slimy, obscene secrets.

Tap, tap, tap. Scott Keegan, tapping a gold cigarette lighter against the metal arm of his folding chair.

O'Hare glanced down at the tape recorder on his desk. The tape had run out, God knows how long ago. He swore under his breath, pulled his nose, and regarded Dr. Collins.

"Let me understand precisely, Dr. Collins. The original — Backing up a bit: Who's Slattery? You struck Dr. Ashenden in the — how'd this Slattery get — "

"I knew! I *knew*!" Dr. Collins sounded stubborn. He shook his head.

O'Hare breathed out a sigh of exasperation. Hopeless. At least for now. Later would have to do.

"Inspector?" Scott Keegan stopped tapping the lighter. "I can help a bit, on that account." He tipped his head to the side, his transparent-looking eyes questioning. His fair hair gleamed like burnished gold.

"Good. *Good!*" Inspector O'Hare looked over the silent room. "Almost half past one. If anyone would like to leave for lunch?"

No one stirred.

70

By chance," Scott Keegan said, "some correspondence fell into my hands. Letters of some years ago. They were between my grandfather and a Danish woman in Copenhagen. Years before, they'd been fellow medical students in Dublin. They'd also been lovers, deeply in love and engaged to be married. Then one night the young woman — let us call her Ingeborg — packed her bags and, leaving no word for her lover, disappeared back to Denmark."

Scott's hand toyed with the lighter. It was a fine hand with polished nails. The narrow wrist bore a thin, flat watch. "Why, I wondered, had she gone, when so in love? And with a happy future in store! Why had Ingeborg so abruptly fled? And with no explanation!

"But reading further in the correspondence — or, I might say, the bitter, accusatory letters — that finally reached Gerald Ashenden from Ingeborg, letters in response to his that had up to then gone unanswered, I" — Scott looked at Inspector O'Hare — "I learned the reason. And I admit to being horrified. And then —"

But there was an interruption. The door to the police station had opened; a wind swirled the papers on Sergeant Bryson's desk before it closed. Two people had come in. Inspector O'Hare recognized Jasper O'Mara in his familiar oatmeal sweater. But the woman with him was a stranger, a pleasant-faced woman, gray-haired, upright, in a tan coat open over a dark blue dress. Nelson rose, wagged his tail, and collapsed down again. Sergeant Bryson unfolded the one remaining chair, and the woman sat down.

"Go on, then, Mr. Keegan," O'Hare said impatiently. Might as well. It would all be in tomorrow's papers anyway, maybe even on tonight's radio and television news after he'd talked to Dublin Castle, so what difference did the presence of these two people make? "Go on, Mr. Keegan."

"It was this," Scott Keegan said, "One afternoon in a pub in Dublin, Ingeborg, happily engaged to Gerald Ashenden, ran into a young fellow she knew, one of the medical crowd from Richmond Hospital. He was drunk, as usual. Name of Slattery, an X-ray technician, always half-drowned in his cups, never mind that he had a wife and two little ones to support. Did extra work for a private doctor, Doc Blair, on O'Connell Street, as did the medical student, Gerald Ashenden. Always broke, was Slattery, but that afternoon he had a pocketful of pounds. He was drunk enough to tell Ingeborg where his windfall had come from. He said—" Scott Keegan's voice stopped.

O'Hare looked sharply at him. Scott was looking over at his mother, sitting beside Mark Temple. Caroline's great hazel eyes looked back at her son. Then, "Darling," Caroline said, "go *on*."

"Yes, Ma." O'Hare could see the glitter of tears in Scott Keegan's eyes.

"Slattery told Ingeborg he'd done a job for Gerald, got fifty pounds for it. 'Innocent as a lamb, the girl, that blue-eyed girl from Ballynagh, believing what Gerald had told her! X ray to see if their baby was going to be a boy or a girl! I'd happened into Doc Blair's office after hours; I'd left a half-pint behind the radiator. And there they were, the pair of them, the girl all delighted, happy. Gerald saw that I'd twigged what he was up to. Made me sick, it did! He knew I knew! We'd been at Barney's pub the Tuesday a week before, me, Ashenden, and a couple of other med students, when Hotchkiss, a fellow med student, came in. He was drunk and excited and began bragging about something he'd done. Hotchkiss bred Cavalier King Charles dogs as a sideline, and his best female cavalier, a Blenheim, had gotten out and become pregnant by a stray. Hotchkiss needed her pregnant quickly by another pedigreed cavalier to have a salable litter by April. "I tried every damned thing — purges, God knows what! — to abort that stray's litter. No luck! Then I remembered something I'd heard from a dog breeder in Cork. He claimed he'd had success with strong doses of radiation. I tried it on my Blenheim bitch and — Glory be! — that did it!" Hotchkiss slapped a handful of pounds down on the bar. "Drinks all around!"

" 'I don't think any of us believed his tale, but we drank and joked about it. I remember, though, Ashenden asking Hotchkiss, "You're sure the X ray did it?" And Hotchkiss said, "Had to be. The breeder in Cork has a brother who's a doctor and had done it more than once before. So I thought, *What the hell! When you're desperate, you'll try anything.*"

" 'So there they were, Ashenden and the girl, and me with my half-pint from behind the radiator. And him knowing I knew what he was going to try, to get clear of the blue-eyed girl from Ballynagh.

" 'But I'd caught him. He knew how to close a fellow's mouth, though: Make him a party to it. "Fifty pounds if you'll do it," he told me. "You do the X ray." Fifty pounds! I could see Nora's eyes go big at that. A pork roast, fried chickens, clothes for the kids. A dinner out, and the rent paid!

"So, drunk, in the pub, Slattery told Ingeborg, waving a

handful of pounds around, 'All to clear the way for you, my pretty!'"

Scott Keegan ended his tale. "Those letters! It was that night that Ingeborg fled in horror from Gerald Ashenden. Fled back to Denmark. She never saw him again."

71

Scott Keegan's voice stopped. At Inspector O'Hare's left, Dr. Collins gave a strangled little cry. He looked from Caroline to Scott with his hidden crippled leg. He looked then at Rowena. "Pregnant!" he said. "My God!" His pudgy body shook with a sudden, violent shudder. "Rowena! You should indeed have ridden him down! Erased him! *Killed* him! Monstrous! *Monstrous!* All those years, friends, playing chess, a drop of brandy. And I, never knowing! Until—" His voice broke. He got to his feet, fumbling the tweed cap onto his balding head. Unsteady with emotion, he turned to Inspector O'Hare. "You'll wish another statement, no doubt, Inspector. I'll be glad to give it! The murder of Gerald Ashenden, I'm proud to say. You'll find me at Collins Court when you're ready. But just now, I've a bit of cod with mayonnaise waiting." His voice quavered on the last words.

On the way out, he blindly fumbled his handkerchief from his pants pocket. Sergeant Bryson hurried to open the door for him. The wind took the door and slammed it shut behind Dr. Collins with a noise like a pistol shot. On the heels of the slammed door, a woman's voice said:

"But that's not true! That X ray! *It never happened!*"

72

A new voice. A clear, Dublin-accented voice, from the Liberties quarter lying behind the Guinness works. A voice now edged with distress. The woman sat back near the door, the center of the semicircle that had Inspector O'Hare's desk at its open side. She was the woman who had come in five minutes earlier with Jasper O'Mara, Torrey Tunet's friend. A stocky woman, rosy-cheeked, gray hair in a bun. She wore a dark blue dress, Her tan coat was on the back of her chair; her purse lay in her lap.

"Never!" the woman repeated. "He didn't!" And to Inspector O'Hare, " 'Tis my late husband you're speaking of. But he didn't! I'm Mrs. McLaughlin — Nora Slattery that was. Widow of Donal Slattery." A look of distress; two lines appeared between her brows. "I knew t'would come to bad. And then, him going to Ballynagh, to Gerald Ashenden. Donal played everything light, that was his trouble. It was his nature. A lovely man but for the drink and taking nothing serious, always a bit of a laugh hidden in his cheek, Donal toying with what it was all about, more a game like. And then, the drink throwing everything off."

Scott Keegan gave a half-hysterical laugh and struck his trousered leg with his fist. "Whoever you are, you're not making sense!" At the same time, Inspector O'Hare said, "The Donal Slattery who . . . who suffocated in the bog?"

At the woman's nod, he leaned forward in his chair and put his elbows on the desk. He had a feeling he would not be surprised if it suddenly started to rain doughnuts. Or frogs. "Well, then, Mrs. McLaughlin?"

"Like I said, Donal didn't do it. 'Made me sick to my stomach, it did,' Donal told me, 'I knew Gerald was in love with Ingeborg. What Gerald was up to was to free himself by killing the fetus so's he could marry Ingeborg.'

"So in the X-ray room my Donal stood the girl in front of the X-ray machine so's she'd think she was being X-rayed. Then he told her the X rays had come out too fuzzy to tell if it was a boy or girl, that the problem was that it was too early to tell. He knew that anyway Gerald didn't care to see any X rays. Gerald didn't want X rays. He wanted a destroyed fetus."

" 'Why didn't I do it, Nora?' Donal asked me, 'Why didn't I X-ray the girl? How could I do such a thing? Sanctity of the church. And a dangerous business. Could've damaged the girl. Or left the fetus alive and damaged. Gerald would've risked it, he was that desperate. But I wouldn't. So I lied to him. I told him I'd done it. But I didn't. And look, here's the fifty pounds.' "

Inspector O'Hare regarded Mrs. McLaughlin. But he was seeing a table laden with a feast of ham and roast of beef, and seated at the table, two small wide-eyed children. He blinked away the image.

"So," Nora McLaughlin heaved a sigh, "Kathleen Brady remained pregnant. Donal told Gerald Ashenden he couldn't understand it, that possibly the X ray hadn't been strong enough."

Someone under his breath whispered, "My God in heaven!" O'Hare pretended not to hear. His gaze was fastened on Mrs. McLaughlin.

She continued, "Then, right after, Ingeborg disappeared."

"Disappeared? Went off, you mean?"

"Off to Denmark, I imagine. Heartbroken, I imagine. In horror at what Donal told her, I guess. Donal in his cups! Loses his head and maybe blabs something to Ingeborg. I asked him, had he said anything. He couldn't remember; he couldn't remember anything he said or did when he was on the drink. Once, a family came to move into our house. They said Donal had sold it to them; they'd given him a down payment. They had it on paper, Donal's signature. Donal couldn't even remember."

A waiting. In her lap, Mrs. McLaughlin began abentmind-edly snapping her purse open and closed. Open, closed . . . *snap, snap* . . . open, closed. There was no other sound in the police station, open, closed. She sat looking off into space. Inspector O'Hare coughed. Mrs. McLaughlin blinked. Her fingers on the purse went still.

She said, "So Gerald Ashenden married Kathleen Brady. Six months later the Ashenden baby was born. Caroline they named her. Poor little thing! Pitiful. Damaged. Bones so weak! I heard of it from Donal.

"But Donal swore to me again that he'd done no X ray on Kathleen Brady." Mrs. McLaughlin was silent. Then, pensively, "Once in a while I'd see a write-up in the papers about Gerald Ashenden getting some medical award at a dinner or banquet. But never any mention of Kathleen and the little girl. Never in all those years."

The little girl. O'Hare tried not to look at Caroline Temple, sitting there beside Mark Temple, but he looked anyway. So did everyone else. Caroline's hazel eyes were gazing dreamily at Mrs. McLaughlin. *As if she is hearing a fairy story,* thought Inspector O'Hare, *Hansel and Gretel in the woods.*

"Never a mention," Mrs. McLaughlin repeated, "never in all those years."

In all those years. Inspector O'Hare drew in a breath. Years. So many years later: death from a strong hand holding down a drunken face in a bog. O'Hare had been a young

232

man, Jimmy Bryson's age, when it had happened. Inspector O'Hare remembered it. In the woods north of Ashenden Manor. The nighttime call, in the dark woods the flashlights crisscrossing the bog, the muck on the man's body. The bulk of Dr. Collins standing nearby. Now, arms folded, Inspector O'Hare waited.

Mrs. McLaughlin said, "But then Donal, after being in AA for sixteen years, went back on the drink. We got desperate again for money. Donal said he'd visit Gerald Ashenden in Ballynagh and get enough money from him to pay what we owed, so he could start over, clean slate, no drink. 'Five hundred pounds,' Donal told me, 'that should clear us.'

"And he told me, 'Nothing to worry about. I'll tell Ashenden I've had a bout of conscience about X-raying Kathleen back then, and I'm going to make a clean breast of it to the law. I'll go all guilty and penitent, Nora, never mind that I had nothing to feel guilty about. But implying at the same time that for five hundred pounds I'd have to reconsider about my conscience.' "

For the first time, Nora McLaughlin looked around at the fascinated faces of the listeners. Then she said to Inspector O'Hare: "I thought how mighty strange it was. Ironic. Because my Donal never did anything wrong except take money from Gerald Ashenden to do a wrong thing he never did. And now Donal was going to try to get more money for the wrong thing he never did. You understand me, Inspector?"

"Yes."

Nora McLaughlin nodded. "Well. So Donal went to Ballynagh, to Ashenden Manor. And they say that Donal got drunk and had a heart attack and fell down in a bog and suffocated. I couldn't make it out. I'd heard of Russian peasants getting drunk and falling down in the snow and freezing to death. But a bog? A heart attack? I couldn't make it out.

"A Dr. Collins had found him. I ask myself often, was

that really what happened to my Donal? But what could I do? Donal and I—we'd never known Donal had a bad heart. Do you have to have a bad heart to have a heart attack?"

"I expect so," O'Hare said.

73

In the silence, a crackle of paper. Then Nelson thumped his tail. Everyone in the room looked around. Sergeant Jimmy Bryson guiltily stopped his noisy opening of the box of dog biscuits. Inspector O'Hare refrained from raising his eyes to heaven.

Scott Keegan was gazing from under his brows at Mrs. McLaughlin. He said bitterly, "Would that your tale were true, Mrs. McLaughlin. That your husband never —"

"But it *is* true! Donal never lied to me!" Nora McLaughlin's rosy face went rosier with indignation.

"Come, now, Mrs. McLaughlin! Look at me!" He slid his trouser leg up for the second time. "D'you think I suffer this brace on my leg to amuse myself? In or out of his cups, your husband Donal had you on. A fabrication. A pretty and lying tale. God knows why!"

Mrs. McLaughlin looked about to cry. "No! I — he wouldn't! Not Donal! Never! He wouldn't —" She half turned and looked up at Jasper O'Mara standing beside her chair. "Please! Please, Mr. O'Mara! You said just tell the truth! And so I did! I did! And that you'd a way to . . . I forget the word."

"Corroborate," Jasper O'Mara said. "From the Latin, *rober*, meaning 'to strengthen.'" He slanted a glance toward Torrey Tunet. "I won't let you down."

Inspector O'Hare for an instant closed his eyes. *Now what?*

74

A somewhat dirty brown envelope the size of typing paper.

Jasper O'Mara shook its contents out onto Inspector O'Hare's desk. Everyone leaned forward to see. "What *is* it?" Sheila Flaxton, who was nearsighted, said fretfully to Winifred Moore, who had eyes sharp as an eagle's.

"Not exactly the crown jewels," Winifred answered. Trinkets. A small, tarnished silver cross on a chain. A few old lace doilies. A Bible with a peeling leather cover. A half dozen yellowing snapshots.

"What's all this?" Inspector O'Hare frowned down at the miscellany.

"Ah," Jasper O'Mara said in his pleasant baritone, "a bit of property that once belonged to a woman named Alice Coggins. Spinster aunt of Kathleen Brady. From the attic of Nolan's Bed-and-Breakfast. Courtesy of Sara Hobbs, who was good enough to allow me . . ." He pushed at the few snapshots. "Family shots of the Bradys. This one," and he slid a snapshot forward.

For a long moment, Inspector O'Hare gazed down at the photograph. A smiling little girl standing alone by a barn. Clean, checked dress, pigtails with bows. The little girl on crutches, a steel brace.

Inspector O'Hare took a breath and closed his eyes. It

had all gotten away from him. He even felt dizzy. He became conscious of Torrey Tunet over there by Nelson. He said, "Mr. O'Mara, I am by no means sure — "

"But I am," Jasper O'Mara said, "An hour ago I called the parish priest in the Brady's village near Galway, out toward Clifden. Yes, he told me, he remembered the Brady family well. Genetic problem. Now and again it surfaced. Too often, alas. A pity."

A vehement whisper, "Winifred, I'm *missing* it. What are they *saying*?" No answer.

Inspector O'Mara looked down one last time at the snapshot in his hand: pigtails, pretty little eager face, one of the Bradys that had drowned. Then reluctantly he handed the snapshot to Caroline Temple. He didn't have the heart to look over at Rowena Keegan, the granddaughter of Kathleen Brady. And pregnant.

75

Caroline Temple gazed down at the snapshot in her hand. "Oh," she whispered. *"Oh!"*

Inspector O'Hare found the moment difficult. Caroline Temple, such a delicate face, and the startled, white-lidded hazel eyes that she now raised to his. Then she said, "Scott," and handed the yellowed photograph to her son who sat on her left, his trousered leg in the brace awkwardly stuck out.

Scott bent his fair head over the snapshot. Then a long, drawn-out breath and, incredulously, *"Christ!"* He thrust the snapshot at Rowena who'd turned startled eyes to him. "Take a look, Rowena! Take a look, for—oh, *Christ!"* He put up his finely manicured hand and rubbed his forehead, shaking his head slowly back and forth. "And all the *time!* The wicked old bastard thought *he'd* done it! All the *time!* He with his damned X ray. And he kept paying me off! Letting me bleed him!"

Inspector O'Hare looked over at Torrey Tunet, who stood at the corner of his desk. She had this morning led to revealing Dr. Collins as a double murderer. But what help could she now be to Caroline Temple and her two children? No help at all. O'Hare felt a wave of pity for the family from Ashenden Manor.

Rowena Keegan, holding the snapshot, ran a fiercely angry hand through her red hair. "Whose *fault* doesn't matter!

I thought it was *his*! So, in the meadow — Either way, any child of mine would be born damaged, Maybe crippled. To suffer. So I won't ever have children. *Never!*"

"Don't fret, Rowena." Scott's voice was so low that O'Hare, hardly a breath away, had to strain to hear. "Dr. Sunshine will light up your life."

But, unbelievably, a soft laugh from Caroline Temple. "Oh, darling!" she said to Rowena. "Not you!" She took a breath. "Not *you*, Rowena! It doesn't apply."

"Ma," Scott said. "For God's sake, Ma, this is *real*. So don't —"

"Scott, be quiet." To Rowena: "When I married Tom Keegan, my father was furious. He carried on about Catholics always wanting children. 'You're not physically able! You'll die in childbirth!' he raged at me. It made Tom afraid for me. I was surprised at my father's solicitude. He acted . . . strange. He proposed that, instead, Tom and I adopt a child. *Now* I understand why. He couldn't bear the thought of another genetically — He said that if Tom and I agreed, I'd inherit Ashenden Manor and all the Wicklow estate. And the child would inherit the Kildare property. But —"

"Ma, what're you —"

"Be *quiet*, Scott. But two provisos: The adoption was to be kept secret. His associates, his friends, *no one* to know. And second: He, with his superior medical knowledge, would select the baby. 'A healthy baby,' he said. 'A perfect little specimen.' "

Caroline's thin shoulders suddenly shook. "I remember thinking then, *Not like me. Not a pained, whining, frail thing like me!* That's what he meant. I knew it. He could have said it aloud: *Not like you.* Hating the sight of me, tortured by it. Because — though how could I have known his secret? — he thought *he* had done it."

Caroline reached over and took the snapshot from Rowena. She gazed down at it. "What a sweet little face! And those pigtails. She must be one of my mother's little sisters.

Yet, my mother, like Rappaccini's daughter, was glowing, a beauty. My beautiful, black-haired mother! But harboring within her — " Caroline's voice quivered. She looked at Scott. "Later, when I became pregnant with Scott, my father was beside himself. But I rebelled. I rebelled even against Tom's fears for me. I wanted to have my baby. Mine and Tom's."

Not a sound in the room. It was as though the listeners held their breath.

"So — " Caroline turned to Rowena, who sat staring at her. "*Anyway*, back then, two years before I had Scott, my father went over there and got you himself and brought you back. You were four months old. The *healthiest* baby."

Rowena said, green eyes wide, "Went over there? Where?" She looked in shock. She pushed her red hair impatiently behind her ears as though to better hear her mother's words.

"To Denmark. He was adamant that the baby come from Denmark. Though why you have red hair, I can't imagine. It's so . . . so *Irish*."

It was Scott who began helplessly to laugh. Then Caroline joined in, then Rowena. They all three laughed so hard that tears came to their eyes, and sometimes too it sounded like sobbing. For some minutes they were unable to stop.

76

At Collins Court, Padraic came into the great hall and without even stopping to take off his jacket or cap went into the drawing room. Because first thing, he had to know.

He went across to the mahogany table where the beautifully inlaid box with the Chinese chess set lay. He opened the box. Carefully, he took out the chess pieces. So exquisite. Each piece both cool and warm to the touch.

And there, at the bottom of the box, was — ah, yes! — the twist of green paper with the pair of wooden knitting needles. He had hidden them here, and here they were.

Padraic shook his head. He couldn't help but smile. That clever Torrey Tunet! Not only clever with words! She'd fooled him. She must've bought another pair of the wooden needles at the Grogan sisters' shop. She'd have given them to Inspector O'Hare. Had she told Inspector O'Hare she'd found them in the garbage at Collins Court? Or what? How much of this had Inspector O'Hare known? In any case, O'Hare had cunningly played out his part.

In the great hall, the clock chimed. Half past two o'clock. Delicious smell of baking from the kitchen, Helen Lavery's scones. And there'd be the cod. After his late lunch, which by now would so late that it would really be a high tea, he'd still have plenty of time. In October it did not get dark until seven.

Half past four o'clock. What a fine feast Helen had given him! First a mushroom soup with bits of carrot. Then the cod. And the cranberry scones with the tea. He'd miss all that.

At his desk in the little surgery, he made out a check to Helen Lavery: A thousand pounds a year for her twenty-two years of service at Collins Court. He put the check in an envelope, with a note.

Next, his confession, for Egan O'Hare. The inspector called it a statement. Weasel word, *statement*. A confession. A confession of murder. Of two murders. But before writing it, he tore up an earlier confession he'd written many days before, just on the chance that Rowena might be found guilty of the knitting needle murder of her grandfather, not that he'd believed Inspector O'Hare would ever have gotten enough evidence against her. Still, he'd slept better.

He wrote the new confession carefully, read it over, and, satisfied, signed and dated it. In the great hall, he put the envelope with the confession on the central round table, propping it against the silver bowl with the Collins family crest, the bowl that had been there since he was a boy. Inspector O'Hare would be coming for him in the morning. Well, this would have to do.

Upstairs in his bedroom he put the envelope addressed to Helen Lavery on his dresser.

Next, he packed a few travel articles. He had money, pounds. He knew what he was about. By the time they found out, he'd be gone. A pity he couldn't take the Chinese chess set, but it was too heavy. There'd be months maybe while he'd be carting it around.

In the bathroom off his dressing room, he squeezed a blob of medium ivory, number 3 makeup base onto his middle finger, dabbed it around his eyes, then carefully smoothed it, blending it in. Fine. At one time, he'd thought of wearing glasses to conceal those ugly brownish circles. But he had perfect vision, and besides, he'd always disliked the look of glasses.

Before going downstairs again, he stood a moment at the tall bedroom windows. He could see the walled kitchen garden below, and rising beyond it the high hills where sheep browsed. At his death, Collins Court would, finally, go to Jeremy Collins, a distant cousin in Australia.

The last thing before he left was to put on the old tweed cap of his father's.

Leaving Collins Court, going through the great hall, he thought what a pity it was to leave his books behind. Still, Tennyson's *Ulysses*, " 'Tis not too late to seek a newer world."

Going out the door into the purpling dusk, he felt a wild surge of ephoria such as he'd never felt before. His new life.

77

Reaching Ashenden Manor with Caroline in the old Rolls, Mark Temple said, "I'll be right down," and went upstairs to his dressing room where he took off his country squire clothes and put on a shirt, sweater, and trousers — all clothes from the old wardrobe he'd brought from Dublin.

"What're you doing?" Caroline in the doorway. Mark went over, took Caroline's hands in his, and sat her down on the bed. He kissed her. "I'm not a country type, my love. I had a romantic notion for a while that Ashenden Manor would fulfill an old dream of mine. But no, it turns out it doesn't."

Caroline said, "I'm glad. I've always hated living here. Tom and I, we dreamed of leaving. But, money. We thought until we had enough *money* —"

"But you've been hanging back about leaving!"

Caroline said, "I thought Scott was sleeping with men for money. I thought if something dreadful happened and he needed me, I could protect him. I couldn't leave him at Ashenden Manor without me."

Mark looked at his wife's delicate frame. Protect her son! How? Then Caroline's hazel eyes met his. Protect her son? Yes, if she had to, she'd find a way. He imagined her pulling a bright sword from its scabbard and launching forward, fair hair flying in the wind.

Downstairs, Scott and Rowena sat at the dining room table going through the yellowed old photographs of the Brady family. Scott after some minutes leaned back and looked at his sister. "What about Flann? Where's he now?"

"I don't know. Jasper wouldn't tell me. Said that was safest." She sighed. "Flann's never been to Ashenden Manor. He couldn't visit me here; you know Grandpa. So no one in Ballynagh knew about him. The thing was—"

"Ah, yes, Grandpa! And Flann a scribbling Irish nobody, son of a stonemason! Cry havoc! To arms! Rowena, his perfect creation, destined for the most aristocratic Anglo-Irish or English marriage! We can't have this raiding Irish fox slipping into the fold and—"

"God! You make it sound so Charles Dickens!"

"Well, isn't it?"

"I guess." Rowena drew lines on the tablecloth with her fork.

"About Padraic," Scott said. "Later, when I'm alone, I'll think about Padraic. For Padraic, a private requiem."

"Yes," Rowena said. They were silent. Rowena gazed down again at the old photographs of the Brady family, a family whose blood was not hers. Then she looked over at Scott. "Any chance of getting our money back from Dr. Sunshine?"

"Please! Can a cat turn into a canary?"

At the Ballynagh police station, at three o'clock, Inspector O'Hare said into the phone to Chief Superintendent O'Reilly at Dublin Castle, "Absolutely, sir! We'll be getting a full confession. We'll be bringing Dr. Collins to Dublin in the morning."

To Sergeant Jimmy Bryson, Inspector O'Hare's face had that full-blooded look it always got with success. His eyes were brighter. His gray hair looked crisper. He lounged back in his chair, phone in hand. "Ah, well, sir! Thank you, thank you."

Inspector O'Hare put down the phone. "So!" He rubbed his chin and looked over at Jimmy. "What a windfall! I called this informal meeting, and voilà! As the French say."

"Right, sir. Voilà."

"We ought to buy chairs of our own, Jimmy, and not have to borrow from the Grogan sisters every time."

"We could do that," Bryson said. "You want lunch, sir? I'm going to Finney's."

"I do, Jimmy. Bring me back a fish sandwich, will you? And some crisps. I'll make tea here." He stretched widely. He could hardly wait for tonight to tell Noreen about it.

Jimmy Bryson gone, O'Hare sat gazing out at Butler Street. Slowly, his satisfaction was draining away. Under his left pants leg, the long scar from the scythe, that time when he'd tripped on a stone, clearing his field. Dr. Collins's careful stitching. Fourteen years ago? Or sixteen. He sighed.

At Castle Moore, Sheila found Winifred standing before the library fire, warming her backside and sipping bourbon.

"Winifred?" Sheila sat down on the fringed hassock beside the fire. "I've been thinking. How *ironic*. Considering that back in the days when Gerald Ashenden tried to abort Kathleen's baby with radiation, the medical profession itself hadn't the least idea that X ray could have any harmful effects on a fetus. Birth defects, for one. They'd no *idea* —"

"A castle's so damn chilly," Winifred said. "Thank God for bourbon! Yes, Sheila, the medical profession didn't yet know. But there's hardly a scientific advance that isn't accompanied by smarmy activities that go on sub rosa. Unethical fringe activities. Such as, in this case those known to a dog breeder in Cork. Then to Hotchkiss. And then, alas, to young Ashenden."

They were silent. The fire crackled. A log shifted and a plume of sparks shot upward. On the hassock, Sheila

246

hunched her shoulders and rubbed her arms. "Then all those years, Ashenden living with what he'd done."

Winifred said, "Oh yes, that. But then, there was Rowena. A compensation? In Gerald Ashenden's head, Rowena was his child. His and that Ingeborg's child. A Scandinavian saga, if ever there was one!"

"*Act*ually," Sheila said, "you might make a sonnet of it, Winifred. A dark kind of Irish sonnet. I could use something like that in *Sisters in Poetry*. I'm short the next issue. Or if not a sonnet—"

"No." Winifred shook her head. "If I were to write anything, it would be a long poem, more romantic than Scott's young Lochinvar who came out of the west." She looked down into her glass. "It would be about Padraic Collins."

At the groundsman's cottage, Jasper said, "Torrey. *Torrey!* What is it?"

Torrey stopped pacing. "Hmmm? I'm just—Nothing." The gypsy. She saw the gypsy's dark face, all crafty and hinting, and heard again, "A reward, is there? You think about it, Missus." But the gypsy'd had the goods on Padraic Collins, no way for him to wriggle out. And he was rich. *Then why come to me?* Something wrong.

78

It was February, and in Dublin a snowfall during the night had slowed the morning traffic. So at half past eleven, Jasper, in Dunleavy's pub around the corner from the Shelbourne, half expected Torrey to be late.

It had been four months. Belfast first, then an investigate bit in the Mideast. Now home to Dublin. Dust on the garaged Jaguar, musty smell in the closed-up apartment. On the bathroom scale, he'd weighed himself. Gained six pounds. That wonderful Turkish food, eggplant in a thousand guises.

"Jasper. Hello."

Torrey sat down and shrugged off a fleecy-looking coat. He saw that she had lost weight. She'd become too thin. It had put shadows under her cheekbones and somehow drew attention to her mouth, which at this moment smiled at him, bewitching him as usual. Her short wavy hair was damp from the snow, as were her short black eyelashes, so that they starred her gray eyes. She had on the same red turtlenecked sweater he remembered. He sighed with pleasure.

"So. Tell me all," he said and took her cold hands in his big warm ones, "Tell me how you are. Did you get my letters? Every time I called the cottage, I got your recording. Frustrating, but at least it was your voice. I had to imagine the rest, you at the laptop, a crackling fire in the fireplace . . ."

"Yes. I tried to buy the cottage from Winifred Moore, but she won't sell. So I'm only renting. But it's cheap. The gypsy's murder in the cottage helped, if you want to be cynical about it. Here's the waiter." They ordered. Hot tea for her, beer for him.

"And the kids' book?"

"I met the deadline. Two weeks later the publishing company went bankrupt." She gave a little shiver of pleasure. "You know, I'm glad? Interpreting's my thing; it fits my skin. Ballynagh's now my base, my jumping-off place. Tomorrow I'm off to Greece, a five-day job. So I'll still eat. Modern Greek is easy. Fascinating too, once you know what it's derived from. I love the Greek tragedies, *Medea*, for instance. Myths and tragedies."

Jasper said, "Speaking of Greek tragedies, any news about Padraic Collins? Have the Gardai caught him yet?" And when Torrey, gazing at him, only shook her head, he said, "Now *there's* a Greek tragedy for you. To kill one's best friend! That's the pity of it."

"Oh," Torrey said, "Padraic Collins didn't kill Dr. Ashenden."

When it was over, and to Inspector O'Hare's mortification Dr. Padraic Collins had slipped from between his fingers, the news media forgot Ballynagh. As Winifred Moore said, "They went baying off after fresher blood."

Torrey was alone, Jasper gone to Belfast. She finished the three-language book and sent it off. She walked the hills with pregnant Rowena, learned Gaelic, restlessly bit her fingernails, and read the *Dublin Times*, the *Sunday Independent*, the *Sunday Tribune*, the *Evening Herald*, and a gaggle of news magazines. She was on edge, searching for something, she didn't know what. Waking in the morning, she would think restlessly, *Something wrong.*

The gypsy woman had been a fellow Romanian. Now, any mention of things Romanian in the news caught Torrey's eye. The Romanian gypsies lately escaping into Ireland had joined the itinerant population of tinkers, those "travelers" who crisscrossed the countryside in painted wagons and caravans, sharpening knives, selling kitchenware, and occasionally stealing. They were largely illiterate. Most pubs barred them from entering, and they were unwelcome in villages; hospitals admitted them only grudgingly. Their caravan camps hung on the fringes of villages, of towns, of cities like Dublin. Torrey read that the Irish government was trying to better the tinkers' situation, even to building housing. But tinkers and gypsies were footloose. Torrey thought of her explorer father and wondered if the Tunets had once been gypsies in Romania.

Then one Sunday morning, over her breakfast of tea and buttered toast, she came upon a small newspaper item. It spoke of an incident in a Romanian gypsy caravan encampment in southwest Ireland, on the outskirts of Clonakilty, a small town near Skibbereen: A gypsy child's arm was nearly severed under a wagon wheel but was saved by one of the Romanian gypsies, an old fellow who surprisingly had some medical knowledge. The gypsy was even said to help with gypsy women in childbirth, generally a woman's job.

Torrey sat back. Her tea grew cold. A gypsy with medical knowledge. A shiver slid down her spine. That night she lay awake.

Four days later, she was driving a rented Toyota west on Route 71 beyond Cork and through Bandon. It was mid-afternoon. A dozen miles ahead lay Clonakilty. Pastures and hills, and a cold salt-smell of the sea; no tourists in winter. Only, on the edge of Clonakilty, a straggling gypsy caravan of three wagons.

Torrey drove slowly into the encampment. There was an air of activity: men and boys harnessing horses, women packing away goods. Departure was almost palpable.

"An hour later, and they'd've been gone," Torrey said to Jasper. She pulled the fleecy-looking coat closer around her shoulders. "I would've missed them. So I was in luck, wasn't I?"

Jasper, sitting with folded arms, staring at her, said, "I don't know yet. Go on."

It was the biggest of the three horse-drawn wagons, really a small trailer. "I went up the steps. He was there."

Padraic Collins. He was sitting up against pillows in a

bunk bed, his legs crossed at the ankle, reading, wearing bifocals. A picture of ease, of comfort, his pouty little belly given freedom — he'd unbuttoned the top button of his worn-looking pants that must once have been orange. He was just the same. Padraic Collins, small, balding, chubby. He took off his reading glasses and looked Torrey over speculatively, as though checking to see if she still had signs of the flu. Then he asked her if she'd like a cup of tea.

They sat at a small table that hinged down from the wall. Padraic had put the kettle on. "I knew you were clever," he told her. "Are you going to turn me in?"

She said she didn't know. She kept looking at him; he still wore the light makeup around his eyes, but some of it had rubbed off, showing darkness.

The stove was kerosene, the blue flame was small under the kettle. "I might've known," Padraic Collins said. "That newspaper item! A clever young woman like you. You fooled me that time in Ballynagh." He sighed and gave her a smile. "You don't let go, do you?" And when she waited, "Might as well tell you."

Sitting opposite her at the hinged table, Padraic, his fingers turning a spoon over and over, said, "It was two days after Gerald Ashenden's death on the bridle path. I couldn't sleep for the horror of it all. By three in the morning, I was exhausted. And, finally, hungry. Helen had baked cranberry scones, my favorite. I knew there were some left. I went down to the kitchen. I got out the scones and butter. I opened a kitchen drawer, I was looking for a knife. And there was the knitting needle with its tip cut off.

"In the morning, I faced Helen Lavery with the knitting needle. She collapsed. She confessed she'd shot the knitting needle tip into Gerald's horse. 'I was afraid for you!' she told me, 'because of what you said when you came home from bandaging his shoulder! That you knew that Dr. Ash-

enden had killed Mr. Slattery in the bog. And that *he knew
you knew.'* "

Padraic Collins glanced around at the kettle over the blue
flame; no steam yet. He put two mugs on the table. "It had
been my mistake, a terrible mistake! Losing my head, shaking with the horror of it, babbling. Blurting out too much
to Helen Lavery! She was always *there*, just the way my
governess had been when I was little, a trusted presence."
Padraic rubbed his eyes, the gesture brushed away even
more of the light makeup. "So she wanted to save me. She'd
shot Ashenden with my old pop gun. She'd found it in the
nursery years ago. It was Swiss made and could shoot pel-
lets a good fifteen feet. She always used it to shoot kidney
beans at the rabbits to drive them out of the kitchen garden.
She'd become an expert shot. Why a knitting needle? She
never thought such a tiny puncture would be discovered.
And it wouldn't likely have been, but for you."

Steam rose from the spout of the teakettle. Padraic turned
off the flame, gave the china teapot a quick rinse, and put
in a handful of tea leaves. He waited; then he carefully filled
the teapot from the kettle.

"The gypsy woman had been nearby in the woods. She
saw Helen Lavery shoot the knitting needle tip into Thor.
So in the kitchen, that morning with Helen, I thought, *Get
rid of this cut-off needle!* It was by then seven or so, the sun
already up. I went outside to the pond by the garden wall
and threw the cut-off needle as far into the pond as I could.
It flew up in an arc, it was steel or aluminum, a good ten
or twelve inches, the sun flashed on it, a pretty sight. Unfortunately witnessed by the gypsy woman who was hanging
about. My second mistake! So she saw. And thought of
course that Helen Lavery and I were in it together, that we'd
murdered Gerald Ashenden."

Padraic Collins carefully poured tea into the chipped
mugs and set out butter and a plate of scones. "That pair of
wooden knitting needles in the twist of green paper? That

the gypsy brought to blackmail me? Naturally me, not Helen Lavery! I being the rich one, owner of Collins Court and eight hundred acres! She even came into my library at Collins Court and threatened me. Blackmail. If she told what she'd seen on the bridle path and that she'd seen me throw the evidence into the pond, Inspector O'Hare might well have the pond dredged. She threatened me with that. And laughed."

Sipping from the mug, Torrey gazed at Padraic, who was absentmindedly running a finger beneath an eyebrow. He said, "Helen Lavery would go to prison! All my fault. I couldn't let that happen. I was tempted to pay off the gypsy woman." But then he'd thought that next year she would be back. And the following year. Blackmail is an open-ended business.

"I couldn't let the gypsy tell Inspector O'Hare what she'd seen on the bridle path! Helen Lavery had done it to save my life! To save me from Gerald. Can you imagine, Ms. Tunet, what it must have cost Helen Lavery to do that? A decent, hardworking, honest woman become a killer? In all my books about romantic heroines with flowing golden hair, I'd never found a one like Helen Lavery."

80

In the pub, waiters were beginning to get tables ready for the noontime crowd. Jasper O'Mara, chin in hand, couldn't take his eyes from Torrey Tunet's intense face.

"So you see," Torrey said and sat back. She ruffled her drying hair.

Jasper said, "And the gypsy? Smothered in your bed. Are you going to tell me now that Helen Lavery also killed the gypsy?"

Torrey shook her head. "Oh, no! It was Padraic Collins killed the gypsy, just as he told Inspector O'Hare. And as Padraic Collins said to me in Clonakilty, in that gypsy trailer, 'Blackmail's like a mushroom growing in the night. It gets bigger and bigger. So I had no choice.'"

"I see." Jasper nodded. "But —"

"Shaw! Back, are you!" A beaming red face, flat blond hair. Jasper introduced him. Matt Quinn, of the *Sunday Independent*. Full of news and questions. Torrey didn't even hear. Clonakilty . . .

Outside the trailer, men's voices, a horse neighing, a radio was playing rock and roll. Inside the trailer, Torrey asked Padraic Collins, "And you have no . . . no guilt over it?"

"Oh, yes! Yes, Ms. Tunet! Guilt is what I live with," Padraic Collins said, "Guilt. And expiation." Again running his fingertips under his eyebrow. "It's mostly the children that need medical care. Hospitals aren't friendly to gypsies and travelers — 'tinkers,' they're called. Ireland is changing, the government is trying, but still . . ."

"Nice meeting you, Ms. Tunet." Matt Quinn departed. It was already noon; customers were shrugging out of parkas and coats, waiters were, beginning to take orders. Jasper blew out a breath and regarded Torrey. "How about lunch? They have a Wednesday special. And a good cook in the kitchen." He paused. "Or would you rather . . . ? I've missed you."

"I'd rather."

After, as they lay near naked side by side on the bed in Jasper's apartment on York Street, Jasper, one arm beneath Torrey's head asked, "Are you going to turn him in? Padraic Collins?"

Torrey was quiet. Then, "From almost the first," she said, "when I came into the trailer, I knew something. Padraic Collins's face. Something about around his eyes. And when he poured tea into the mugs, and I looked more closely, there came into my head, *The Assyrian came down like the wolf on the fold, / And his cohorts were gleaming in purple and gold.*"

"Blake? Kipling? But why?"

"Byron. It was the word *wolf*. At first I didn't know. Then I did."

"Know what?"

"That Padraic Collins had been concealing something else. Out of vanity, likely . . . *I* don't know."

It was like a mask that Padraic Collins had tried to hide. So faint, but clear, the wolflike shape of that darkness, when Collins, absentmindedly brushing fingertips around his eyes, had rubbed away the makeup, and she saw. And at first, was puzzled.

Now, lying beside Jasper, she sought out his hand and

laced her fingers with his, as though to hold onto his strength. She said, "Jasper? In the trailer, looking at Padraic Collins while he talked, I thought at first: In Greek, *wolf* is *lykos*. Then I thought: And in Latin, *wolf* is *lupus*. The wolf-like shadow, like a mask across the eyes."

Jasper's fingers, after an instant, tightened on hers. "Lupus. Lupus erythematosus." He was silent. After a moment, he slid an arm beneath Torrey's head and drew her close. "Is that why you didn't turn him in to the Gardai?"

Torrey nodded. "How could I? Padraic, in his late seventies, and on the run, living a gypsy life and doctoring whoever needed medical help. And with lupus! Lupus demands proper care. How long could he last without it? Collins knew it was risky. But he made his choice. And you know"—she tipped up her head within Jasper's encircling arm—"I love him for it."

81

It was after seven and dark when Torrey got off the bus beside the break in the hedge that led to the groundsman's cottage. In Jasper's apartment, lying in bed, between talking, napping, and making love, hours had passed. Then in his state-of-the-art kitchen, Jasper had made them a high tea of a Turkish dish that was mostly eggplant and was indescribably delicious. At six o'clock he'd gone to an editorial meeting and Torrey had taken the bus.

A crusty snow crackled under her feet when she stepped down from the bus. She drew a deep breath of the pure cold country air. She could see the few lights of Ballynagh down the road. What was Ballynagh anyway, that she was in love with it? Nothing but a few streets and cottages and two or three manor houses and a castle owned by an ironic poet. Nothing but Nelson of the gold-brown eyes and wagging tail, and the smell of dark beer from O'Malley's pub, and Finney's crisp-fried cod and the white fluffs that were sheep grazing on the high hills. Nothing but the drawing in of a breath of air that was like a drink of pure, cool water. And the way, last night at dusk, the sun slanted across the mountains so that they became violet, then deep purple.

In the cottage, she turned on lamps. She knew that it was not over with Jasper O'Mara, or should she say Jasper Shaw? She was happy about that: Their lives crisscrossing, she going off on interpreting jobs, Jasper on investigative jobs.

But there were some things she wasn't ever going to tell her darling investigative reporter, Jasper Shaw. For instance, what she knew about Helen Lavery having gone to live on her brother's farm in Meath and a few weeks later reported to have disappeared. What she, Torrey, knew? Or did not quite know. But there in the gypsy trailer, at the hinged table across from Padraic Collins, she had suddenly asked, "Where is Helen Lavery?" her question startling herself.

Padraic was spreading butter on one of the scones. He didn't even look up. "I've no idea," he said. He put down the knife and bit blissfully into the cranberry scone.

So, no. Some things Jasper Shaw was never to know. And there was at least one thing she herself didn't know and now never would. Why *had* the Romanian gypsy woman, drunk, thrown out that tantalizing hint? *A gypsy's words, they might be smoke. A lady like you is different, could make something of it.* A backup? In case Dr. Collins resisted blackmail, and Inspector O'Hare wouldn't likely believe a roving gypsy's tale as against Dr. Collins's word? Not believe it enough to have the pond dredged? Likely, that. But no way now to know.

Torrey looked at the clock. Getting late. She'd better pack a bag and go to bed. She was leaving for Greece at eight in the morning. Rowena's husband, Flann, would drive her to Dublin; he had to be at his desk at the *Irish Times* early tomorrow. A month ago, after he'd appeared again in Dublin, there was always a car following his. Flann had glimpsed it in the rearview mirror. But no more. Whatever had been was over. Torrey forced herself not to ask of Flann, "Then your father, Rory. Is he safe, somewhere?" Flann and Rowena were living at Ashenden Manor. Rowena had passed her vet exams. Later, after the baby was born, they'd move to Rowena's property in Kildare.

As for Ashenden Manor, Scott, hired by his mother, was totally absorbed in working with an architect and contractor on plans that would turn the manor into a country estate guest house with landscaped gardens, tennis, golf, riding, and a superior cuisine.

Her bag packed, Torrey set the alarm. She should go to bed. But then, looking around the fireplace kitchen with voluptuous pleasure, she couldn't resist: She put on her heavy striped apron, spread some newspaper on the floor, and with a paint scraper began to scrape the peeling brown paint from the old kitchen chair. Later, she'd sand it, rub in an apple green tint, then wax it. When she returned from Athens, she'd also buy chintz for the shabby-looking couch beside the fireplace.

For the bare breath of an instant, she thought of Inspector Egan O'Hare and of the two false gypsies moving in a caravan somewhere along the roads of Ireland.

Rightly or wrongly, she decided, scraping off the old paint, she was content with her conscience.